YOU
BET
YOUR
HEART

YOU BET YOUR HEART

Danielle Parker

joy revolution

Text copyright © 2023 by Danielle Parker
Jacket art copyright © 2023 by Kgabo Mametja
Title page art, dedication page art, and camera art on pages 14, 46, 58, 114, 135, 166, 190, 207, 230, and 262 copyright © 2023 by Kgabo Mametja
All other interior art used under license from Shutterstock.com

All rights reserved. Published in the United States by Joy Revolution, an imprint of Random House Children's Books, a division of Penguin Random House LLC, New York.

Joy Revolution is a registered trademark and the colophon is a trademark of Penguin Random House LLC.

GetUnderlined.com

Educators and librarians, for a variety of teaching tools, visit us at RHTeachersLibrarians.com

Library of Congress Cataloging-in-Publication Data is available upon request.
ISBN 978-0-593-56527-8 (trade) — ISBN 978-0-593-56529-2 (ebook) — ISBN 978-0-593-70578-0 (international ed.)

The text of this book is set in 11.5-point Apollo MT Pro.
Interior design by Cathy Bobak

Printed in the United States of America
10 9 8 7 6 5 4 3 2 1
First Edition

To Betty K. Parker

CHAPTER 1

I'VE BEEN SUMMONED.

Every student at Skyline High School knows the principal's calling card—that infamous wallet-sized light green piece of paper. So when Marcus Scott, the self-declared Hermes of school messengers, busts into my AP English class like he's walking onto a Broadway stage, I don't pay him any mind. Instead, I grow an inch taller in my seat, extending my raised hand high in the air.

"Why, Sasha, yes, please," Mrs. Gregg says. Her eyes dart between Marcus and me. She nods for me to proceed and we both smile. We've been doing this exchange all senior year. She asks the tough questions, and while other students are thinking, I stay ready to answer. Like right now, my fingertips flutter in the air as I wait to respond to her question about Shakespeare and his influence on modern media.

But that moment never comes, because Marcus walks up to Mrs. Gregg, hands her the summons slip, and then points at me. It's not until Marcus leaves that Mrs. Gregg slides the flimsy paper across my desk and I realize what's happening. All eyes in the room shift to me, and my body stiffens. I know what they're thinking, because it's what I'm thinking too: What the hell is this about?

I've been called to the principal's office all of once, and it was because my perfect-attendance certificate needed to be picked up. Without making too much of a fuss, I grab my bag and place my pencils, pens, and highlighters in their respective pouches—yes, they each have their own homes. Then I gather the rest of my things and go. Quickly. Trying not to overanalyze how the word *now* is circled three times in black ink.

In the main office, a small bell on the door dings, announcing my presence. I take another step and am met with a mix of familiarity—I've been going to Skyline since freshman year, and the school is like my second home—and newness, because I'm never actually in the main office. The walls are adorned with student photos from the last three decades, with a sea star, a sea otter, a sea lion, and my personal favorite, waves (because we are, you know, making waves here as the second-best public high school in Monterey), as a backdrop. When you go to school this close to the Pacific Ocean, the themes are always gonna be nautical. Mrs. Brown, the world's nicest office attendant, perks up.

"There's our number-one girl," she calls from behind the counter. "Sasha, sweetie, it's so nice to see you. Whatcha doing here?"

I inch toward her and hold up my summons slip so she can see I've been *called* to the office—I'm not just walking around, loitering, wasting class time. As if I would do that anyway. Her eyes dart across the paper and then back at me before breaking into a warm smile, like the sun. I swear, if every high school in America had a Mrs. Brown, student productivity would increase by, like, a lot. People would just be better.

"Have a seat, honey. Principal Newton is finishing up a meeting and then he'll be right with you." She leans on the counter, closing the space between us. Up close, her brown skin glistens. Her straight black hair is in her signature short bob, and her bangs have a streak of gray that makes her look badass, like how I imagine Storm would be in her fifties. Or forties, or thirties? Maybe? Mrs. B is one of those women with flawless skin and a playful personality who seem to defy age.

I try to return her kindness with a smile.

"Knowing you, I bet this is something good—exceptional, even." Then she flashes me a wink.

I can't help but feel . . . thrilled. Being swept out of class to the principal's office. I've been on point all senior year—scratch that, my whole high school career—and maybe this meeting is about that.

For once, the main office is empty, so I take the seat closest to Principal Newton's door. I shut my eyes and savor the peace. Silence. A little mental vacation, if you will. But as soon as I begin to relax, the bell rings.

"There she is. Hey, Mrs. B—that's B for *beautiful*." A deep voice interrupts my peace. Moment gone. I open my eyes and turn my head.

Mrs. B rests her elbows on the counter. "Here you go," she says, that infectious smile still on her face. "Ezra, honey, you've been called to the office? Don't tell me you're in trouble, now."

From my chair, he doesn't see me, but I have a full view of him. He's wearing a fitted white tee and white jeans, which make his brown skin pop. His curly black hair is pulled up in a small but high ponytail, and he's got a medium-sized gold chain around his neck that lies on top of his shirt. A small diamond sparkles from his ear, and his black camera hangs across his chest like the sheath of a sword. I take one last gaze and notice the outline of his face, his nose and jaw, which are prominent. He stands so tall and straight it makes the bones in my back follow. I really need to work on my posture.

Ezra.

He must be able to sense me staring at him, because he does a small pivot, and our eyes connect like magnets. I blink nervously and avert my gaze.

He turns and holds up his summons. "I was hoping you could tell me. You know what this is about, Mrs. B?" he asks, his voice a lot deeper than I remember.

"No idea, honey. But go ahead and have a seat by Sasha. Shouldn't be long now." She motions for Ezra to sit in one of the two empty chairs next to me. Ezra gives them a quick glance, but decides against it. Instead, he stands awkwardly, lingering by the doorway.

If Ezra is Mr. Fashionista right now, I'm the opposite. I have a strong urge to slink down in my seat and blend in with the wooly fabric. Today I'm in my black Nikes—but not like sneaker head Air Maxes or Jordans, just regular, degular, old-man running shoes with worn laces tied a little too tight. My long locs are pulled back in a messy bun, giving end-of-school-day vibes. I didn't have time to do anything special with my hair this morning. Okay, I never do. Who has that much time? I'm too busy with school. I mean, this isn't New York Fashion Week, right? Who cares that I'm not wearing makeup? I huff and catch a whiff of . . . Wait . . . am I wearing deodorant?

I'm in my favorite baggy, ripped blue jeans and a black tank top, layered underneath a holey, loose green-and-red flannel with the sleeves rolled up. I give myself a quick once-over and . . . what am I? Going to go work on the railroad? What is this—pioneer chic? Not that I care what Ezra thinks, but I know I have better outfits than this. I peek down at my arms, my umber skin is a little, okay, maybe a lot, dry, with tiny white flakes speckled across my arms. Did I put on lotion? Out of habit, I pat the side of my hair. *This is fine, I am fine.*

I gaze back to Ezra, who hooks his thumbs in the front of his pockets.

Has he been staring at me this whole time?

He raises his eyebrows and says, his voice soft and deep, "Hey, you."

CHAPTER 2

MY CHEST TIGHTENS. I WISH I HAD MY HEADPHONES ON, SO I could pretend to be listening to NPR and avoid any type of conversation with him. Before I can respond, two tearstained freshmen walk out of Principal Newton's office.

"All righty, then. Who's next?" Principal Newton's voice bounces off the walls. That just happens to be his energy— he's like the Energizer Bunny, but with eyeglasses and a big smile. Skyline High is totally his Disneyland, the happiest place on earth. But I guess if you're going to be working with kids, it's the right kind of energy to have. He appears, then holds open the door and makes a big "come on in" gesture with his other hand. I blink out of my trance and stand. Ezra takes a step back, and I scoot past him.

"Oh, you too, Ezra. Both of you, come inside. Have a seat, please," Principal Newton says.

Come again?

Both of us?

We enter his office, which consists of four large black chairs, a tall lamp, and a desk that is an absolute mess, with multiple piles of papers, pens, and books in disarray. I cannot with this chaotic energy. Just give me five minutes in here, some color-coded folders, and a label maker and I know I could make this room shine. Sparkle. Sing. But that's not why I'm here, so I snag a seat and ignore the mess.

"Sasha, this is Ezra. Ezra, this is Sasha, another senior. Do you two know each other?" Principal Newton asks.

"No." "Yes." We speak at the same time.

"No," I say again, with a little more authority in my voice.

So maybe that's not entirely true. I guess if we're going to get technical about it, Ezra and I have met. We *used* to be friends—best friends, actually—but that was years ago. I don't know him now. I *knew* him. Past tense.

"Okay, fine. We've met," I say, doing my best to ignore the glare I know Ezra is giving me.

Ezra sits down, leaving an empty spot between us. Principal Newton tugs at his green bow tie and then rubs his bald head. He smiles as he sits up in his big, rolly chair. He clears his throat, and his cheeks turn a light pink.

"Is this where the kids would say 'it's complicated'? Is that the relationship status update here? Verified? Green check mark?" His voice booms as he laughs at his own joke and welcomes us to do the same. I wait for Ezra to respond, but he doesn't. So I don't either. At least we both can agree on silence.

"Well, then." He coughs, annoyed by our lack of enthusiasm for his comedy routine. He brings his face to his laptop screen as he pecks at the keys with his index fingers. He finds what he needs because he presses his hands together and his eyes light up. "Let's talk about why you're both here." He leans away from his screen, his blue eyes dart from me to Ezra. The only sound in the room is the fluorescent lights from above, crackling as if insects are being fried inside.

"As you know, it's late April, and senior year is wrapping up. There are several things on my radar, of course." Principal Newton takes a long pause. Apparently, he's a master of the art of suspense. "Teachers and administrators are beginning to prepare for end-of-the-year activities and whatnot. You both know that senior year has lots of moving parts, don't you?" He perks up in his chair, waiting for an answer. I'm doing everything in my power not to scream, so I keep quiet. I'm not one for surprises. Ezra just shakes his head like he has no idea, like he's genuinely interested in this buildup.

"Yes, lots of moving parts, lots to plan. Prom, Senior Legacy Night, and, of course, graduation. This is a special time for seniors, so much happening, there's so much good stuff on the horizon. But I digress. This is all to say that, as of today, we have two people tied for the position of valedictorian and the accompanying scholarship."

Okay, now I'm really listening.

The scholarship. $30,000.

"This is new for Skyline High School and for me. I've never seen such rigor academically. Same classes, same grades, two different people." Mr. Newton points to me and then Ezra. "One, two."

"What?!" The shout comes louder than I'd like, but his words awaken everything inside of me. I've never missed a day of school, I've never turned in a late assignment, I've made sure to give everything the proverbial 110 percent.

Before either of us can utter another word, Principal Newton continues, his voice becoming more serious, like he's about to give a lecture . . . or a eulogy. "This is rare, of course, and anything can happen by June, but I wanted to let you two know because—"

Ezra shifts in his seat, agitated. "I'm sorry. Are you sure?"

"Positive. I actually wanted to discuss this with you both today so that we can—" But before Principal Newton can finish, I'm on my feet, backpack falling on the floor.

"It should be me!" The words fly out.

"Excuse me?" Principal Newton slides back, his chair squeaking.

"With all due respect, Principal Newton"—I lower my tone and sit down again—"it should be me for valedictorian. I've worked extremely hard these last four years and . . . and . . . when is the last time the school has had a valedictorian who was not only a woman, but Black and Korean? I think I—"

Ezra jumps in and cuts me off. "Whoa, whoa. Hold up. You think *you* should get it because of your gender and ethnicity?" He fakes a laugh, the space between us narrowing. Our brown eyes lock. "In that case, I think *I'm* more deserving. Being both Black and Jewish, I can say that I am very underrepresented, not only in—"

"Oh my god, you can't be serious right now," I clap back.

Ezra's eyes widen, the incredulousness on his face hard to ignore. "Serious about how I identify? Yeah, actually, I am. It's literally what you did three seconds ago," Ezra replies.

"Okay, but it's different—"

"How is it different?"

"Enough," Principal Newton barks. The room goes painfully silent. "The last thing I want to do is get either of you upset or worked up about what *could be*. There are lots of hypotheticals here. So please, let me continue." He pauses and softens his voice. "I am so proud of you both. You've done something amazing, truly. Your hard work is a testament to this, to your grades. Absolutely outstanding. Historically, the person with the highest GPA is valedictorian, and the second highest is salutatorian. Both positions are, again, very impressive, and both people will have the opportunity to speak at graduation." The energy in the room is heavy. "But unfortunately, per the stipulations of the award, only one wins the scholarship," he says.

The scholarship. The one thing that means everything to me.

My central nervous system shudders, and I dig my nails into the arm of the chair. I'm suddenly faint, queasy. This is not the good news I was anticipating; this is certainly not something exceptionally good. This is its evil twin. Tied? With Ezra? Of all twenty-five hundred students at Skyline, I'm tied with *him*? I bite the inside of my lip so hard I'm sure I draw blood.

Principal Newton gazes at me. "I know, Sasha, that this isn't what you were expecting to hear."

I blink away the tears building in my eyes.

All I can see is the scholarship.

It's not just any scholarship; it is symbolic to me and my journey. I'll be the first in my family to walk across the stage and receive my diploma. I'll be the first in my family to attend college. The way I've grinded these last four years, I want to be ranked first in our high school class and win this award. I want to see my face in the local newspaper, and I want to give a speech on the graduation stage. So hell no, we can't be tied months before graduation. This must be a bad dream. I need to wake up. I need to get out of here.

For a moment, we sit in silence. Dreadful, humid silence. My breathing is slow, like a computer on rest mode. I keep waiting for my brain, which is normally so sharp, fast, witty, to say something, to do something, but nothing comes.

Thankfully, after another moment, my system reboots.

"Principal Newton, Ezra didn't go to school here for all four years! Do the classes from his other school even transfer? Doesn't that mean something? It *should* mean something. Plus, he's always late. Does attendance count for this? He doesn't bring pencils to class!" I exclaim, racking my brain for any reason I can think of to make my case.

Before Mr. Newton can answer, Ezra cuts in.

"Oh, word, SJ? This is what you're doing right now?" he scoffs.

I shrug as Ezra glares at me, like I should answer his question. But I simply won't. I said what I said.

He puffs out his chest and clears his throat. "Since you

want specifics, I attended Forest Grove Preparatory, which is private. And, if we're stating facts, one of the best schools in New York City, if not the country. Come to think of it, Forest Grove is probably more rigorous and ranked higher in overall school standings than Skyline." Ezra turns to Mr. Newton. "No offense, Mr. Newton." Then he whips his head back toward me. "One might argue that the grades *I* received at Forest Grove weigh more heavily than the grades *you* received at Skyline, thus making me more qualified to be valedictorian and win the scholarship." Ezra finishes and smiles, showing the small gap between his two bright white upper front teeth. "And hey, thanks for bringing up my personal life."

I'm too shocked to retort. I wasn't trying to press sensitive buttons by bringing up Ezra's business, including his parents' divorce. It's just fact. He didn't always go to Skyline. His parents were separated by the end of eighth grade, and just like that, he was on a plane, living with his father in New York.

He moved back to California junior year and began attending Skyline, with us both operating under the unspoken agreement that we would pick up where we left off, as ex–best friends. I swerved him in the halls, and in class he pretended he never knew I existed. Our history behind us. Until now.

"Okay, you two. Let's settle down. This is not how I had anticipated this meeting going. I think we are missing the bigger picture—"

Ezra grunts. I fold my arms across my chest.

What exactly is the bigger picture? It takes everything in

me not to ask, so I press my lips shut. Not the right time for inquisitiveness, Sasha.

All the late nights of studying, all the parties I missed out on, not to mention what my parents missed out on. This title and the scholarship—it's not only about me. My mom has had to give up just as much of herself to ensure I get here. All that stress comes back and sits heavy in my stomach and in my throat. I want to retch.

The final bell rings its familiar sound, dismissing hordes of students. A small walkie-talkie on Principal Newton's desk starts to blink and buzz, shaking the papers underneath. He grabs it and turns down the volume as he stands.

He waits for us both to get the hint, and then we stand too.

But it can't end like this! I want to blurt, but my mind is moving too slow. Or everything around me is moving too fast. I don't know. Shit!

"That was the bell, so I've got to go. Let's table this conversation. I will stay abreast of the situation, and I'm certain everything will be okay."

I nod, my shoulders hanging. Ezra says nothing but narrows his eyes.

We leave Newton's office in silence. When we reach the main hall, he scurries away, leaving Ezra and me in his wake.

Ezra Philip Davis-Goldberg is officially trying to ruin my life.

I've got to stop him.

CHAPTER 3

BUT FIRST, I'M GOING TO NEED A MINUTE TO RECOVER OR A GLASS of water. Hell, maybe even a snack or some essential oils.

The walls around me get blurry as I rub my weary eyes, my academic career suddenly on the line.

"One hundred and eighty-six school days per year for the last four years . . . ," I mumble.

"Equals seven hundred and forty-four days of a state-sanctioned high school education," Ezra responds on beat.

". . . times eight hours a day? Not including after-school work, weekends, and . . ." My voice trails off. The math is getting a little too . . . mathy.

"Okay, slow down. I'm good, but let me catch up. Seven hundred—"

I blink back to reality. "Wait, huh?"

Ezra shrugs. "I'm helping you. What, you counting the hours you spent studying? Every moment leading up to this—"

I hold up a hand to stop his talking—it's interrupting my thinking. I mean, he's right, but he needs to quit. "I don't need your help with that." I sound more flustered than I'd like.

Ezra rolls his eyes. He's still here. "Hi, Ezra. It's nice to see you too, Ezra. Been a long time, Ezra. And now we're tied for this thing, Ezra? Kinda wild, right, Ezra?"

I huff and the words fall out. "Wild? No, actually. I hate this. I don't want to be tied with you."

Ezra's face goes flat; the light in his eyes flickers out. "Ouch. Damn, SJ. Come on. It's not that bad, is it?"

I swallow, annoyed to be so close to him. And frustrated that he's comfortable enough to call me SJ—no one calls me that anymore, not since my dad. Where do I even begin? A tie feels worse than coming in second. How do I tell him without hurting his feelings that he's a jerk and we aren't friends and being tied with him feels like I'm being pushed off a very high cliff? Okay, fine, I guess that's impossible. But then I remind myself that I don't care about his feelings. I did once, but I promised myself I wouldn't ever again.

I let out a dramatic sigh, my lips in a pout. "To me, it is that bad. I just don't want to be tied with you . . . or anyone, for that matter." Maybe he'll understand that.

Ezra huffs. "I guess that explains why you're bringing up my attendance to the principal. And telling him that I 'don't bring pencils to class'?" he says, using air quotes.

The stark comparison of us—two different people who have arrived at the same milestone—makes my insides tighten.

"Am I wrong? It's kinda insulting to those of us who show up on time. You're always taking up class time asking around for supplies that you're supposed to bring. That's, like, your thing, or whatever."

Ezra's mouth falls open. "Honestly, I'm surprised you even noticed me. You're like this"—he brings his open palm to the tip of his nose and squints, then bounces his hand off his face like a trampoline—"you're so damn close to the board—"

I gasp. "Hey! I *choose* to sit up front. I *like* sitting up front. It gets me good grades," I ramble, my hands now on my hips.

Ezra just shakes his head. "You must be seething right now, knowing that the person who is currently tied for the same coveted position as you doesn't bring his own pencils to school, huh? That I can sit in the back of class and still earn the same grades as you? I guess your Hello Kitty pencil pouch with the matching Post-it notes and your smelly highlighters ain't the winning combination you thought it was. . . ."

My jaw drops, unhinging itself. Ezra pauses, his face lights up, and a grin appears as he savors my reaction.

Did he just come for my stationery? And my highlighters that happen to smell like tropical fruit?!

"Okay, too far. Now you're just being rude!" I shriek.

"Me? What about you? Do you hear yourself right now?" His mouth opens and closes.

"You can't just waltz back in here and try to ruin my life," I mumble just loud enough for him to hear.

"Waltz back in here and ruin your life?" Ezra's facial expressions go through a flurry of emotions before he lands on a proper stank eye. "All right, Hollywood. Dramatic much?!"

"*I'm* dramatic? This, coming from the boy who only ate red foods for a whole year?"

"You really wanna take it there?" Ezra retorts, frown lines appearing around his eyes and on his forehead. Technically, I did pinky-promise to never ever speak of his red-food obsession. He made me swear on Hello Kitty. I guess he was embarrassed that at the age of eleven, he was still oddly particular about the color of the foods he ate.

I know better than to answer him. This tit for tat could go on for days—we've got way too much history. And I'll pass on revisiting any more of it today. "I'm . . . I'm going to destroy you," I sputter. I don't think before I speak, because I've certainly never thought about destroying anyone, and if I did, I wouldn't say it out loud—definitely feels like something you'd keep secret or in a journal. But Ezra has got to go.

We stand in silence. I do my best to hold his gaze, to try to read his face.

After a long pause, he responds. "Not exactly what I was hoping to hear in our first real conversation in like four years, but crazier things could happen, I guess. If that's how you feel, though . . . bet." He smirks mischievously and then walks away from me. He does a quick spin on his heels, and the sight of him, the expression that hangs on his full lips, jolts me just a bit. He's always had one of those smiles that can make you forget why you're sad or what you were just thinking about, features warm enough to light up a room. And I hate it.

"See you in class, SJ," Ezra says as he waves goodbye.

Here, right now, is where I should say something witty like they do in the movies, but nothing comes.

Mrs. Brown peers from the side of the office door. "What's all this noise in my hallway?"

I fake a smile and soften my voice. "Sorry, Mrs. Brown. It's all over." But that doesn't feel true. Thankfully, she just nods and heads back inside.

I stand there so long I swear a tumbleweed blows by. Hmph. Ezra. *That guy.*

There was a time in my life, after our big fallout, when I wondered about Ezra. What was he up to? How was life treating him? We spent so much time together as kids, it was only natural to think about him, even if our friendship was over. I used to speculate about his life and the kind of person he'd turn into. I think I have my answer.

Some people get better with time, and some just get worse. I know which category he's in.

CHAPTER 4

MY PHONE VIBRATES IN MY BAG, BRINGING ME BACK TO LIFE.

THE TRILOGY GROUP CHAT

Chance 3:25 p.m.: Don't forget we switched tutoring
this week—happening now!

Priscilla 3:25 p.m.: Be there in two.

I read the words and send my response, and after a moment, muscle memory kicks in and carries me away. I've got
places to go. Outside, the after-school energy is buzzing, contagious, even. Students have already changed from their school
clothes (hip, trendy, fun) into their various sports uniforms
(way too much green and gold). I make my way through the
various landscapes, from the long line of cars eagerly rushing out of the student lot to the main entrance, where bright
yellow buses wait to take students home. We're like ants,

marching in line to our next destination. I shoulder through the chaos of the main walkway, which is as full as the 101 freeway at five p.m. on a Friday.

I take a detour from the action, a salmon swimming upstream.

While I walk, Principal Newton's words bounce around my brain. But there's one that sticks out.

Tied. Tied. Tied.

Ezra and I are *tied.*

I take a second to gather myself outside of Ms. T's—she's our ethnic studies teacher—classroom. Inside, the kids are already there, books open on top of their desks.

"You're late, Miss Sasha," Ben calls out. I can always count on middle schoolers to be honest.

"Sorry, sorry. I got caught up." *In some bullshit,* I want to add, but can't. Wrong audience. I head to the front of the room, where Priscilla, my best friend, is already sitting in her assigned desk. Today her thick brown hair is pulled up in a high ponytail and she's wearing bright red lipstick. Priscilla sits next to Chance, the final member of our best-friends-forever-unbreakable trio. Chance, at six foot two and 220 pounds, wiggles to get comfortable in one of these tiny desks. His body twists and turns like he's in some sort of maze. He's got dark brown skin that is always glowing and honey-brown eyes to match. He's a big guy, sure, but what's most impressive about Chance is his brain. I can practically hear him reminding me, "It's called eidetic memory, and I've got it." More commonly called photographic memory. He's the only person

I know who can memorize, well, almost anything. Don't ask him how much of pi he knows because it will take him at least three minutes, and once he's started talking, he won't stop. It's both exciting and terrifying.

"Base coat," Priscilla says, motioning to the red polish bottle as she applies the paint to her fingernails. Chance covers his nose at the smell. I slump into the desk next to hers.

Our tutoring club isn't official, it just kind of happened and turned into a regular thing. Sophomore year after school, I'd hang out in Ms. T's room to do homework while Priscilla would be at a student council meeting. One afternoon I went in to find some kids from the middle school down the street hanging around too. Apparently, they were waiting for their older siblings from Skyline to get out of practice or rehearsal and had found their way into Ms. T's room.

At the time, three sixth graders were chilling on desks, swiping away on their phones. Ms. T had been in and out of the room, and a girl named Khadijah, frustrated by the math in front of her, slammed down her pencil.

I couldn't help but notice.

"Mind if I check it out?" I asked. She'd pushed her paper toward me reluctantly. It wasn't long before I was at the whiteboard, eraser in hand, going over the basics of algebra. The two other students, Marquese and Juan, had followed Khadijah's lead, taking notes and asking questions.

Then we just kind of made it a regular thing. We began to meet on Thursdays to help one another out. Plus, I get to put this on my college app, and the kids make pretty good grades.

They may be small in size, but they are mighty in jokes and always down to dance in one of my WeTalk videos. Sometimes, if we're lucky, Ms. T brings us snacks. Other times we don't work at all, we just shoot the shit and giggle. But whatever we do, it must be working, because although eighth grade is challenging, Khadijah is top of her class, and Juan is right behind her.

Of all the things I've done at Skyline, which, okay, outside of my schoolwork isn't much, I'm most proud of this. What good is all my knowledge and learning if I can't share it with others? Yeah, my grades are stellar, and I am proud of what I've been able to accomplish, but seeing kids like me succeed, especially those that schools often push to the side, fills my soul in a way that nothing else can. I'm not going to miss my classes, I won't miss the outdated textbooks or these uncomfortable desks, but I'll miss our tutoring club. With my whole heart.

"Hot fries?" Khadijah offers up the open bag of red wonder in her hand, pulling me out of my reverie. Tempting, ever so tempting, but I shake my head. With the tumultuous afternoon my stomach has had, I don't know if I could handle any more spice. Khadijah makes a face to say "Suit yourself" and grabs two like a crab with pincers.

Priscilla blows on her nails and the strong scent of polish travels up my nostrils. I wince.

"Are you okay?" she asks, a small dent of worry forming in her brow.

I nod, doing my best to fake a grin.

Juan scribbles something on his paper and then peers up at us from his notebook. "We gotta interview high schoolers in preparation for our big transition next fall. What advice you got for us?"

"Oh yeah, good call, Juan. I haven't started either," Khadijah chimes in. "Tell us everything we need to know and keep it one hundred. What works? What doesn't?"

Priscilla is eager to speak. "Don't fall in love. Don't date in high school. Well, date, but keep it light. Don't get caught up, if you know what I mean."

Chance rolls his eyes. "I think she means to try and find a healthy balance between school and crushes." Chance makes eyes at Priscilla for approval as she nods. "But also, don't get caught up."

"You know I already got that covered. Trust," Juan says. "I've been in and out of two relationships this month, and we stayed friends after." Khadijah peers up from her paper, eyebrows arched and neck bent, a glare that means she doesn't believe him, and I'm not sure I do either, but I'm not gonna press.

There's a small window of silence, so I jump in. "I'd say stay focused. Ask questions. Get tutoring; don't be afraid to ask for help when you need it. Because we all need it. Remember who you are and where you come from. School is important, but so are you. Take care of yourself, challenge yourself, but also, love yourself in the process," I tell them as

I scan the room for nods of approval. A little cheesy, yes, but true. I wish I'd had someone to tell me these things when I started here.

"Oh, here are some more goodies." Chance leans in. "Most of the books you need to buy are free online. Use SparkNotes to help you *understand* the text, not to write the actual essay. Do not plagiarize, because that's dumb lazy and you'll end up doing double, if not triple, the work. And you will almost always get caught. If you get Mr. McDaniel for a teacher, ask to switch classes. Immediately."

The students scribble down our words.

"Dope, thanks. I'm finna get an A on this last project," Juan says, closing his notebook.

Khadijah tilts her head, her short braids framing her face. "What are we gonna do next year without y'all?"

Priscilla leans back as she closes her nail polish bottle. "You're going to keep going. You've gotta keep thriving, no matter what."

No matter what.

My eyes close and my mind travels back to freshman year, when Mr. McDaniel made me come to the front of the classroom with several other students, mostly white, to teach about affirmative action, using my body as a prop. The awkwardness of that day is imprinted in my body.

I wish I could say that was the first time I'd had a teacher ask me to do something moronic and hateful in front of the class, but it's not. It's yet another reason why I'm committed to being the best inside these school walls. I've had everyone look at me, and everyone look through me. As one of the only Black students in my honors classes, it's been mostly me having to set the bar and be a spokesperson, while also being a teenager just figuring life out.

Like in tenth grade, when Jake Longfellow started wearing a Confederate flag hat to school because . . . why, again? It took all my courage and weeks' worth of anxiety to finally ask him about it. When I did, he said something about Southern pride. Right. I pointed to the ocean, the Pacific Ocean, the one we can smell in our noses and see from all our school windows.

Or in eleventh grade, when our AP English teacher, Mr. Remington, insinuated that I plagiarized an essay. As if my genius couldn't be my own. I scored a five on the AP Literature exam just to spite him—and, okay, to remind myself of who I am and what I'm capable of.

"Annnnnnd on that note, I propose a Super Smash Bros. tournament!" Chance calls out, the bright red handheld controllers already on desks. There's a small explosion of claps and giggles. I nod, not that the group needs my approval. Quickly, everyone huddles in the front of the room, ready to play. It's so obvious from the laughter and the ease that in this moment, the group is happy.

Not everything at Skyline has been bad. I've got the perfect example right in front of me.

CHAPTER 5

AS SOON AS TUTORING ENDS AND THE STUDENTS ARE OUT OF earshot, Chance packs up his Switch and narrows his eyes on me.

"Spill it, Johnson-Sun. The tension, the teenage angst, is written all over your face."

I hesitate.

"Something's off with you. I can feel it. It's about a boy, isn't it?" Chance's eyes dart to Priscilla for some type of confirmation. Not like she would know better than him. I tell both everything, equally.

Priscilla shrugs. "That kind of droopy body language is almost always about a boy. Honestly, I don't know why y'all mess with them." Priscilla shifts in her seat, and together their eyes land on me like lasers. I wasn't aware that my countenance was so telling. Yeah, I still feel off, and if anyone could pick up on my energy, it's these two.

Chance raises his eyebrows at Priscilla. "Um, watch yourself. What would Luka Dupont think?"

Priscilla sticks out the tip of her tongue, her signature move. "Luka and me . . . it was just one night of . . . vibes, you know? Besides, that was my pre-Gina era. I don't know if it really counts."

"Luka counts," I chime in. "If you match energy with someone, why discredit it? Not to mention, you were so cheery after Luka. I think love is always a good thing, no? No matter how short-lived."

"Ugh, you're right. I was blissed out for a whole month. Luka and I were on some cosmic connection–type shit. Our romance was destined. Short, sweet, but written in the stars. Romeo and Juliet could never."

We all giggle, because Priscilla and Luka had forty-eight hours of a wild romance at some intensive weekend drama workshop in the Santa Cruz mountains. Priscilla came back a changed person, to say the least. After a moment, the room falls quiet, and my sad-face slouch is back.

"Okay, Sasha. What's up?" Priscilla asks.

I frown. "Ezra Philip Davis-Goldberg," is all I can get out, hoping I can make his government name sound menacing. When I think about him, my heartbeat starts to pick up and my body is tense again.

"What? Why? Do you like Ezra?" She stretches the last part of his name like taffy. Chance perks up.

"No, not at all. Not likeable. Not cute." I cross my arms

on my chest. Not that Priscilla asked if I thought he was cute or whatever, because he's not, but I should probably clarify regardless, right? Fine, maybe Ezra did grow into his face. And so what he finally learned to style his hair? None of that matters. Only one thing is of importance to me, and it's not his high cheekbones.

Priscilla flutters her long eyelashes at me. I don't think she believes me.

"I had chemistry with him junior year. He's chill. He's got that whole artist thing going on. Very messy-sexy. I can see how that'd charm people. You might be into it," she says.

Chance snorts. "What the hell is *messy-sexy*?"

I don't know where to begin or how to answer, so I just blurt out the most crucial information. "Hello! We are tied for valedictorian!"

"Oh no. No, no, no," Priscilla mutters. Chance rubs his chin.

I continue. "It's ridiculous, right? I knew there'd be competition, but I wasn't expecting it to be him. He doesn't care about the position or the scholarship. And here we are—tied." I could burst at the seams. "Plus he only comes to class—if he comes at all—to turn in work." I pause and catch Chance's eye.

He just shrugs. "What? I can respect that." Priscilla and I let out a simultaneous groan. Of all the students at Skyline, Chance should be in the running for valedictorian. He's smarter than me, scratch that—he's smarter than everyone (teachers included)—but he doesn't have "the drive," as admin likes to say. Chance comes and goes to class as he pleases, like school is optional instead of mandatory. Priscilla and I have tried to talk to him about, ya know, showing up more, playing the game, but according to Chance, his attendance is not up for debate.

Months before graduation and my friends know all about the scholarship. *My scholarship.* The one I've been working so hard to win. My tribute to those who've sacrificed for me to just exist. My legacy.

Chance shifts in his desk and in a calm voice asks, "What are you going to do?"

"That's the thing. I've been too upset to think. He doesn't care about any of this. Not like I do. Trust me, I know him."

"You do?" Priscilla asks. "How? You've never uttered his name. Secrets don't make friends."

I can't help but roll my eyes. "Because he's not worth mentioning." I pause, but they aren't satisfied. I let out another huff before my brain rewinds. "We went to the same elementary and middle schools. We bonded in the third grade over having long, hyphenated last names and being biracial . . . and we'd share books or whatever. You think I read a lot? You should have seen Ezra. He's a big nerd, like 'finish a book a day, write the author'–type dork. When we were young, I don't know—we just clicked, became friends or whatever, blah, blah, blah."

Priscilla unleashes excited golf claps. "Oh my gosh, shut up? That is really sweet."

"Priscilla, no! We were like eight. Who cares? I promise he's not someone you want to keep close."

"Fine. But I think it's cute that you had a friend like that as a little bun. I didn't have my first real best friend until sixth grade, and that fell apart by seventh, so, you know," Priscilla says. She leans toward me, the color draining from her face. "Wait—he's not going to replace us as your best friend, is he?"

"Are you listening to me? I hate him. We *were* friends. Like, another lifetime, a thousand years ago, Sasha version 1.0, when I didn't know any better. We cannot and will not be friends ever again." I pause as a heaviness fills my chest at recalling that part of my life. "Plus, we had such a messy falling-out."

"Why? What happened?" Priscilla asks quickly.

"You don't need to answer that," Chance says even faster, "but of course, inquiring minds want to know. Friendship breakups are taboo, but so common. I wish we talked about them more. I would bet that these types of breakups are just as traumatic as the romantic kind." He rubs his chin again, always philosophical and thoughtful.

I observe my people. My friends through thick and thin. We tell each other everything, so I let the memories of Ezra and me bubble to the surface. "It's just, he's a lot. Unreliable. Hurtful. I don't want to remember the specifics, but I think it was over a party, and he threw our friendship away."

I straighten and lift my chin, ready to deliver the one piece of info I've never gotten over. "And the worst part? He called me the b-word! To my face!"

In disappointed unison, they both gasp.

"Yeesh," Chance groans.

Priscilla flashes her nails at us. "Ugh. Thumbs down, dislike."

"Yes, exactly. Dislike," I say for emphasis.

It's shocking how fast the memories of Ezra and me flood to my brain. I hadn't thought about him, or that time in my life, in forever. And now, here they are, in full color. I see us as awkward little kids, huddled over a copy of Fullmetal Alchemist. Sometimes he'd read out loud in these ridiculous character voices that always caused us both to grab our stomachs as we giggled. He'd always save me the last cookie or chip in his lunch bag. He'd tell me to make a wish when the clock was 1:11 or 3:33. He was my first friend to get AirPods, and whenever he'd listen to music, he'd let me listen too.

This is the same person who, later, knew how to cause irreparable damage to our sacred friendship. I hear us fighting, yelling. Goose bumps flood my skin when I think about our falling-out, because no one is meaner than an angry thirteen-year-old. On that shitty breakup day, we were a special type of cruel. We knew exactly what to say to hurt each other in that fight, our one and only.

Priscilla pats my hand; I can tell she wants to hear more.

I frown. "This is so frustrating. I've had to work so hard, and I don't mean just my schoolwork. You know how difficult these spaces can be for people who look like us." Chance nods. I keep going. "To get this far and possibly be second?

31

No—hell no. I don't want to be second. That position, that scholarship—they're mine."

My eyes begin to mist when I think about who all my hard work is for. I can practically hear my dad's mom, my grandmother, her stories of struggle and sacrifice to put my father through school. They were poor, and life was never easy for her—working several jobs, raising children, existing in a world that may not have always loved or cared for her back. And then there's my father's rendition of the same story, just a generation later, the opportunities he still didn't have, the same doors that remained closed, that would probably never open for Black men. My family has never been shy about expressing our struggles. There's beauty in it all, of course, but there's also rage. I can feel that weight plus all the nonsense I've had to endure at Skyline just to survive. I think I'm about to drown in these emotions.

Priscilla's face is stone cold. "What are you going to do about it?"

Her words shock me back to life, like I'm a kid who has put her wet hands in the wall socket.

What *am* I going to do about it?

The verb *do* in English is one of my favorites. It's currently reminding me that I have agency. Is this title yours, Sasha? Or are you going to let that guy take it from you? The familiar voice, the one that gets me up in the morning, the one that pushes me to try again, the one that won't let me settle, brings me back to life.

"I'm going to beat him, take what's mine. I won't let this opportunity slip away." I lift my chin.

Priscilla nods, her earrings bouncing as she moves. She and Chance smirk. "That's our girl." She pats my arm. "And we're here to help you."

CHAPTER 6

AFTER TUTORING, PRISCILLA DROPS ME OFF AT HOME. INSIDE, there's a stillness that is comforting, no matter what kind of day I've had. Peace. As soon I cross the threshold, I kick off my shoes at the door, drop my backpack, and head straight to the kitchen. Food first, always.

"Hello? Is anybody here?" I call out, my voice bouncing off our empty off-white walls.

Our apartment is a quaint two-bedroom, one bathroom that my aunt found for my mom right after my dad died. It's like one minute you're living in a house that is big and full of life and possibility, and the next minute you're in a U-Haul, your stuff scattered in heavy brown boxes, and you're doing your best to remember where everything is, how everything fits together.

I walk through our small living room, past the old blue sofa, and turn the corner to the small but functional kitchen.

"Oh, Jesus!" I cry out.

My mom lifts her hand, and my pulse slows. I let out a shaky exhale.

"Language," she whispers, eyes shut, body relaxed.

"You almost gave me a heart attack." I stand next to her. "Didn't know you were home." She's always doing that, standing like a statue and scaring me.

The living room, next to the kitchen, is our favorite part of the house. There's a small, sturdy black bookshelf that holds the pictures of those who protect us, as my mom likes to say. My most treasured photo is a large sepia pic of my dad in the military. In it he's eighteen, like me. He's not smiling; his full lips are straight, sealed shut, like he's holding in a secret. But if you look close enough, you'll notice the magic, the twinkle in his eyes. He didn't formally graduate high school; he said he was too eager to see the world. So as soon as he turned eighteen, he got his GED, dragged my grandmother down to the army recruitment center, and joined the service, two months shy of what would've been his official high school graduation date.

"I was praying." Mom grabs my hand, her touch warm. I don't have to ask to whom because I already know. My mom is the one who is always letting the family—my dad, her parents, an uncle, and a few distant cousins—know that I've received an award, or that I've gotten good grades. She lights the candles and incense and talks to the photos and leaves out all sorts of fruit for them as offerings. Meanwhile, I study. I grind. I work hard to get the best grades, for them. For us. And if I can just focus, if I can bring home one more achievement—the valedictorian title with its scholarship—this win will be the ultimate cherry on top. Then I can attend Monterey University, the local private college. Monterey University isn't as glamorous as Stanford and it's not my dream school, NYU, but it's got strong programs, including a kick-ass data science department that I've already researched. Not to mention it's affordable, *plus* they're giving me a nice chunk of change to go there. And lastly, of course, I'll be near Mom.

"But why didn't you say anything?" I ask, trying to break her trance.

"I was praying," she repeats, unbothered.

When she's finished, she opens her eyes, examines me, and smiles. My Korean mom is barely five feet, and everything about her is quaint; delicate, even. Whereas I'm tall and lanky, like my dad. Physically, I'm just like him—his full lips, his thick black hair. But she's half of me too—my mom's eyes sit above my cheeks, and we have the same long black eyelashes, small ears, and quirky mannerisms. And something I've gotten from both of my folks is our commitment to the things and the people we love.

"You finished with work for the day?" I give her hand a small squeeze, then head into the kitchen, where I grab a coffee mug and put my phone in it. Who needs a fancy Bluetooth speaker when porcelain mugs exist? I pull up my afternoon mix, entitled Baddies O'Clock, which is lots of Billie Eilish and Olivia Rodrigo, and turn the volume low.

"Not yet. I just need a quick break before two clients'

houses. The Hawkins family started renting out their pool house, very messy. After I handle that, I'll be done for the night."

"Hungry?" I ask. She nods. "I'll cook something for us," I say. Mom hesitates, unable to hide the uncertainty on her face. I overcooked rice one time (in the rice cooker, no less, truly shameful), and she's doubted my "skills" ever since. I couldn't step in the kitchen for two whole months after the rice debacle. She's not wrong, though—I can't do much outside of boil water.

"Sit, Mommy." It's not often that she listens to me, but today she folds into the counter-height chair, and her feet dangle above the footrest. I reach inside the various brown cabinets to grab what I need. My specialty, basically the only edible dish I can put together, is good old Shin ramen, but I jazz it up like it's from an expensive restaurant. The key is the additions—kimchi, corn, eggs, green onion, and, if I'm really feeling fancy, a slice of that yellow Kraft cheesy wonder on top.

"How was school today?" my mom asks.

A simple question, but my insides twist. I give my focus to the thin stalks of green, slicing slowly, turning them into small Os. I don't know how to answer her, so I don't. I pretend I'm too deep in my task.

When I'm finished cooking, I place a bowl, a spoon, and chopsticks in front of her, then sit down across from her. I take a moment to savor the hot steam that escapes the noodles and warms my face like a sauna. I know I should wait for it to cool, but I'm impatient. My fingers twirl the noodles around the slender sticks, and I bring them to my mouth.

"So? How was it? School?"

I slurp my noodles. My tongue burns, but I don't care. I twirl more ramen, hoping to evade her question.

She blows her noodles, waiting for her food and me to cool down. I put my spoon and chopsticks on top of the bowl, the red broth stormy underneath.

This question is like a multiple-choice test. Do I:

A. Tell her my problems as they relate to Ezra;

B. Have an emotional breakdown and describe the stress of senior year—scratch that, the stress of my high school career; or

C. Pretend everything is fine?

I think . . . I will go with C. Final answer.

"It's okay. I don't know, the usual. Nothing out of the ordinary." The words almost sound convincing. I examine the table, my chopsticks, my soup—anything to avoid her eyes. "How's work?"

She mimics my movements, twirling the noodles around her chopsticks but with much more grace. "It's okay. The usual." She grins. Maybe she means it.

Mom didn't plan to clean houses forever. This work was supposed to be a layover, a short stop on the road to bigger and better things in America. She immigrated to this country, fresh off a flight from South Korea, and needed a job fast. Preferably one where her thick accent, the one that slurred the Rs and made lazy Ls, wouldn't be a problem. The Plan, also known as her dream, was to go to school, get a degree in accounting, embrace new possibilities and opportunities that only education could provide.

At first, The Plan worked. She received her GED when I was eight. After many years of my dad and me helping her with flashcards, she took the test and passed. I remember that celebration because it wasn't a birthday or an anniversary, but a reason for us to go to a fancy restaurant and order whatever we wanted. A reason to put on our nice clothes and smile at everyone: our lives were unfolding according to The Plan. We went to Sushi Time, our usual place, and I got two drinks to mark the occasion—an orange juice and a Sprite with a cherry.

Immediately after receiving her degree, she started community college. She'd work and clean houses during the day and attend school at night, as detailed in The Plan, Phase Two.

When I got a little older, I also got a job of importance. "You think you can handle this, SJ?" my dad asked me as he placed the spare silver house key in my hand. Not only could I handle taking care of myself, but I welcomed the responsibility; this would be my way of contributing to The Plan. Maybe I was a little young to be home alone from three p.m. to nine p.m., but I could practice the recorder and read fantasy and romance books in peace. I would take care of me, so they could take care of *us*. The Plan would require a little time, but in the end, The Plan would evolve into The Dream aka The Best Life Ever.

But overnight, that all changed. Everything changed. You spend all your time thinking you live in one world, only to realize you don't. Maybe you never did.

Because Dad died unexpectedly.

It was too much for my mom to take care of me, to work, and to go to school. She had to quit something, so she dropped her classes. The one thing she wanted most for her life, she gave up for mine. So yeah, the very least I can do is go to school and kick ass.

"That was yummy. You're getting good." My mom's voice brings me back to the present moment.

"Do you need help tonight?" I keep my eyes low, secretly hoping she says no. It's not uncommon for me to help her on school nights when she really needs it. But tonight, I need to prepare for tomorrow's ethnic studies seminar. Seminar points are awarded by participation, so if I can dedicate a solid chunk of time to forming my arguments, I'll be ahead for tomorrow. I can't start slipping in school, not in the eleventh hour, not with today's news. But it's already five p.m., and if my mom has two more houses to clean, it's going to be a late one for her alone.

She frowns. "No. No. I'll be all right. Will you?"

I feel a little guilty over how much relief her response brings me.

"I'll be fine. I have a lot of schoolwork anyway."

On the table, her phone buzzes, and a picture of a woman who is eerily similar to my mom, if my mom were to wear dark lipstick and have an eighties style perm with bangs, appears. Kun emo, or my mom's sister, or big aunt. I nod and my mom answers.

"Unh . . . unh . . . unh . . ." is all she says into the speaker. One word that has multiple meanings, enough to sustain a conversation with the right person. I try to pick up on something, anything really, but I can't make out Kun emo's Korean; it's too fast.

Kun emo lives in Los Angeles, where being Korean American is cool and trendy. Well, cooler than in Monterey. Whenever we visit, I marvel at how many non-Koreans chill in Koreatown, how many of them are at KBBQ, chopsticks in hands, bright red kimchi dishes on their tables, like natives. When my dad died, Kun emo begged my mom to move to LA. She said there'd be better job opportunities for my mom, better for us to be around more Koreans. But my mom never budged. *There's more family here,* Kun emo said, referring to my mom and their two sisters.

Two years ago, Kun emo tried to get my mom and me to move to Los Angeles for the millionth time under new, more alluring circumstances. She was opening a dessert café with boba named after famous actors and cake slices that cost fifteen dollars (Yes! Fifteen!) and changing weekly decor. Without consulting me, my mom gave her a firm no. When I questioned her about why she was so intent on staying here, she said that she and Dad had planned to move to Monterey so they could retire by the beach, as a part of "The Plan," the ultimate, final phase.

But now, Kun emo's café is so popular she's opened another location, this time in a fancier part of town, charging more for her desserts. And people are paying. Scratch that—people are lining up around the corner to visit her café. My mom's housecleaning business? Maybe not so much.

My mom hangs up the phone and gently pats my hand.

"Emo says she and the other aunties got tickets for graduation. She said she's excited for you and your speech." Her eyes glisten. "We're proud of you, you know that, right?" My head bobs as I chew the inside of my cheek. *The valedictorian speech.*

Mom clears her throat and stares at the clock on the microwave, then at the dishes, and then back at me.

I know this look; a clean kitchen is her sanctuary. "Don't worry. I'll do them," I say. She pushes her bowl forward and then begins to get up. "Anything else you need?"

"No. I think this will do. Thanks, honey." She takes a big gulp of water. "Oh, actually, can you grab my black coat from the hallway? The nights are starting to get so chilly."

I glide to the closet, and there I can't help but notice one thing: a bulky floral backpack from her time in school, her textbooks probably still inside. It sits in the back, next to a broken golf umbrella and a tennis racket from two failed lessons (Dad thought I could be the next Serena Williams before he learned of my irrational fear of flying yellow balls). This is the place where the things we can't bring ourselves

42

to throw away end up, waiting for us to someday rediscover their usefulness, waiting to be reminded that they exist. I hesitate before reaching for her coat.

Maybe she can't attend school anymore, but I can. Maybe she doesn't have the chance, but I do. This small bump—Ezra—won't knock me off course.

I pass her the old black coat. "Don't work too hard," I say as she gives me a quick kiss goodbye.

Then I gather my backpack and my phone, and I go to my room to get ready for battle.

♡♡♡

My mom comes home around ten p.m. and lets herself into my room as I'm watching a YouTube video on gentrification and redlining in California. I've read the articles from class a million times and have made at least two million color-coded annotations. I find myself so immersed in this history and how it affects the present. Redlining shows us how the government created areas within cities that they deemed "safe" to insure mortgages for people to buy homes. Oftentimes, the Black neighborhoods were colored red, meaning they were too "risky" to insure mortgages, or to let Black folks buy houses. I'm confident in the material, but I end up falling down a rabbit hole. The issues facing my people aren't just gentrification and redlining. Now it's asthma. Specifically, the link between redlining and asthma disproportionately affecting communities of color. I jot down more information in the margin of my notebook. Why aren't we talking about these connections in class?

"You need a break," Mom says near me.

"Soon. I'm almost done," I say.

Midnight comes, and I take a dance break to help clear my mind. I'm not ashamed to admit I learn all the WeTalk dances the second they drop. I become obsessed with watching professional dance videos, mimicking the movements as best I can, and after thirty minutes of clicking end up on the Alvin Ailey American Dance Theater official account. I'm captivated by the company's skill, grace, and dedication. They began performing in 1958, a group of talented Black dancers on the road, trying to leave their mark. Unlike other dance companies that were white focused, Alvin Ailey created a sanctuary for Blackness and Black dancers. Since that first tour, the company has become one of the most popular and most important in the world. In fifth grade, we went to a show for a field trip during Black History Month, and my obsession with dancing began. To this day, dancing is my way to let go and regroup when words in a textbook begin to blur.

Sensing that my solo dance party has ended, Mom comes into my room with a plate of peeled oranges and an apple cut into small bits shaped like lips, grapes, and a spoon full of peanut butter. If tidying is her respite, nourishment is her love language. We don't speak. Instead, I accept the colorful plate and smile.

It's late, but I'm feeling reenergized and need just a teensy bit more studying. Ten more minutes. No, okay, fifteen, tops.

At one in the morning, my eyes start to sag, and my eyelids get heavy. *Keep going,* I tell myself. I do ten quick jumping jacks to get my blood flowing again. At my desk, I drink water and let my mom's fruit fuel me for another thirty minutes.

Then I stand in front of my mirror and say, "Respectfully, I disagree." I know it's a simple phrase, but it's a powerful one, especially in prepping for class discussions. And tomorrow I'm not letting anyone, or anything, get in my way.

Especially Ezra Philip Davis-Goldberg.

I devour the last of the oranges before falling asleep a little before two a.m.

CHAPTER 7

THE FOG WRAPS ME IN A COOL BLANKET AS I WAIT OUTSIDE OUR apartment complex for Priscilla to pick me up. I love the way Monterey feels in the morning—misty and fresh, with a tinge of horror movie vibes, like that moment right before something goes wrong. But the fog always burns off, and sunshine always breaks through.

Although I went to bed late last night, I got up early this morning, taking the time to make sure I'm my best self for today's seminar. Look good, feel good, perform good. I'm in my favorite black skinny jeans and a black T-shirt with a purple-and-white cropped tie-dye hoodie on top. Unlike yesterday when I felt like a mess, this morning I took the time to re-twist my locs and put my hair in a high bun. I even put on some makeup—a little bit of blush, some mascara, and eyeliner. I tried to do a somewhat decent winged eyeliner, but I'm horrible at that. So after the third attempt, I decide on a basic fill—your girl is back and feeling good.

I hear Priscilla's techno music before seeing Golden Girl, her faded gold VW Beetle, turn the corner and stop in front of me.

"Morning, sunshine!" Priscilla says as I slide into the back seat.

"Morning, best friends!" I say. "I love it when we are all together in the a.m.! Totally starts my day off right."

"You two are way too chipper this morning," Chance says as he grabs my hand and squeezes as a hello from the passenger seat.

"I'll go to one class before heading downtown. I need to get a passport." He winks. Chance has been talking about a European excursion all senior year. There was a short time in life when he thought he might take classes at the local community college, but he decided against it. He "wants the world to be his teacher," so he's starting with a one-way flight to Europe, a passport, and a backpack, with the intention of visiting as many countries as possible before moving on to the next continent. I envy him.

"I'm excited for you. It's all happening so soon," Priscilla chirps, and I nod in agreement.

The heater is on full blast, so I open my hoodie, doing my best to adjust to the temperature. Priscilla sips something from a bright yellow Starbucks mug. I put my seat belt on and take out my offering, akin to gas money.

"I made breakfast, a sandwich. My specialty—egg, ham, and cheese."

"Oooh. Someone's on overdrive." She grabs the steering wheel; the car takes off.

I nod my head. "Umm, yeah—I plan to crush seminar today."

Priscilla flashes me a goofy smirk, likely a mirror of my own, while taking a sharp right turn, and the car tires kiss the curb just a bit. I unwrap the sandwich and try to fit it into her free hand.

"You're so sweet, but I can't." Priscilla takes another swig of her beverage. My face curls up in shock. Our relationship is practically built on three Cs: carbs, chocolate, and cheese.

"What do you mean, you can't?"

"I'm a vegan now," she says.

I snort. "You're a vegan now? Since when?"

"Since yesterday." She smirks and raises one eyebrow high as we all laugh. Priscilla's long brown hair is lightly curled today and bounces around as she shimmies in her seat, her upper body dancing to some Bad Bunny in the background. She's made it her signature to always wear fun makeup, like ridiculously long eyelashes or bright eyeliner. Her nails, which are always done, now have gold glitter on top of yesterday's red. And on each of her fingers is a ring of some sort, mostly thin gold bands, but today I notice a purple crystal and a mood ring.

Chance is in his quintessential Chance uniform: a vintage T-shirt of an obscure band, dark blue jeans, and his black slip-on Vans. If he's feeling quirky, he'll wear colored tube socks, but I don't see any, so it must be a basic Thursday.

Of the three of us, Priscilla's style is loudest, but we all balance each other.

"I'll take it," Chance says, his hands already on the sandwich.

"So, I was thinking about your situation," Priscilla says. We bounce as the car rolls over something I'm sure she could have avoided. Chance and I know better than to remind Priscilla of stationary objects as she drives. Riding with her feels like we are in a game of Mario Kart. I have my license but no whip, so until something major happens, like Mom wins the lotto, free rides in the Kart with Princess Peach it is.

"Okay, P. Keep going," I say, watching the outside world wake up.

"We need to know exactly who and what we're dealing with."

"Pardon?" I call out as we drive past the wharf and the various piers, the ocean waves spraying against the rocks.

"You knew Ezra as a kid, big deal. But yeah, you've both changed. We all have. What are we working with now? Who exactly is this person? And what is he capable of? How much do we *really* know? We need intel, like in those true crime documentaries."

"Like . . ." *Huh?*

Chance turns to me. "Reconnaissance work. P failed to mention that this was my idea."

I frown. "Recon? For what?"

His head peeks between the front and back seats. "Have you not read *The Art of War*? You need to get on that. It's legendary."

Priscilla's eyes dart to mine in the rearview mirror. "Wasn't that required reading sophomore year?"

"No," Chance and I say in unison. Priscilla lets out a giggle.

I relax my face. "I guess it's not a terrible idea. What exactly—"

The moment the light turns red, the car rolls over the crosswalk line to a stop and Priscilla tosses two large ziplock bags to me and Chance. They are fluffy, like an oversized marshmallow.

Chance is faster than me at opening his. "Oh no. Not these again." He frowns, holding up a black beret, matching scarf, and cat-eye sunglasses with fake diamonds on the side. Sophomore year Priscilla and her family went to Paris for spring break, and she came back with berets for me and Chance, plus an additional thirty just in case. I wore mine every day for a month as homage to that beautiful city. Instead, everyone at school thought I was imitating the Black Panthers. Especially when I raised my hand.

Priscilla leans into the steering wheel, her foot heavy on the gas as we take off again. "Rule one. We can't go on this mission in regular clothes, we need a disguise."

"You really think this is gonna hide who I am?" Chance flexes his arm muscles. He has a point.

"Hear me out," Priscilla says. "We'll ask to use the restroom and meet on the D side of the building ten minutes into every class, in our gear. Then, we'll pass by Ezra's classes, see what we can uncover. Where does he sit? What does he do? What is he about?"

Just the mention of his name makes me huff. "That sounds like a lot of work."

"And how does that help her win? I don't understand the connection," Chance says as we approach school grounds.

We sit in silence for a moment, and before we know it, Priscilla parks the car in the lot and we slide out, backpacks on. Within several feet we are lined up, in our formation, from tallest to shortest. I'm in the middle.

I give it a little thought. "Nah. He's not worth the energy," I say to the group, but mostly to myself.

"Your loss," Priscilla lets out. Her hands rush to cover her mouth. "I mean, not a loss, you know what I mean. It's a saying that we could, you know . . ." She's trying to find a way to erase her words; she's the superstitious type, not wanting to put anything negative in our space.

"I know what you're saying, and I appreciate your help, it's just not gonna happen. Win or lose, I know I'll be good. But I'm going to do what I've been doing and just . . . beat him. Besides, we have one class together, and he's rarely in it. And when he does come, he just sits there, zoned out." I pause and shake my head. I can't lie and say that the idea of losing hasn't crossed my mind. I thought about what it would mean to take an "L" last night before drifting off to sleep. Yeah, I'd be fine without the scholarship, Monterey University's financial aid package is generous. But life with the scholarship? Now, that's something to dream about. With the scholarship, I could afford to get a new laptop—I've had my current once since middle school—and maybe I wouldn't have to take on a campus job. I could enjoy freshman year at Monterey more. I could save a little money. The scholarship would be a nice safety net, ya know, for when life inevitably turns up the heat.

Priscilla's eyebrow is arched high; Chance cocks his head. I stand up straight.

"Seriously, I'm fine. I've got this. He's all right, but I'm better. Trust me," I say, turning toward class before either can respond.

CHAPTER 8

WHEN I ENTER FIRST PERIOD, I ALMOST TRIP OVER MYSELF. IT'S HIM.

Ezra's in class . . . before me? He's . . . here?

He's never on time. But right now, he's bright-eyed and bushy-tailed, sitting on top of his desk with a pencil tucked in his curls. As if this is the most normal thing in the world.

He must have some type of Spidey sense, because he turns, and we catch each other's eyes, and then his lips split in a grin. Ezra waves and pulls the pencil from his hair, his curly black strands falling out of place as he gives his head a small toss, like he's in a freaking shampoo commercial. He's trying to be cute! I bite my lip, ignoring a small giggle that wants to escape.

"Okay, to your seats. Let's get this show started," Ms. T commands. "Who would like to begin?" she asks, her clipboard and pen ready to go. We all scramble to a desk.

I raise my hand, but Ezra blurts out first, his voice strong, "I got it, Ms. T."

Ms. T nods, and Ezra begins.

"So, this unit has been about redlining and gentrification, right? But a lot of these articles leave out one big piece, in my opinion, and that's intersectionality. I think we'd be remiss if we didn't frame these topics with that in mind. Environmental racism is affecting communities of color disproportionately—there's a link, an overlap. These are not just single-subject issues; they are all intertwined. The sooner we start addressing them as such, especially as the neighborhoods around us change so rapidly, the better we'll be. I mean, just research how fast Seaside is changing. Hell, even Los Angeles, or the Bay Area. I don't recognize these cities anymore. They're the perfect example of gentrification before our eyes."

"But neighborhood change is good." Without fail, Stacey Clemens jumps in for the retort, like she's some pundit on Fox News. "Besides, it's not like people lived there before. You make it sound like—"

Hello! Of course there were! My chest tightens and I lean forward, ready to speak. My brain revs up, and I give it a try. "Yes, actually I . . ." But my voice is meek. I know what I want to say, but my mouth is stuck, full of peanut butter. Something about hearing Ezra has poked a hole in my plan. This never happens. I am normally way better than this. I lock eyes with Alicia Martin, the other Black girl in the room. We communicate to one another silently, like "Who's gonna tell them? You or me?" But before either of us can, that deep voice pipes up again.

"It's absurd to think that these neighborhoods never had residents before," Ezra says, right on beat. The confidence in his voice bounces in our circle. "There were people that created flourishing, rich neighborhoods, probably because they were denied access to common suburbs. Then, these same people got priced out or driven out of the same neighborhoods they helped build, because some developer thinks the location is hot. And let's be real, we're primarily talking about people of color."

"So what? People can't move?" Stacey answers back. "Neighborhoods can't change? What about economic growth? I don't know if I agree that it's *always* race related—change seems to be a part of the natural progression of societies, ours included."

Ezra leans back in his chair but shakes his head. Ms. T scribbles on her clipboard, letting the discussion evolve. Ezra's voice, his presence, is messing with my head. His ideas are like academic adrenaline—I'm not used to having to deal with any more than a random chime-in from him. This—this is brand-new. His contributions to the discussion are . . . *good.*

"Respectfully, I disagree with Stacey," I say just like I rehearsed, resting my elbows on the table. The words from last night blur in my brain. Okay, but why do I disagree? Follow it up. *Think, Sasha, think.*

Stacey tilts her head, as if she's preparing to fire back. The eyes in the circle shift to me, but nothing comes. The room goes quiet for a beat.

"Why do you disagree, Sasha?" Ms. T asks.

"I—I just do," I answer, still fumbling for a good argument. *Yeesh.*

"I got this, Sasha," Ezra says, spotting an opening. He gives me a thumbs-up. Several students snort and chuckle.

I shrink in my seat. The voice I thought I had, the one I practiced with, is gone. Vanished. Disappeared.

All I hear is Ezra. Ezra. Ezra. Every time someone poses a question, or tries to rebut, Ezra's there. He speaks over two students twice. He's got statistics like he's Siri. Ms. T asks a question to the group that I should be able to answer in my sleep, but it's intercepted by—guess who? Ezra. He calls Tommy out after Tommy complains about reverse racism. Ezra delivers a small lecture on the topic, taking the words out of my mouth. Except they aren't my words. They are just my thoughts.

It doesn't take long before I'm rubbing my clammy hands on my thighs, my jeans chafing against my skin. I don't recognize myself. I've never been this tongue-tied in class.

I try my best to get it together, but before I can utter a word, the bell blares, and the intensity of the room dissolves. That's a wrap on today's seminar.

"Okay, everyone. Great job, good work today. Especially you, Ezra. Nice to have you so involved." Ms. T beams.

Ezra takes his time exiting the classroom, like he's waiting for me. I stomp over to him, but he turns his broad shoulder when I'm inches away. He takes two quick steps toward the door, and I hurry to catch up with him.

"Hey, hey! Ezra," I say. Finally, my voice is back.

Ezra pivots to face me, but he doesn't speak. A silent standoff.

Here I go.

"What the hell was that?"

CHAPTER 9

WE WALK INTO THE HALLWAY AS A MISCHIEVOUS GRIN SPREADS on Ezra's face, like the Grinch right before he steals Christmas.

"What do you mean?" he asks.

"You know what I'm talking about. What were you doing in there?"

Ezra chews his bottom lip, revealing a prominent dimple on his left cheek.

I sigh, glancing away. Dimples have been known to weaken my judgement.

"This is school, and that in there was class. I was participating. You should try it sometime." The sarcasm in his voice burns my skin.

"I—I know what this is—"

"Where's your head at, SJ? You better get it together if you want to be valedictorian." He lets out a little laugh.

My eyes widen. "Oh my god—you're doing this on purpose." The realization is cold and shocking, like that time Priscilla dared me to jump into the ocean one night.

Ezra pauses, making me wait a thousand years for his response. "Uh, yeah. I guess I am. With more intention, anyway. You know, I usually don't think too hard about school, but finding out that I'm on the verge of becoming valedictorian kind of inspired me. An increase in effort could be worth my time. Plus, you are a worthy adversary." Ezra fiddles with his camera, and my heartbeat begins to pick up. A *worthy adversary*? He hits a button, and a hissing sound fills the silence. "Also, talk about the scholarship. Now, that's a nice bag. The Doc will be pleased."

"Your dad?" I ask.

"Uh-huh. Guess who was also—"

"Valedictorian?" I take the word from Ezra's mouth. My chest tightens. Ezra's dad, Dr. Davis, is the first and only doctor I know personally. He's a brilliant surgeon, one of the youngest to graduate from medical school. I knew he went to Skyline too, but I had no idea he was class valedictorian. But, duh. Of course he was; he's number one in everything he does. Dr. Davis is the prototype for Black excellence and achievement. Suddenly it all begins to add up.

"Bingo," Ezra says in a flat voice. I can see Ezra's father's office now—the many degrees on the wall framed in heavy, brown wood; the energy of the space—academic yet still personal. Sometimes his dad would come home from the hospital and tell us awe-inspiring stories of the day's operations. Other times he'd bring mystery samples and let us explore them using his microscopes, prodding us with questions about what we saw and what we could infer. He made learning feel like this fun, exciting experience. Meanwhile, Ezra's mom is a classically trained pianist and opera singer. My young mind absorbed so much at Ezra's house—it was always the perfect mix of science, music, math, art, and entertainment.

Ezra nods. "Yeah, this will get my dad off my case and satisfy my mom since I didn't apply to a traditional college or art school. Or anywhere, for that matter." He chuckles to himself and then fiddles with his camera again.

Ezra is speaking, but his words don't make sense. Is that laugh for real? He's didn't apply to college . . . his parents care but he doesn't . . . what?

"The title's mine!" I screech, realizing none of Ezra's business is my concern.

Ezra makes a smug face, his lips forming into a half smile as he lets out a soft tsk. "I hate to mansplain here, but technically, at this very moment, the title belongs to no one, we just happen to be tied. So really, it's anyone's prize. Including mine." There it is—the one-two punch. If this were a boxing match, it would be the blow that would knock me dizzy, almost end me. I can practically see stars. Everything begins spinning beneath me, blurry.

But I get back up.

I swallow hard and close my eyes. Think, brain. Say something, do something.

"Let's settle this between us, right now. Whoever got

the highest SAT score, how about that? We can tell Newton we've figured it out, and there doesn't need to be a tie. He'll be happy we settled this for him, save him some trouble," I rattle off. Good, good. I crushed the SAT, which I better have, considering all the time, energy, and money I put into that damn test. I sold candy bars all sophomore year and recycled cans from summer festivals at the fairgrounds to pay for that overpriced prep class tuition.

Ezra presses his face to the back of his camera and points the long lens up toward the ceiling. *Click.* He stands on his toes, finding something worthy to capture that I just don't see. *Click. Click.*

"No can do," he says, his eye in the viewfinder while his hand adjusts the lens.

"Why not?"

"Didn't take it." His voice is nonchalant.

Click.

Dammit!

"You didn't take the SAT? What about the ACT? Why not?" My voice is high and scratchy. Ezra just shrugs like I've asked him something mundane about the weather.

I frown. "You're kidding, right? The counselors and teachers pushed them so hard on us—"

"I'm sorry, are they mandatory? Are they required to be valedictorian? Besides, you don't even need them to get into some colleges. They won't define me. And don't get me started on the financial aspect of those stupid tests—practically a Ponzi scheme. What a joke."

All I can do is gawk at him. I know we haven't spoken in years, besides yesterday, but this doesn't sound like him. Every senior I know is wildly excited about leaving home and starting a new chapter in their lives. Whether they are moving to a new state, or moving to a new country, or simply moving out of their parent's house, everyone's eager for what's up next. Or if they aren't going to college, they're motivated to start working full-time, to have their own money, to be free from the shackles of high school, eager to plan their days doing what they want, when they want, how they want. I'm not making this up; the energy is palpable, you can't ignore it—the senior year buzz.

Around us, a second bell rings. We are officially late to class. Then an idea pops into my brain.

"I'll bet you for it," I say.

"Excuse me?" He lowers his camera, letting the gadget hang around his neck, and his face gets pensive; his eyebrows pinch together.

My brain hasn't fully processed my words, but I can't back down. I tilt my neck from side to side. My feet are suddenly light in my shoes. I can do this. Float like a butterfly, sting like a bee.

There's a spark in my throat, and my legs are strong, rooting me. "You heard me. I'll bet you for it. The position, the scholarship, everything. Otherwise, we'll remain tied like we are now. Let's take matters into our own hands and settle this."

I can practically hear the calculations running through

Ezra's mind as his eyes dart back and forth. System processing, challenge loading.

"You want to bet for the title? *You?*"

"Yeah, you heard me. The title, the scholarship, all of it."

Ezra rubs his chin. "I call bullshit. There's no way you'd do that. You're too . . ." Ezra steps to me, his face near mine, and I notice the small brown freckles scattered on his cheeks, the deep brown of his eyes. My heart beats faster and I can feel my temperature rise. I can't help but watch his mouth as he speaks. He licks his bottom lip. "What's the word? You're too . . ." His voice is smooth like a late-night radio DJs, but I don't let it charm me.

"I'm serious. I'd rather lose than be tied with you."

He steps back, and whatever energy was building between us is gone.

"Why would I want to bet? I could just show out in class like I did today. How would the bet be any different?"

Ugh. It's a good question and a bad reminder of my blunder in first period. I haven't gotten that far, but I need Ezra out of my way.

"This is different because, um, the loser will throw—I'm talking C range—an agreed-upon assignment. Like, totally flop on an essay or whatever." My stomach drops. Ask for extra credit, yes. Attend office hours, obviously. But intentionally do badly? Throw an assignment? That doesn't compute. But I can't let him call my bluff, so I lift my chin and stand up straight.

Ezra licks his lips and that dimple returns.

"Make it D range, like completely tanks, goes to the depths of hell, visits Hades and never returns to this here dimension."

Yeesh, okay, take it easy. I pull at my collar, stretching my already loose T-shirt.

"Fine, D range. Best two out of three wins it all. Loser makes sure to *lose*." I puff up my chest even though my armpits begin to sweat. What would happen if I got a D? No, I couldn't get a D, could I? Teachers would know that something was off, right? They'd let me redo an assignment, certainly. . . .

Ezra interrupts my thoughts. "Beautiful. I love it. No sharing the title, no collaborating. We can end this contest . . . swiftly." His voice sounds almost sinister, with a tone I've never heard from him. Maybe Priscilla was right. Maybe I should have done some reconnaissance work.

"I'm ready," I say, squaring my shoulders. Ezra starts to speak, but I jump back in. "This is how it's going to happen: Whoever scores highest on each assignment wins that bet. Best two out of three. The defeated will bow out and give up their pursuit of valedictorian."

Ezra rubs his chin. "I'm game. I'll let you suggest the first bet."

"First bet is our *Hamlet* essay."

He doesn't blink. "The one that's due tomorrow?"

I nod.

"She wastes no time." He smirks. "Young Hammy of Denmark? Easy. Too easy."

I just roll my eyes. "Deal?"

"Deal."

Ezra lifts his broad shoulders before speaking. "My turn. The second bet is our civics presentation in two weeks," he says.

"Great. I'm not worried." I tie a knot in my T-shirt behind my back, a sliver of skin now visible. Ezra's eyes lower, stealing a view of my stomach. I can't process that because civics is my lowest grade. A 96, I think. Okay, so not like failing low, but you know. Lower than I'd like. It's not my best subject, but I make do.

He leans in and bats his long eyelashes. "You sure? I would be a little bit worried if I were you." Is that sympathy in his face? Or is he being cocky?

"Pfft," I say. "That's two bets. Which I'll win, and we won't need a third."

"You can only hope to get that far, SJ," Ezra says.

"On the off chance you survive, the third and final bet can be—" I pause, unsure of what else to wager.

"To spice up Senior Legacy Night with some type of challenge?" he blurts out.

"No!" I shout. Confusion covers Ezra's face. If I was playing it cool and confident before, I may have just blown my own cover.

Goose bumps sprout on my arms. Senior Legacy Night is

a big deal for our school—the administration rents out space downtown, we're expected to dress up, alumni and parents are allowed to come and witness us declare our futures through our legacy presentations. Our last hurrah before graduation. The project is intended to be tender and a little emotional. We're asked to examine our lives, where we've been, and where we are going. And most importantly, we must think about our legacy, what we want to leave behind at Skyline. I've attended every Legacy Night since I've been at school here, and it's always a big adrenaline rush. Even though seniors tend to complain about doing the work during the school year, the actual night of the event is super inspiring, with folks speaking their dreams into the universe, hopeful. I want to follow in those footsteps.

Only Priscilla and Chance know this, but I've planned to dedicate my senior legacy project in honor of my father, specifically, dedicating valedictorian and this prestigious scholarship, which I know I'm going to get, to him. I'm claiming the win. My legacy, what I come from and where I'm going, they're all intertwined in this award. My grades, my life, my family—all one intricate web of being. When I cross the graduation stage, it's not just me. I'll be taking my family with me; this is our award. To be a literal first in *my* family, and in more ways than one. But I can't tell Ezra this now; he wouldn't understand. If anything, he'd just discover my Achilles' heel and use it against me.

"The third bet should be, um . . . something like . . . ," I start, still searching for an alternative.

Ezra scans my face, and I hold my stance to keep my composure.

He closes the gap between us. "I think I get you. You want to do something non-academic to break the tie, is that it?"

What? I haven't wrapped my mind around the possibility of there being *another* tie.

"No, that's not exactly what I was going to say. I just don't think we need to decide bet three right now. I'm already late for class," I mutter.

He lets out a little chuckle, like he's slightly annoyed. "Fine. No need to decide that now. And honestly, I doubt we'll get that far. Two ties? Don't think so," Ezra says. His words are calm and confident, while my knees feel a little unsteady. I wince, trying to remember if he's always been this self-assured.

He holds up a finger.

I lift my eyebrows. *What now?*

"Though we do need a pièce de résistance, if you will." Ezra tilts his head, and a new idea clearly pops into it. "I think the winner of each individual bet should get *a thing* if they win," he says. I narrow my eyes.

"A thing? The winner gets the scholarship."

"Yeah, duh, but I think the winner of each round—for example, the English essay—deserves a small prize. I mean, someone will have earned it, right?"

"Like, what?" I press my lips together. I hadn't thought this far ahead, and here Ezra is, layered, calculated.

"Hmm . . . I could probably use a scribe for a day, or someone to carry my books around, or someone to fan me and feed me grapes at lunch, something like that." Ezra flashes a flirty grin. A strength from deep inside helps me resist this new, lame attempt at charm.

He nods to himself, pleased. "The winner would get help with one activity of their choice, max three-hour time commitment." That mischievous grin reappears on his face.

"Three hours?" I yelp. That could mean the loss of valuable work time.

Skrrt. I need a time-out, maybe a pro-con list, something to help me think before I answer. I hate making decisions just on the fly like this. I feel reckless around him, and I don't like it.

"You want the bets? I want this extra provision. It's the art of negotiation," he says. He must want me to back down.

He obviously doesn't know me now either. "Sure, Ezra. Sounds great."

Ezra directs his gaze at me, so strong and heavy I think I can feel the electricity in his brain transmit to mine. I want to turn away, but I can't.

"So we have a deal? Winner of the first bet can claim his—"

"Or her," I jump in.

"Right. Winner of the first bet can claim his or *her* prize after the scores are in."

Ezra extends one of his large hands. I'm having an out-of-body experience as I shake it. His touch is warm, and I let him hold on a little longer than necessary. I feel a little floaty. His gaze too is steady, observant. He's searching for something in me, but I'm not sure what. After another lengthy moment, he breaks our grip and runs a hand through his hair, then flashes a smile. My legs wobble when I take a step back, and I attempt to shake off whatever that was.

I savor one last view of him as he fiddles with his camera and then flings it on his back like a professional. And at the same time, it's like I'm staring into a split mirror. I see eight-year-old Ezra, the one who loved meatless chick'n nuggets, who would secretly read anime in class, who was a math whiz and terrible at the recorder. The one who used to be my best friend.

Until we became enemies.

I adjust my backpack, then say with total seriousness, "You know, you're going to regret betting against me, Ezra Philip Davis-Goldberg."

CHAPTER 10

AFTER THE FINAL BELL RINGS AND SCHOOL RELEASES US FROM ITS tight grip, I head to my absolute favorite spot—the school library. Once my right foot crosses its threshold, my jaw loosens and my shoulders drop. Yes, right. Hello. There is balance in the world, and it can be found here.

"Hiya, Sasha," Mrs. Maka, our librarian, calls from behind the counter. She flashes me a bright smile, and I mirror her reaction. Mrs. Maka is this dope young librarian who is always recommending new books for me to check out or talking to me about the importance of libraries and historical archives.

"Is this okay?" I ask, but I'm already walking toward the back corner of the room, to my treasured desk, an old, wide, wooden thing where I can spread out my books, notebooks, and Post-its, and my left hand can be free to write without worry of falling off the edge of the table.

"Of course, it's okay," she says. "But only until five.

Five-fifteen at the latest. Then we both need to go and have lives outside of these walls."

I nod. It's three-thirty now. There's a lot of damage that I can do in an hour and a half. The Skyline Library isn't anything special, but I like to hang out here because most students don't. The back room is lined with outdated computers that students are always playing games on or switching the keys on the keyboards. It has chunky, black printers that often work, but never on the days when you need to turn in an assignment. Above all, there are lots and lots of books.

Shout-out to the architect of this building because to me, the best thing, the thing that doesn't get enough credit is the large, expansive windows that make up the far wall. On a clear day, you can see the whole bay, all the way to Santa Cruz. On a foggy one, you're immersed in an enchanted forest, floating in the clouds. Beautiful either way.

I take several steps toward my table and then: "You've got to be kidding me," I mumble under my breath. I pause, unsure of what to do next, though my body weight is already shifting on my heels, like I should back up and go.

Ezra turns around, his black camera in hand. "Go ahead, there's enough space, I don't mind." His head tilts, pointing to the table. *My table.* I scan the library, sitting at another desk just feels like betrayal; the other ones are too small. Plus, that's bad energy, right? I've done some of my best work in this spot. If I start changing things up last minute, what might happen?

Fine.

Without another thought, I grab the chair across from Ezra on the farthest end, which is still too close.

He holds the camera, shuts one eye, and *click,* snaps a picture.

I ignore him and dig into my backpack, pulling out all I need for this session. I take a moment to set up, sensing his gaze still on me. I place my headphones on the table, just in case I need to escape a conversation.

I clear my throat. "I always sit here, this is the largest table, so—"

"Left-handed things. Gotcha." He takes a photo, and I shy away.

"Why— What are you doing here?" I ask, trying to prevent another impromptu pic. Out of habit, my pen twirls in my hand, looping in circles like a figure eight.

"This just happens to be my second favorite place on campus." Ezra's voice is cheerful. "I was just thinking about how incredible libraries are. Like the backbone of a great society, ya know? Where else can you go, chill, read a book for free, and not be expected to buy anything? Straight anti-capitalist vibes."

I can't help myself, so I add on. "You're not wrong. But why aren't there more taco trucks at libraries? Or maybe a café in the back of the building? Not a lot of food, just nibbles. Doesn't have to be pricey, but you know, snacks." I get hungry using all my brain power.

"Now you're describing a bookstore with a cafe. But the

taco truck thing—that has potential." He sounds sincere, which makes me grin.

So I add, "I kinda feel like taco trucks attached to anything is—"

"Fucking epic? Should I get out a piece of paper, and we can write up a business plan? Like we used to do, back in the day? We can call it Textbook Tacos!"

We both let out a relaxed laugh. Ezra holds my gaze the entire time, reminding me that, oh yeah, we used to bullshit like this—casually, freely, without any judgement. The sun pours in through the window, and the diamond in his ear is sparkling.

He leans in and his long arms reach across the tabletop, and I can't help but notice his hands. His fingers are slender, and his nails are trimmed like he just had a manicure or something.

"Remember when you thought you invented—" he starts.

"Aht, aht, stop right there. How was I supposed to know . . ." I cover my face with my hands. I know what Ezra's gonna bring up, and it's downright embarrassing. I guess I've forgotten how silly— how *ridiculous* we were as kids. Well, I was the silly one. He was more serious. Funny how things change.

"You thought I forgot, didn't you?" Ezra arches his eyebrows.

I don't know what I thought, honestly. I haven't thought much about Ezra except for—

"Ez, you ready?" A voice cuts in, loud and self-assured.

I drop my hands into my lap, suddenly embarrassed. I'm not sure why. Kerry Patterson stands behind Ezra and rests one hand on his broad shoulder, all formal and oddly possessive. He doesn't flinch, so I keep a straight face too, even though the moment is strange.

Kerry is not really an enemy, not really a friend. Since freshmen year, we've had way too many classes together, never really understanding one another. Which is fine, I know I won't get along with everyone, but it's still a little uncomfortable knowing that someone may actively dislike you.

Ezra stands up, and the camera twirls around his torso. "Taco trucks, SJ. Taco trucks." He pushes in his chair, and they walk away together.

I tap my finger on top of my notebook, remembering how Ezra and I used to hang. But then I shake away any brewing thoughts and remember why I came here, and it has nothing to do with taco trucks.

I check the clock—I have just enough time to tighten up my *Hamlet* essay and add to my legacy project. I put my phone on Do Not Disturb and dive into the big questions. For me, legacy is simple: legacy is how I honor my family, the work I do now to make my family proud. Yes, I know I'll dedicate the scholarship and award to my family, but the other legacy questions loom over me—I don't want to make a mistake. I think more about the prompts attached to the assignment.

What defines you?

Think about who you want to be in the future.

Your future is up to you, what does it look like?

What stands out as the biggest learning experience you've had in high school?

The questions stare back at me, expecting an answer that I don't quite have. I know the biggest defining moments in my life so far—the way life can change unexpectedly, the way a world can get shaken up, like a snow globe, in an instant.

Nothing. Okay, then, next question.

What does my future look like?

That's easy. Bachelor's, master's, doctorate in data science, so school, school, and more school. I'm good at fact-based, data-driven decision-making. I also want to help my mom and my family as best as I can. Make them proud.

I sigh. Not because I don't want to help them, because I do, but because . . . What else can I say about the future? A small voice calls out to me: *I . . . I don't know.* What else is there to do in my life? Do people just go around knowing this?

I exhale sharply.

This isn't going so well. Let's change it up.

I check my watch again. Shoot. I don't have much time left. This hasn't been as productive as I'd anticipated. I stand and stretch, blood rushing to my legs. I wobble, then head to the front of the library to ask Mrs. Maka about some of the readers and resources for Mr. Mendoza's class.

Hopefully, she has a few minutes to spare and I can run through a few ideas with her. Our civics presentation is to research and analyze how civic engagement can be seen as social justice. I'm doing something a little off the beaten path and want to incorporate the fundamentals of civics and philosophy. But I need more information to bring it all together.

"Mrs. Maka?" I ask in my sweetest voice.

She tilts her head. "Ten minutes, Sasha. You have ten minutes."

"Thank you, I only need five." Ten would be ideal, but I don't want to push it. "Do you have the books Mr. Mendoza left for us? For civics?"

Mrs. Maka shuffles behind the desk and then slides a large, spiral-bound book my way.

"Thanks." I tuck the book under my arm and walk back to my desk. Once seated, I flip through the book quickly; the sound of paper rustling shivers through me like inspiration.

The article for next week's lecture is on page 102. I let my fingers flip through the pages, and when I get there, it—

"What the actual hell?" I squeal. Pages 102 to 108 are gone. Where the text should be —instead a perfect cutout, like someone used a knife and removed the text. Missing. I've seen students tag or leave graffiti in books, fine. Pen-15 Club, I see you. But take the whole article out of a book? Who would do such a thing? Who has the time and the energy and the foresight to be so villainous?

I narrow my eyes at where *he* was sitting earlier, my blood boiling. Mr. Mendoza only leaves one book in the library to help us practice our research skills. Ezra? Ezra took out the article he knew I'd need for the civics presentation, for the second bet. I cross my arms and my head shakes in disappointment. This is vandalism. Petty theft?

I swivel my head in both directions, scanning for him. I imagine he's probably still watching me from some obscure hiding point, cackling at my expense. I snatch up my things, too irritated to place them in their respective pouches. So much for using this time to get ahead. I stomp out of the library, plans foiled.

CHAPTER 11

FRIDAY ROLLS AROUND, AND I'M FEELING PRETTY GOOD UNTIL IT'S time to actually turn in our first bet. I stand, biting my nails, in front of the black metal box on the teacher's desk. My *Hamlet* essay is in hand, ready to be released.

Dear Essay Gods, I think, *I know I call on you a lot. Maybe too much . . . Okay, I know it's too much. Specifically thinking about that time I brought some of Priscilla's crystals and sage to school to ensure a good grade on a paper and someone thought it was weed so the class had to be searched and we got a massive lecture on the risks of cannabis. But please. Right now. A favor. My last favor. I won't ask again. I . . . I can't let Ezra beat me. Not on this assignment. Too much is at stake. Please, please, please, I need your help. I need to start off strong. I need to crush him out of the gate. I need to win.*

The bell rings and I drop my essay in, hoping, praying, wishing on a star for the best, because I feel . . . nervous. Like, the most fucking nervous I've ever felt in my life.

♡♡♡

After school, Chance, Priscilla, and I gather for our weekly Fry-Date, our standing friend gathering where we share fries and feelings. Today we're seated at Spudsy, this new restaurant in downtown Monterey that has dedicated itself to the only vegetable that matters—the potato. Their whole thing is bright white walls with pink neon lights and big dialogue boxes with overly animated potatoes saying things like "You don't know till you Fry-it" and "I only have Fries for you."

"God, I love a good food pun." Chance slides into the booth and grabs an oversized laminated menu at the end of the table.

"Yes, these are so punny," Priscilla says in amusement. Chance mimes like he's hitting a snare drum. "Hey, before I forget, Lisbeth is having a party tonight. Any takers? Her parents have a hot tub."

"I'll go if Sasha goes," Chance says, knowing that I'll never go. I'm tired.

I bite my lip and grab a menu though I already know what I want—fries, extra salty, and a Coke. Then I shake my head without making eye contact.

"Boring, but fine." Priscilla gives me a playful glare.

"I got some facul-*tea*," I say.

"Ba-dum bum!" Chance hollers. "Now, that, that is a good pun. Brava."

I take a small bow, closing my eyes and sweeping my hand

across my chest. "Thank you, thank you. I've been saving it all week."

"Okay, so spill it!" Priscilla says.

"Last week, on Senior Ditch Day, I was in class—"

"You know senior ditch days are practically sanctioned by the staff, don't you?" Priscilla leans in. Most of the seniors took off that day to meet at the paddle boats downtown, near Dennis the Menace Park, and have a picnic. Priscilla went to the picnic, Chance stayed at home playing video games, and I went to class.

"That is absolutely not true," I reply, laughing. "Anyway, did y'all know Ms. T rides a motorcycle? And that Mendoza has a back tattoo? Like, a huge one? These are the things that we talked about when most of the senior class was gone."

"That's your tea?" Chance asks.

I clap. "My facul-*tea*," I say again. "Get it more now? Whatever, at least it was funny the first time around."

Chance pats my hand, and I snatch it away. I can be hilarious!

We pause our conversation as a young server in a white shirt and jean jacket with too much flair for a fry-and-burger spot comes to our table. We order our usual—two large baskets of regular shoestring and sweet potato waffle fries. I order my Coke, Priscilla gets a strawberry milkshake, and Chance just sticks with water, no ice, and a lemon wedge.

As soon as the server leaves, Chance drums the table. "Okay, good things . . . Who wants to start? Let's go," he says. I try to think of something good from the week. We started this tradition of sharing what's good in our lives sometime during junior year, after we noticed all our conversations were getting incredibly bleak and existential. I blame the amount of AP classes we were taking. This was also around the time Chance started to give his classes and grades the bare—and I'm talking bare like a tree in the dead of winter—minimum. He didn't understand all the hoop jumping, all the stress we were enduring for some exam scores.

Priscilla lights up. "I'll start! Prom committee met the other day and finalized our theme, which is great because there was a lot of back-and-forth about the general aesthetic, and I was worried we wouldn't be able to get it together in time. But we decided today! Who wants to hear?"

"No," Chance and I say in unison.

"Oh, come on! Is it because you want to be surprised when you attend prom?"

"Ain't happening," Chance says, wagging a finger. "Besides, Newton says I can say goodbye to prom and graduation if I don't get my act together."

I bend his menu, making him pay attention to me. "Chance Robert Bell the third. You might not graduate? I thought we moved on from this. You have to walk the stage with us, don't you dare."

Chance smirks, but it only fires up my anxiety.

"I need you at graduation," I plead. "No matter what your feelings are on the archaic nature of letter grades and the lack of holistic care for the student as an individual, we need you at graduation. We've gone through too much together these last four years to not have this last celebration. Together." He holds my gaze. I can tell by the stillness in his face that he's letting my words sink in.

Chance inches closer. "But am I wrong? Are grades a true indication of one's learning? Keep it one hundred, Sasha."

I let out a small huff. "Priscilla, weigh in."

She nods, one hand across her heart. "I second all of what Sasha said. I'd also like to humbly ask that we keep this same energy for prom. A hoorah before the last hoorah, if you will—"

Chance and I avoid locking eyes with Priscilla as he says what I'm thinking: "Absolutely not."

Priscilla frowns. "But you can't make me go alone—"

"What do you mean? You have Gina," I ask.

Priscilla stares out the window, "About Gina. Let's just say I better save that for *after* our good things." Priscilla fidgets with her hands and then clears her throat. Gina is Priscilla's first and only girlfriend, the love of her life, Priscilla's words. Priscilla has mentioned that they've been having some issues, but nothing that she didn't think couldn't be resolved. Maybe that's not the case anymore. If I've learned anything in the past few years, it's that a lot can change in a week.

"Do you, um, want to expand upon this?" Chance asks.

"Absolutely not. I want to push it down for as long as I can until my repressed feelings finally burst to the surface at some extremely random and unrelated time, preferably around my parents and not you two," Priscilla says.

"That's not healthy. Are you sure you don't want to talk about it more? We are always here, you know," I say, leaning in close to her.

She nods. "I'm positive. Besides, before I forget to mention, Emerson Jones is searching for a date."

I roll my eyes and take a long sip of my drink. Emerson Jones was the one and only guy to express interest in me in tenth grade, and Priscilla hasn't forgotten. She thinks I'm never going to find love and that if I don't snag him, I'll be doomed to be alone for as long as I walk this earth. Emerson is nice and all, but he's a total try-hard who likes to shoot finger guns unironically and winks—a lot. Priscilla won't admit it, but I'm pretty sure she thinks I'm an alien because I've never gone on a date or to a school dance. But there's no spark between me and Emerson, not even a little kindling.

I'll date and find love after graduation. Yeah, after grad school, I'll make time to pursue a romantic interest. High school guys are so bleh, and from what I've heard (mostly from the internet, which is just as reliable a source as any other), I'm not sure they get any better in college.

"No way. Don't start with prom *or* Emerson. Like I need another distraction right now." I throw my hands up as my shoulders slump. "However, this does lead me to my good thing," I say. The same server returns, sliding overstuffed red baskets of fries across our table.

"I figured out how to get Ezra out of the way. After class yesterday, I *challenged* him."

Priscilla does a shimmy, and her eyes widen so much that she could almost be one of the characters on the restaurant wall. "Oh my gosh, yes! To a duel?"

"A duel?! WHAT?"

Chance perks up. "It's a form of combat from the Middle Ages. I believe it began in Germany. You know, where two people—"

"Chance don't indulge her. Priscilla, you've watched *Hamilton* one too many times. No one is going to be dueling," I tell them. Priscilla laughs while Chance shrugs.

"As I was say-ing"—I wiggle my eyebrows—"I told Ezra we could bet for the title. We only have a few big assignments left that'll really impact our final grades. I don't know . . . I just came up with the idea on the spot. We agreed to figure things out ourselves by betting for the position and the scholarship." I take a sip of my water and notice something unusual on Priscilla's face. A frown.

"What's happening? What did I miss?" I ask.

"You can't gamble on something like that! Don't bet on the scholarship. This isn't Vegas," she utters.

"What do you mean? Why not?"

"*Why not?* Because you've worked too hard, Sasha. You just can't." Priscilla and Chance make eye contact; then Chance peers up at me.

"I don't like it. Not when you've come this far. I think there are other, more concrete ways to ensure you win the scholarship. Plus, you need to finish your legacy project and we need to plan our summer trips."

All school year I've been planning my legacy project and my graduation speech. Not only am I dedicating the award to my father—who was always reminding me how important education is because as Black people, we're so often denied it—but I want to do a deep dive into what it means to be *the first*. Starting with being the first in my family to break so many educational barriers. But I don't want to stop there— what does it mean to be the first in a field, the first person to desegregate a school, the first to walk on the moon? I want to not only analyze how these firsts help push and shape society, but how they are scary as hell too. Am I excited to be the first person in my family to go to a university full-time? Hell yeah. Am I scared as hell too? Duh.

We sit in silence while the restaurant behind us bustles, the after-work Friday crowd coming to join the fun.

I can't deny the truth in their argument, and I know they only have my best interests at heart.

"I hear what you both are saying, and you're right. Ideally, I wouldn't have to bet him. But graduation is in two months and I need to take care of this now. I can't have the constant stress of 'what-if' haunting me. I can focus on a few assignments with Ezra while still banging out all others, et voilà. Besides . . . as much as it pains me to admit, he's really smart. Hence, our current predicament." Ezra's annoyingly confident voice in seminar fills my ears. "And when he decides to apply himself, he'll be relentless. Neither of us will give up. We've played days' worth of Mario Kart before. Days. Trust. So then what? Teachers decide? Principal Newton flips a coin or something? Not happening. I'd rather get him out of the way on my terms. I'm going all in and I'm betting on myself."

My body warms as the words linger in the air. The words feel like they have power behind them. *I can do this.*

"Are you sure?" Priscilla asks.

"I'm . . . I'm sure of me."

"You don't sound sure," Chance says, eating a fry. My stomach tightens just a bit.

"But I gotta try, don't I? Not to mention, Ezra and I already agreed to the bets. I can't be the one to back out when it was my idea."

I twist a fry from both ends as it splits in the middle. Priscilla breaks the silence.

"Okay, Chance. You're up. What's your good thing this week?"

Chance rubs his fingers together, the salt falling like snow, then reaches for our hands, connecting us in a circle like a coven. "Ladies, I got my passport today. I'm going to Europe the second we graduate! Following in James Baldwin's footsteps."

"Bestie!" Priscilla rubs his arm. "I love this for you! And we support your decision. Hundo percent. Whatever happens, we've got each other. Always and forever. Deal?" Priscilla smiles from ear to ear. I push down the inevitable change that the last months of high school is forcing upon me.

Chance beams. "We'll be by your side with Gina. We'll be by your side with the bets."

"And we are all walking that stage together, dammit."

Priscilla looks between us, eyes big and sincere, and I focus on this moment. My chest fills up from the love that is happening now.

"Deal," I say, holding out my pinkie. Maybe some things in my future aren't so certain, but with these two there for me, I know I have a better shot at winning.

CHAPTER 12

"TODAY WE HAVE A NEW CLIENT," MY MOM SAYS, ONE HAND ON the steering wheel, the other on her favorite black coffee mug. The words WORLD'S BEST MOM hang in a bubbly cursive, a Mother's Day gift I picked up from Home Goods some six years ago. It's Saturday morning, which means one thing: cleaning houses.

"Big house, don't get lost." She smirks as I attempt to be pleasant. For a moment my mind starts to wander about having a Saturday morning all to myself. But I stop that thought. It ain't happening. My weekends spent watching cartoons with cereal are over. I try to find something to be grateful for—at least it will be a beautiful day by the water.

We ride in silence as the sunlight warms the inside of our brown Camry, the old car seats comforting against my body. Some eighties pop music fills the background as my mom dances, just slightly off beat. I sneak a glance at her, and I spot several new patches of gray sprinkled in her black hair.

She's aging. Beautifully, but it means I am too. High school is almost over. Win the scholarship, stay local. Four years of college and then two years of graduate school and then I can work for us both and get her out of this. No more cleaning up after other people. No more folding their laundry and ironing their clothes and picking up their trash. No more long hours, no more special Epsom salt baths for her tired hands and back.

I place my hand on hers and give it a squeeze.

"What are you thinking about over there?" my mom asks playfully.

"What am I not?" I joke back. Seriously, my brain is constantly working, like a twenty-four-hour diner. What's the need for the new client? Worry tries to creep up my body, but I push it down. My mom doesn't know, but I keep a document detailing her clients, our income, and our budget. It makes me feel better knowing that we are covered. Like, literally covered, with a roof over our heads. If we weren't, I dunno, I'd get a side job or something.

She takes a sharp left turn, and from my seat, I have a full panoramic view of the bright blue ocean, the gray rocks, the seagulls flying, the coast that I call home.

"You resemble your father so much when you make that thinking face," she says. I can't help but peer at myself in the side mirror, and she's right, I see him too. My eyes prickle with joyous tears, and I let my body relax as we cruise along.

We've only been driving for five minutes, and it's incredible how fast the neighborhoods change. From simple apartment buildings like ours to one-story family homes to gated mansions with three cars parked in the driveway. Each time I blink, every block gets better and nicer than the one before.

My mom parks our car in the driveway of a large brick house. The manicured lawn is meticulous, the grass almost blue it's so green. From the outside, it is unassuming, but I can tell that it's massive inside. All the houses are around here. It's like this weird disguise tactic: average exterior, ridiculously lavish interior.

"You ready?" my mom asks, grabbing a container of cleaning supplies.

I nod, double-checking that I have my headphones. We walk to the front door together.

Inside, the house is enormous, just as I thought. There are not one but two spiraling staircases, on each side of the living room, and the ceilings are . . . where the hell are the ceilings? Ah, found them, next to heaven. A black grand piano welcomes us to the left, and to the right is a sitting area and a kitchen. The latter has fancy appliances with smart screens, a massive marble island, crystal chandelier, gold picture frames, and elaborate trinkets. Yeah, this house is going to take forever to clean.

Without saying much, my mom and I begin. Mom immediately sets out to grab the linens, starting with the wash. Per usual, I grab the dusting cloths.

Dusting is one of those things that takes time, that you absolutely cannot rush. From far away, you may not notice the dust, but up close, it's there. Waiting to be discovered. I used to try to rush dusting, but my mom would call me back. *You missed a spot,* she'd say coolly. Dusting taught me that things take time.

I begin in the large living room with several floral print chairs. I run the soft, yellow cloth over the wooden arms and legs, my body contracting as I get down low, then stretching toward the sun as I reach up high. I dust everything that I can touch, that my eyes can see. I move with slow, calculated precision, making sure to never miss a spot and to return everything to where it should be.

When I finally peer up, I see it, almost tripping over my own feet. In a large, ornate wooden frame, a family picture hangs on the wall. There are three of them, but their bodies, their connection practically blends into one. The vibrant red hair of the mother and daughter, one standing, and one sitting, their resemblance undeniable.

The Pattersons.

Kerry Patterson.

This is her house? *House* isn't the right word—there's enough space to put our apartment in here, what? Three? Four times? At least.

The yellow dusting cloth drops from my hand. Suddenly everything in the room is more magical, more magnificent than before. Does Kerry study here? Is this where she does her best work? Jealousy and wonder fill me at the same time.

"You okay? Big house, eh?" My mom. Her voice snaps me out of this daydream. She's got her yellow latex gloves on and she's energetic, despite the workload.

"I'm . . . yeah, I'm fine."

"I have an idea," she says, fiddling with her hands, "so we can talk, you know. Girl time. Chat chat—"

"*Chitchat.*"

Someone once mentioned my mom's accent and, at first, I didn't know what they were talking about. *What accent? I don't hear it.* But sometimes, like now, I'm reminded that English is her second language and idioms are hard to remember.

"Chitchat. Yes. You can help me with the laundry. We can fold and iron together."

I force a smile, but my mind is already doing the calculations. This is a big house. And we are just two people. What would make the most sense? What would be the most efficient? What would yield the best results? More importantly, what would get me home the fastest to study?

"I don't know, Mommy. This place is huge. I think it's best, um, more efficient, if we divide and conquer. I think we should work separately." I don't have it in me to make eye contact.

"Hmmm. Are you sure? I can tell you about that new drama I'm watching."

I nod, but I don't miss how her shoulders slump in disappointment. I turn to dust a large glass vase before my mom can respond.

Two hours pass while my brain oscillates between thoughts of how ridiculous Kerry's house is, my excellent take on feminism in the *Hamlet* essay, and how good it's going to feel to destroy Ezra. By the time I'm dusting the top level of a cabinet, my body starts to ache, and pools of sweat build up in my armpits.

Finally, after four intense hours, my mom says the magic word. "Ready?" I nod and grab my bag and the last of her cleaning products before heading to the car.

Outside, a white Mercedes pulls up and Kerry hops out as I'm stuffing the last of our supplies into the trunk.

Kerry carries a tennis racket in one hand. "Hey," she says as she reaches her front door. If she's surprised to see me, she doesn't show it.

"Hey," I respond, and then slide into the passenger seat.

♡♡♡

On the drive home, I'm so deep in the same thoughts that I don't notice the detour my mom takes.

"Where are we going? This isn't the right way," I say, uncomfortable in my seat.

"It's a surprise." She smiles. Except I really hate surprises. Maybe it's the Virgo in me, but I like to plan; I like control. The car slows, and before I can register anything, she's parked in front of an old but familiar brown brick building.

"Anna's Boutique?" The signature white daisies in barrels and the large chalk sandwich board outside the storefront answer my question. My chest tightens. "Why did you park? I don't—"

My mom reaches across and tries to grab my arm. "I

thought we could go check out some dresses. You know, for prom."

I sink into my seat.

"I've been driving by," she continues, "and that dress in the window, that one. That's your favorite color, isn't it?"

She points out a long lace dress practically floating in the window. And yeah, it is my color—lilac, purple's more chill cousin. I love how lilac complements my brown skin, that it's dainty and soft and understated but still very beautiful.

"Why don't you try it on? Let's go in."

But I can't. Last time I was inside Anna's, I was with both my mom and dad. Some places, some memories are just too delicate to remember; there are parts of the past that hurt too much when you bring them back into the present.

"I'm not even sure I'm going to prom." I can't face her. "So that means I don't need a dress." That came out so bratty. I know she's trying to help, but this isn't how to do it.

"What? Why not? Priscilla is going, right? She said so. You should go. Have good times. Find a boy"—my mom leans over —"or a girl, or a person, you know, to dance with. You go. Have fun. Make time in your life for new memories."

Her eyes are like lasers, focused in on me. I blink, but she keeps trying.

"I thought you would like to at least see the dress, you know, at least try it on. I remember when you and your father—"

"That was a long time ago, okay? No. No way." I don't mean to sound nasty; I know it's the pressure from school and life and my need to hold it all together. But if I don't, what would happen to me? What would happen to us? My mom relies on me to be . . . collected.

She stares out the window, and I can practically hear her thoughts. For the eighth-grade father-daughter dance, I *begged* my parents to let me get a dress from Anna's. Anna's is the only place in town that is actually stylish, unlike most of the prudish stores around here that are at least four seasons behind in trends. When they finally agreed to let me peep in Anna's, I found the most perfect dress, in lilac, of course. My mom frowned when she saw the price tag, but my dad just shrugged. I try to push the memory out, but it refuses to budge. Instead, it only appears more clearly, more focused.

My dad and I went to the dance, and it was perfect, like all the excitement and best things in my life wrapped up in one night. I remember the indescribable energy of getting dressed up and feeling *beautiful*. I remember my parents beaming, each of us excited to celebrate a special occasion just for me. My life was full of possibility. I can see the handmade decorations of hearts and stars on the wall of the middle school gym. Two weeks before the dance, my dad and I learned all the popular social media dances. And when those songs played, we went right to the middle of the dance floor and moved like we were about to win *America's Got Talent*. We had talent, and then some. We had so much fun that night, just the two of us. Together. Doing our thing.

I swallow.

But that was then.

This is now.

And I don't really dance anymore.

"Can't we just go home?" I whine. "Plus, we're all smelly from cleaning houses."

It is a low blow, but that gets my mom to tighten up. If there's one thing she hates, it's the residual smell from housework, the way vinegar and bleach stick to her skin and permeate her hair. The way cleaning up after someone else makes you so dirty.

We commence a stare-off. I do my best to hold my stance with my cold eyes and stern face, though I know she's about to speak again. To insist. To make her motherly case. A small part of me knows I should let her be right. But not tonight.

Eventually, she backs down. She fakes a smile, then turns the car back on. I exhale.

CHAPTER 13

THE TRILOGY GROUP CHAT

Priscilla 9:15 a.m.: Why are Mondays so tragic?

Chance 9:17 a.m.: Truly do not recommend. 0/10. Nothing could get me out of bed this morning. I'll be on campus after lunch.

Sasha 10:15 a.m.: How are y'all so good at texting in class and not getting caught?

Priscilla 10:16 a.m.: Years of practice, bb.

MONDAY DOES ITS USUAL THING. LATER ON IN THE DAY I'M IN AP Calculus, swimming in these derivatives like there's an ancient mystery hidden somewhere on the page, when Marcus Scott swings the door open so urgently I jump out of my skin. Everyone turns to him in surprise. Why is he always doing this? With his hands behind his back, he lingers in the doorway. *Oh no, please no—not again, no more summons.* Once he has everyone's undivided attention, he brings a pink box out from behind him and strides into the room while holding the box like an offering.

"What do we have here?" asks Mr. Walsh, my other favorite teacher (he and Ms. T are tied, but I would never tell them that), beaming as he walks to meet Marcus in the middle of the room.

"I want one!" "Let me get one!" students beg in earnest.

Correction: *The* Pink Box.

Everyone at Skyline knows what's in them—donuts. I'm not sure how or why, but there is always a large, bright pink box of donuts from Red's, the most delicious local bakery, floating around in one classroom or another. Someone is either bringing them in or giving them away or both because they are always here. Donuts, lots and lots of donuts. Not that I'm complaining. Usually they're for the teachers, but if you get someone like Mr. Walsh, who is generous enough, the donuts become for the students, too. Like a big kid, he can't resist indulging in colorful sprinkles on a chocolate cake donut and is selfless enough to share in the joy of sugar.

Marcus walks by me and out of the corner of his mouth says, "Check your phone," in a voice that is deep and dramatic. Fitting.

My phone is buried in my pencil pouch, on Do Not Disturb. I pull it out and see a text from Ezra. My heart stops.

> **Ezra 2:25 p.m.:** Ask to get out of class, meet me at your lunch tree. By the vending machines.

I read the text once, and then one more time to make sure I'm not hallucinating. Leave class? Like calculus right now? Not happening. How'd he get my number? Stalker.

I take a moment and check for Mr. Walsh, who is doing some sort of joyful teacher dance, his shoulders shimmy and he's got one index finger in the air, staring at his half-eaten donut like it's a diamond. Jason Tanaka hops out of his seat with his phone in hand and says, "Yo, Mr. Walsh, let me show you a funny video! You gonna die." Jason is trying to derail the lesson even more, and by the grin on Mr. Walsh's face, he just might succeed. On his way out, Marcus raises his eyebrows and mouths "phone" one more time for emphasis.

Usually, Mr. Walsh wouldn't allow videos of grandparents lip-syncing to rap songs to steal his valuable class time. But today? Right now? The power of the donut, coupled with the end-of-year fever, has won. He raises his eyebrows at Jason's screen. The phone's light reflects off his face.

"Okay, three minutes," he tells Jason, who has already pressed play.

I wouldn't normally leave during class, but maybe this is about the bets. Say, if I did need to go, now seems like as good a time as any. I have three minutes. I can be back in time before he's finished another donut. Should I . . .

Go?

Stay?

No.

Hmm.

Sarah Hawkins takes out her phone and says, "I've got one too!" ushering in what will inevitably be a storm of WeTalk videos to avoid actual learning. Senioritis is real.

I exhale.

Just this once.

"Mr. Walsh? Can I, um . . . can I use the restroom?" I ask him, but I'm already standing.

"Make it quick," he says. I force myself to walk slowly, trying not to seem too eager, my breath coming in little bursts.

Ezra is standing at the tree—*my tree*—watching me walk toward him. His hair is pulled into a small bun at the top of his head in a white scrunchie, and he's wearing a bright pink tie-dye shirt with the sleeves rolled up and fitted dark jeans that are frayed at the bottom. When I get closer to him, I see it—that smile, those freckles. My stomach flips.

His fit may be nice, but I'm not here to ogle. This is strictly business. I clear my throat.

Ezra straightens up, his long body propped up against the tree. "Hey, you," he says, a small twinkle in his eye. I swear the brown changes depending on his mood.

I pull at my hair, unsure of what to say or how to be, the nervousness surprising. I mean it's just Ezra, for heaven's sake. I used to roller-blade in his driveway in a helmet and matching knee and elbow pads. This nervous energy should be reserved for someone else, like Michael B. Jordan, a man I plan to meet and marry one day.

Ezra steps forward, shortening the distance between us. "I've been meaning to tell you, your locs are great. They were so short in eighth grade and now you're over here giving Chloe and Halle vibes." He takes a confident stance, nodding to himself.

My voice is stuck. I drop my hands from my hair. The sun breaks through a cloud, and the heat begins to pool on my face. "I, um, thanks." Wait—what's going on here? From the compliment to the way he eyed me as I walked over. I refocus. "How'd you get my number?"

Ezra continues, batting his long eyelashes. "Does it matter? I wanted to talk to you, that's all. I been thinking about us as kids, a lot of memories came up." One of his curls breaks free and flutters across his forehead. Ezra brushes it away, delicately, while holding my gaze.

"Ezra, why am I out here? I should be in class. Wait. How did you know what class I had?"

"Come on, SJ. I can deduce your whole schedule. That's child's play. Walsh only teaches two sections of AP Calculus, so if you're not in mine, you must be in the other. Same students, same classes, remember? We're like the pot and kettle, or something." A silly grin emerges on his face, one that says he likes being right. My cheeks begin to warm, aware of the strong eye contact we are making.

He lifts his arm over his head, does a small stretch, and

then slides his camera to the front of his chest, all in one motion, like a yoga move.

"You should let me take your photo." His eyes light up.

"I'm sorry?"

"Your portraits. The light is so dope right now. You're here, I'm here, this tree is here. You wouldn't think so, but Skyline actually has some excellent backdrops for pics."

My heart drops into my stomach, and when it bounces back up again, I blink rapidly and clear my throat. "This is not what class time is for. I have very important things to do and a scholarship to win."

"That's really all that's on your mind, isn't it?" Ezra drops the camera, and it dangles from his neck. "I knew you were hyper focused, but—"

"This—school, valedictorian, the scholarship—all of it is important to me, okay? Some call it a five-year plan, others call it goals, but I have things I want to do in my life, things I want to accomplish, and I can't let anyone, or anything, get in the way of that."

"Ha!" Ezra lets out a chuckle, which begins to upset me. Once he realizes that, he rubs a hand against his head. "Dead ass?"

"Yes, I'm serious. This is my shit, and you're out here messing things up."

"That would hurt my feelings if I didn't have a better plan. And I'll share it for free."

I roll my eyes but wait for him to continue.

"My plan is no plan. Just catch whatever life throws, ya know?" His eyes widen with excitement.

Ezra's unplan is the most ridiculous thing I've heard in a long time, and last week I was in a group discussion that morphed into a debate over the existence of extraterrestrial life, and it got really weird, really fast. I just shrug. There's no way we can be the pot and the kettle—maybe a long time ago, but it's obvious we are complete opposites now.

Ezra straightens his back and tilts his chin toward the sky. "Remember in seventh grade when you beat me at the science fair?"

I hadn't thought about that in a minute, but he's unlocked a memory, like he's pulled up a live photo on my phone, and I can see and hear us so clearly. It's funny how memories hide. Do they eagerly wait until someone seeks them out again? And yeah, I beat him, but it was never a competition. Right after the fair, we went and got pizza, celebrating together.

"What can I say? Folks love an osmosis project."

He nods. "They really do. And you were cooler, you had a leg up on me."

What? Is he for real?

Ezra shrugs. "Just thinking. It's been interesting to recall how we used to be . . . best friends," he says calmly.

"That was a long time ago. Before you . . . Never mind."

"What? Say it?"

I take a deep breath. "Before you threw our friendship away. You know what you did."

Ezra shakes his head. "Hey, there were two people in that fight."

"It's whatever now. We're not the same. I've changed, you've changed. Life goes on. I've moved forward."

Ezra leans in, like he's examining my face for the first time. "Have you, though?"

I take a nervous breath as Ezra checks his watch, a bulky silver thing with diamonds surrounding the blue face. He squints away and waves to someone in the distance.

"I'm going now, Ezra."

Ezra raises his eyebrows. "Oh! Before I forget—do you want a donut?"

Ezra bends down, and under his backpack he has another pink box. "Chocolate with sprinkles still your go-to?" He lifts the lid and reveals the beautiful creation.

It's just like the one Marcus had, only smaller and . . . Oh my god. My heart does a somersault. How long have I been out here listening to him ramble?

Shit.

Before Ezra can stand, I'm on my heels, running back to class. I check my phone. There are two minutes left until the bell rings. This wasn't supposed to take so long.

At Mr. Walsh's classroom door, I inhale before walking in. I don't want to pull a Marcus. I grab the cold handle and open the door, taken aback by what I see.

I know this scene; I know this sound. Pencils and pens furiously scramble across wooden desks. Students are in a trance as they rush to get their answers down on paper, the clock ticking loudly before time's up. IT'S A POP QUIZ.

Pressure builds in my chest, behind my eyes, like I'm being pumped up with too much air.

Fuuuu— "Mr. Walsh?" I whisper as I walk toward his desk.

"I need the quiz? Can I take it?" I ask. I point to the students and my desk, then throw my hands together, begging.

He finishes the last piece of a new donut, small white crumbs collecting in his beard. The bell rings.

Oh no. No, no, no.

"Where did you go, Sasha? What took so long?"

Shit. I don't have a good reason. I was baited. Maybe I should lie. But I don't have it in me to lie. Damn my goody-goody nature.

He shakes his head in what I can only imagine is disappointment, further crushing my spirit. "Short answer is no; you can't take the quiz. Long answer is please don't leave class for an extended period of time if you don't want to miss important work. Being present matters. You know this." His facial expression is stern.

"But I . . ." I want to beg and plead and tell him that I was outside taking care of this annoying bet, that Ezra is currently ruining my life. But as soon as the thought appears, I realize how ridiculous that sounds.

"Come on, Sasha," Kerry Patterson chimes in as if I asked. She slings her tiny black leather backpack over her shoulder. "You know the rules. You aren't exempt. Only excused absences get a pass."

I grit my teeth and resist the urge to roll my neck and glare at her in front of Mr. Walsh.

Mr. Walsh nods his head in agreement.

Eck.

Fine.

I turn to exit and spot the pink box, folded into a blue recycling bin. It hits me hard, like bricks, like a bucket of ice-cold water in my face. My vision flares red. My neck burns. It's all stacking up. This wasn't a coincidence, it was . . .

A planned distraction? Decoy and all!

Ezra and Marcus and the donuts . . . He knew we'd have a quiz, he knew my schedule . . . He planned it all just to make me miss a few points? To get on his soapbox and lecture me about my life? I pinch the skin around my fingernail.

Mr. Walsh collects quizzes from students as they leave while I stand by his desk, too livid to speak. I finally grab the last of my things and head out the door. My feet stomp on the tiled floors, my hands turning into fists.

Back outside, the sun is bright, almost blinding. I jog back to the tree, but Ezra's not there.

I take out my phone and my thumbs press down with so much vengeance, I can barely see the words I'm typing.

> Sasha 3:11 p.m.: Did you just make me miss a quiz? On PURPOSE?

It doesn't take long before the three dots appear at the bottom of the screen.

> Ezra 3:11 p.m.: The donut was the thing (Hamlet reference).

> **Sasha 3:12 p.m.:** Why would you do that?
> I would never do that to you.

Ezra 3:12 p.m.: That's kind of the whole point. . . .

Ezra 3:12 p.m.: All is fair in love and war.

I take deep breaths, my pulse racing. I feel like I'm Elmer Fudd and maybe Ezra is Bugs Bunny. Maybe he's in some corner, watching steam burst from the top of my head. *Touché, Ezra. Touché.*

Okay, think through this, Sasha. Missing one quiz can't knock me *so* far off my path, right? It's ten points, twenty at most. But then last week's seminar comes to mind, the one where I just sat there, like a bump on a log, and my throat starts to clamp. If I'm missing points in my classes, maybe I won't be able to keep my rank. If I'm not tied for first, then how does that factor into all this? Maybe Ezra doesn't need the bets. Is that his motive here? Is that what he's doing, confusing me by batting his stupid eyelashes so I put up less of a fight?

I close my eyes and I do my best to picture my family in the audience at graduation and me onstage. I strain, trying to see them, all of us together, celebrating my victory. But the image is fuzzy. Ever since Ezra's shown back up in my life, the position seems out of reach. He's solely to blame. How else can I explain today?

CHAPTER 14

SCHOOL ON TUESDAY IS PLEASINGLY PREDICTABLE (AND TRULY, I wouldn't have it any other way). So by Wednesday afternoon, when Mrs. Gregg says the unexpected words "Okay, everyone, the moment you've all been waiting for. I'm going to hand back your *Hamlet* essays," I almost fall out of my chair.

Will the winner of Bet #1 please stand up?

I straighten as my foot continues to do that nervous tap inside of my shoe. She saunters past me three times before finally sliding my paper across my desk. As fast as my fingers can move, I'm flipping through the pages to the last one.

Ah, here it is.

I let out a sigh of relief. I could cry, the grade on the paper is so lovely, so beautiful. Has anything as marvelous ever existed?

A ninety-nine.

Damn near perfect. One point off, but I'll take it. There's

no way Ezra scored higher. I bet he's a ninety-five, on a good day. My body relaxes. I'm beaming.

I skim the essay, rereading the comments, relishing in the smiley face on the last page, and the knot in my stomach loosens a bit. Priscilla gets her essay, checks out the score, and heads over to me.

She holds up her paper in the air like a trophy. "I got an eighty-four! No lie, I did the essay the morning it was due. I hate to admit how good I'm getting at this whole procrastination thing. Hear me out—maybe this is actually a life skill that school is meant to teach us."

"It's definitely not," Mrs. Gregg says, sliding past her.

P snorts, and I chuckle. "Well, if that's the secret of high school, then what have I been doing this entire time? Wait—don't answer that." She smirks, her dark purple lipstick making her look more mischievous than ever. The way Priscilla procrastinates and leaves things up to chance stresses me out. But she's my best friend, and I love her regardless. Besides, she hates when I deliver what she calls my "unsolicited guidance counselor tirade." Which I can't help but roll my eyes at, because let's be honest, the guidance counselors at this school rarely give sound advice. Like when I was instructed to only apply to one college because I'm a "shoo-in." I applied to twelve, just to be safe.

Together we walk out of Mrs. Gregg's classroom, and I hold the essay in my hand like a battle sword.

"Do you want a ride home?" she asks.

"I don't think so. I need to find Ezra and show him what he's in for." I wave my 99 percent–worthy paper high.

"Oh, duh. Ezra. Do you want me to wait for you? I don't mind. We could hang after, go try that new dessert place," Priscilla asks. I tilt my chin up at the sky to assess the weather. It's nice, blue skies with floaty white clouds. A perfect day to celebrate a win.

Everything around me is lovelier, more pleasant. Has the world always been this beautiful? "I'm okay, thanks. I'll wait for him and then walk home; the fresh air will be good for me."

Priscilla shrugs. "Suit yourself. Call me or text and let me know what happens. You are amazing. You're a big, beautiful brain with long legs." She nudges me as we approach our lunch spot, lifting her chin toward our tree. Ezra is already there, leaning against the bark. He's wearing a loose tank top, and his arms have much more shape than I remember. They're muscly, but not in a bad way. He's in long basketball shorts and high-top sneakers. His hair is wild; the black curls on his forehead get in his eyes as he bats them away.

I take a deep breath in and out, suddenly aware of the need to steady myself.

"Let's do this," I say as I approach.

"Well, hello to you too, SJ." He laughs and digs into his backpack, pulling out his own paper. "How should we do the big reveal?"

My body feels like Jell-O as I try to keep my composure.

I'm a little nervous, but there's no way he beat my ninety-nine. I lift my chin. "Let's just say our grade on three."

"You sure?"

"Yes, yes, I'm sure." My palms sweat a little.

"Okay, who's going to count? You want to do the honors?" he asks. His smile is so big, it's practically blinding.

"Fine." I wipe my hands on my hoodie. "I will. Let's do this. One, two—"

"One hundred and one!" Ezra blurts.

"Hey! That's early!"

He lets out a heartier laugh this time, then grabs my elbow and holds it, for just a second. The touch is light and warm, but I can't concentrate on that because the ground is falling out from underneath me.

"Now tell me what you got." He lets go of my elbow and a cloud covers the sun.

"I got a ninety-nine," I mutter.

I lost.

Shit.

"Ah. Yeah, um. That's a good score too." Ezra pulls at his tank top neck. He's such a bad liar.

My ninety-nine wasn't good enough. I'm doing my best to try to understand what's happening currently, this strange and unknown feeling, because until now, everything I've ever worked on, everything I've ever turned in, has been just the right amount of amazing.

"Let me see your paper," I demand, one hand on my hip

and the other stretched out. He hands me his essay, and my eyes do a quick skim at the words screaming out in bright red ink. *"Bravo . . . Great analysis . . . I hadn't thought of that . . . Wonderful nuance . . . You do a great job of connecting gender and social class in Elizabethan England,"* I read under my breath. *"This critique is surely on a college level."* Goose bumps cover my arms.

I give the pages another skim. No way.

This guy?

Someone who was never on my radar while at Skyline until I was called into the principal's office for the second time.

I'm light-headed.

"I can't believe this, I just . . ." I hand the essay back to him, disgust written all over my face.

"What can't you believe? That I can write? That I scored higher than you?" His neck does a small swivel, and his eyebrows rise as if to say, *really?* Then he frowns like he may be insulted.

"No, I can't believe any of this. She never gives higher than a ninety-nine, she . . . ," I fumble, and take a seat on the ground. My body sinks into the earth, which should probably just swallow me whole.

"I knew you'd come with the heat, so I made sure to put in extra effort." Ezra grins.

So this is it. 1–0. He's up.

Ezra brings his face close to mine.

"I hate to interrupt whatever it is that you're having, but

I gotta go. If I win the next one, it's all over. A clean sweep, as they say."

Okay, Sasha. Refocus. You're not out of this . . . yet.

Win the next bet, tie things up. There's still a chance.

Our faces are damn near touching; my eyes are having a difficult time seeing straight.

"Per my victory," Ezra continues, "I have won your assistance. Tomorrow, after school in the darkroom." I swallow, because it's the only bodily function I seem to still have control over, as he continues: "Hello? Earth to Sasha? Do you understand? Blink once if you can hear me."

I blink. At least I can still do that.

"Awesome. So I'll see you tomorrow, then?"

It takes everything inside of me to move my neck. I nod yes.

Two points. Two measly points.

Ezra springs up, like a jack-in-the-box. "Go, Ezra; go, Ezra; go," he singsongs to himself. His arms move around and then he does a dab. He's animated, like out of a video game. "This is going swimmingly."

CHAPTER 15

"YOU'RE LATE AGAIN," BEN CALLS TO ME AS SOON AS I ENTER Ms. T's room. "That means you owe me chips, Khadijah." He holds out his hand to her.

"I'm only, like, two minutes late," I say, but the afternoon tutoring session has already begun. I had to pick a book up from the library since it'll be closed by the time Ezra and I are done today. "Should I be offended that you bet against me?"

"Not even. I think it's a good sign, shows how much I really know you," Ben replies, dimples appearing in both of his squishy cheeks when he smiles. Khadijah reaches in her bag and throws Juan an unopened bag of Hot Cheetos.

"Don't kill me, but I actually have to go," I mutter, taking two steps backward.

"What? Why?" Juan asks.

I pause. How do I explain? "I have to . . . do this thing . . . in the darkroom."

Khadijah perks up. "There's a darkroom here?"

My thoughts exactly but with less enthusiasm.

"Chance? Priscilla?" I whimper. *Please tell me you can handle this,* I think. Chance lifts a hand and immediately shoos me away.

"I'll be here next week, I promise." I turn on my heels before they can finish saying bye.

I trek across campus into unknown territory to be Ezra's serf. There's the usual commotion of campus after school—students on skateboards, a group of sophomore girls getting ready for JV volleyball practice, and the distinct sound of rubber basketballs bouncing on the hardwood gym floor. School gives total Dr. Jekyll and Mr. Hyde vibes. During the day, it's all business and learning and overthinking. But after school it's organized chaos, a thrilling combination of energy and excitement and pent-up aggression. For some, that is.

The closer I get, the more my feet begin to drag. Ugh. I'd rather be anywhere else in the world right now, but a bet is a bet.

The photography room sits by itself, an old building near the small basketball gym, neither of which I ever go to. I guess there are still some things here that I've yet to experience. I've been so busy just trying to do well in my own classes that I've never thought about all that Skyline has to offer or how Skyline ranks in terms of other schools, not until Ezra mentioned it. But it's true, not all schools are created equally. I guess I'm lucky to have access to the programs we have here, even though it's kind of too late to use them. There are some great things available for seniors, like the valedictorian scholarship, for example. Yes, it's still on my brain. How could it not be?

When I reach the photo room, I give the heavy antique door a big push to enter. The space is empty, scattered only with worn-down wooden desks. On the wall across from the door hangs an old, painted sign that says DARKROOM in faded green letters with an arrow. I follow the sign to another door. When I open it, I'm surrounded by complete darkness, which I suppose I should've expected. Instinctively, I reach out in front of me. Please, please, don't let anyone jump out or prank me now because I'm certain I would faint or pee myself.

Thankfully, a soft black curtain greets me. I find my way through its various folds and slowly stumble inside a small hallway. It's pitch-black, darker than I ever imagined, and yet I'm surprised at how well I can move without light. Then my hands meet another large black felt curtain. I shuffle through heavy curtains, almost comfortable now, until I finally find another door handle.

When I open the door, I freeze, my lips parting. The darkroom is . . . stunning.

My eyes take a moment to adjust and all the black fades to the softest, most beautiful red. Silky. Soft. Sexy.

Honestly, I'm sort of in awe.

The workspace feels comfortable, with just enough room to fit six students. In the middle of it there are several sinks attached to plastic tubs. Water flows through the tubs, giving the room a soft echo, like a running stream. It's peaceful. Lining the walls there are large machines and small desks.

Black-and-white photos in different shapes and sizes hang above the water tubs on clothespins. Directly across the room is Ezra.

I don't move. I'm held in place by this indescribable feeling.

The space is calming. I take a breath, a pause. The worry from the past week begins to fade—it slows down like a song and then just stops. My heartbeat slows, and I relax.

Ezra stretches and straightens like a cat. He's wearing a long apron over his clothes, and he has on round, wiry glasses. Ezra in glasses! I haven't seen that since, what, sixth grade? Before he got contacts and became middle school cool and started going by "Ez." I try my best to control a giggle, but it's hard. When we were younger, he was always losing his glasses (even though they were on top of his head, hiding in his curls) or, on cold mornings, fogging them up while trying to warm up his hands.

He places whatever he was holding down and pushes his glasses up on his nose. "Hey, you. I wasn't sure you'd show up."

I raise my eyebrows, the last of today's tension leaving my body. "This is . . ." I try to find the right words for what I'm feeling, but I can't. That's the mark of something truly special. Magical, even. When there aren't words to describe the emotion because it's deeper than language.

"Well, now that you're here, I need you to insert those test strips into those plastic, projector sheets. Watch out for fingerprints—last thing I need is fingerprints on them. Once they're all in sleeves, they go in the binders. But make sure you keep them in order. Right now, they're in chronological order, and I'd like to keep them that way."

Oooh-kay.

"Good to see you too," I murmur as I find my way to the chair and toss my backpack on the floor.

"Sorry, there's just a lot to do," he says, gesturing to the pile of—what? Two hundred? Five hundred?—test strips to stuff. I sigh. I lost the first bet. Let's add each strip to the long list of reasons why I will NOT lose another.

"You could have been doing something way worse, you know. Trust me, I thought about it," he calls from his corner. "But I figure losing is bad enough. Plus, I need the help."

Ezra turns to face me and runs a hand through his hair. "I guess I got behind on my work. Old habits die hard."

My lips half frown; for me, or the work, or his habits, I'm not quite sure.

I slouch in the chair and get started. Ezra and I work in complete silence. Every three minutes or so he moves around the room in a circular motion, like the hands on a clock. Every two minutes, a timer goes off and he scoots over to a water bath to remove a large print. Sometimes I think I can feel him staring at me. Other times I pause to watch him move so fluidly, like a dancer. He's focused, I can tell by his breathing and his pacing. When he can't seem to figure something out, he pushes his thin glasses up his nose and tugs on his ear. He stands with perfect posture and occasionally puts his hand to his chin, like it helps him think. It's endearing.

I know that expression. That's me during a final. That's me creating the most beautiful presentation ever. That's me readying the kids in tutoring club for a test. That's the zone. And Ezra is in it. As much as I hate him, I can't hate on his dedication. So I continue to stare for a moment or two; the glow of the room makes him look, well, nice, attractive.

He must sense my eyes on him, because he turns to face me and breaks the silence.

"How's it going over there? All finished?" He walks toward me, then stops in the middle of the room, near the baths.

"Ezra. I just started. I've been in here for what, ten minutes, max? Give me a break."

"What? You need to create an outline first? Where are your Post-it notes, anyway? And that pink fluffy pen that's shaped like a bird? Or a cat, I'm not sure."

I smirk. "I see you've been noticing me." As soon as the words leave my mouth, I want to take them back. I don't wait for him to respond. "It's a flamingo, and don't start with my stationery. Not right now. I'm finding this to be really—"

A relaxed smile takes over Ezra's face. "Zen?" The mockery has drained from his voice.

"Actually, yeah." Like a sunset on a warm evening. Towels, hot and fluffy straight out of the dryer. He smiles again; the red hues behind him create a glow on his white T-shirt, making the brown of his skin glow.

I don't know if it's his calm demeanor or that I get to catch a breath, but my words come out soft. "You're lucky you get to work in here, that this exists for you whenever you want.

It's like a little sanctuary." Everyone needs a safe space where they can go and simply . . . be. I'm a tad jealous that Ezra has his. I wonder what something like this could be for me. I have the library, but somehow, it's not the same. The library is still connected back to work and school, which I'm good at, but I don't know. It's not freeing or calming. Not like this.

"Right? I knew you'd get it." He drums his fingers on the table. "My dad got me my first film camera when we moved to New York as a distraction-from-divorce gift. From the first pic, I was hooked, practically obsessed. It kind of helped me make sense of a new city and my new life. Helped me to see things in a fresh way. My sidekick." He pushes the glasses up on his nose again and beams. "This is my refuge. The port of calm in a storm. All the other senior photographers stay in the computer lab. They're addicted to Photoshop and digitizing anything they can. Don't get me wrong, Photoshop is great, and memes are fun to make every once in a while and all, but this—making prints here—this is magic. My magic." His dimple appears.

"I can tell. Even by these," I say, pointing to the large stack in front of me. "This is . . . impressive."

Ezra chuckles. "Yeah, you're not wrong. I found a lot of my parents' old negatives from the eighties and nineties. I've been working with them a bit, reprinting some. Wanna see something new? You gotta check this out, I think you'll appreciate it."

Ezra wipes his hands on his apron and walks over to my desk. Before I can move, he's behind me, his chest practically on my back. His arms, which are long and shapely, square me in. His face leans down and he flips through the binder. His arm brushes mine. His skin is delicate and warm. I freeze, wondering if I'm the only one who notices how physically close we are. I can practically hear his heart beating. When he finds what he wants to show me, he reaches into his pocket, pulls out a small black viewfinder, and hands it to me.

"Here. Use this." He takes two steps back. I unfreeze, doing my best to not fixate on his smell—jasmine and sandalwood, intoxicating together. When I bring the plastic up to my eye, everything I see is suddenly more resolute, crispy. In front of me are small squares of black-and-white pictures. There are some of his father, in locations that are unfamiliar to me. The next photos are of his mother. At first view, the pictures seem the same, but they're subtle differences.

She stands in their backyard, her hand on her stomach, blades of grass behind her. The tones create a deep contrast of light and dark in all the right places—her skin, her hair, the sky. In the first pictures, there's not much you can see outside of her frame; but as the portraits progress, the variation is there. In her face, her demeanor, the energy that Ezra is able to capture around her. And of course, the change in her growing uterus. Growth. Transformation.

Life is both happening now and being created.

"Whatcha think? Be honest." His voice is eager.

"They're absolutely beautiful. You developed these?" I turn and our eyes lock. He nods shyly. He's proud.

"And your mom?"

Instantly, I'm transported back to their classic Victorian house, in the nicer part of town, where almost every home is a two-story with a full view of the Bay. I can see her, at their Steinway piano, eyes closed and fingers lightly on top of the white keys. She'd practice her vocal warm-ups, arpeggios that became the soundtrack to us running up and down their stairs. I can hear her soft and sweet voice, asking if I'd like to stay over for Shabbat dinner. I can see her bright blue eyes in the rearview mirror of her car when she'd drop me off at home after an afternoon of play.

She's . . .

"Pregnant. About seven months. She remarried a year ago. I'm going to be a big brother." The excitement in Ezra's voice is electric. Even his eyes seem bright.

"Wow. Congratulations to you all. Mazel tov, right?"

He rubs the back of his neck and huffs out a laugh. "Yeah—I mean, yes—that's right. Thank you."

I soften imagining his mom, and I can't help but ruminate over mine. I've never thought about my mom dating again. Would she date? Could she get remarried? Would she want to have more kids? Could I be a big sister? Or would I be too jealous? Bigger yet, has she moved on from grief? Have I?

Last winter, we had a massive thunderstorm on the Peninsula that knocked down the power lines in our neighborhood for a night. In the morning, my mom opened the fridge to check if any of the contents had survived. When she opened the freezer door, she let out a yell so raw and sharp it pulled me into another world. She sank to the floor, crying, in palpable pain.

Before he died, my dad made a pan of lasagna and stuffed it in the freezer with his other creations. He was always doing that, making food and freezing it *just in case*. Even though we moved across town, my mom made sure to save his last meal, his last physical gift to us. But the storm, the loss of power, the aluminum couldn't keep the lasagna from going soft, spoiling, sagging into itself. For an hour, my mom deliberated about what to do. Keep it? Throw it away? Back and forth, back and forth. Finally, she threw it in the kitchen trash can, and I took the trash to the dumpster.

My chin drops and in a low voice I say, "She's so happy."

Ezra squints at me through his glasses, his eyes almost disappear.

"Sure, yeah. She's happy, so I'm happy." His voice quavers.

"That's the most important thing, right? Happiness in life?"

Ezra's mouth drops open, and there is a new level of incredulousness in his face that I've never seen.

"Don't take this the wrong way, but you're kidding me, right?" He glides over to me.

"Huh? No. What do you mean?"

"Are you happy, SJ? Like, is happiness something you actively seek in your life? Because from what I've seen, you're obsessed with one thing and one thing only—"

"That's not true," I cut in.

"Oh yeah? Quick, without thinking, what's the last movie you saw?"

"I—"

"What's the last concert you went to?"

"Okay, you're being—"

"I said without thinking. Just on the fly. When's the last time you went to a dance? Are you going to prom?"

My arms cross in front of my chest. "This is a false equivalency—just because you think—"

"Just answer me this: When's the last time you went on a date? Kissed?"

Ezra's hands are on his hips and he's staring at me like he knows, all too well, my secrets . . . or lack thereof.

I don't feel good anymore. The room is suddenly too compact and stuffy. Are there windows in this place? I need actual sunlight. No amount of red light can make me calm again.

"I know what you're trying to do," I say, "or what you're trying to insinuate and that is absolutely not fair. I am dedicated to my work. Succeeding brings me joy. That's my prerogative and how I show my dedication—"

"Oh my gosh, you been talking to my dad?" Ezra says, pinching the bridge of his nose.

"What's that supposed to mean?" I ask. He doesn't respond, so I continue. "Seriously, tell me. Because from what I remember, your dad is, like, a brilliant, nice, kind, *dedicated* guy, so thank you? Do you know how lucky you are to have him in your life? As a role model?"

Ezra stops, and his face goes flat. "My bad, I didn't mean anything by that. I just—"

"I know." I force the words out, but my throat is suddenly sore.

When my dad died, we had a small funeral, and Ezra was my only friend to attend. Okay, ex-friend. I guess when you're thirteen funerals aren't the most exciting place to be. None of my other classmates made it out, and I didn't have Priscilla or Chance yet. But Ezra and his dad showed up.

The mood in the darkroom plummets. We are both standing on eggshells, unsure how to maneuver with each other. We could be on the brink of extreme vulnerability, sharing it all; or we could ignore the past and how that colors our present and pretend we don't know each other's history.

Ezra stops and stares at me so intently it makes me nervous. Nothing on his face or body seems to move, while I'm suddenly so aware of every hair on mine.

"What?" I squeak, somewhat self-conscious of just existing.

"Now I'm genuinely curious. Are you going to prom? Do you have a date?"

"I . . ." My throat tightens. My cheeks burn.

He continues. "Last concert?"

I drop my eyes to the tile floor of small black-and-white checkers.

"Mm-hmm," he says, like he's vindicated or something.

"The things that make you happy don't have to, you know, make me happy or whatever." The words tumble out of my mouth, but they don't sound convincing.

"Okay, maybe that came out wrong. You should be happy. I think you deserve to be happy, that's all I'm trying to say."

"Cheesy much?" I say, but smirk. Ezra grins, then turns back to his station as we work in silence for another twenty minutes. I try not to stare at his test strips and prints, but it's hard. The curiosity I have for this part of him oscillates between convincing myself I hate it (and by extension, him) and marveling at his talent despite everything (him ruining my afternoon and possibly my future).

I think about my mom, and how much I'd love to have our sacred moments captured like this, physical, something to hold on to. There are so many memories and keepsakes of life that I wish I could capture and save because our memories are often so unreliable. I wish I had more pictures of my dad. I know I should try harder to make more memories with my mom.

After a moment, I soften, and my curiosity gets the best of me. "Are these photos for your legacy project?"

Ezra frowns. "Absolutely not. No way. I'm not doing that."

"No, you're not using the photos? Or no, you're not doing the project?"

"Your choice. The legacy project is kinda wack, if you ask me. I shouldn't be forced to know what kind of legacy I want to leave on the world. At least not yet. Let me breathe. Additional requirements to graduate outside of my regular classes? Seems sketch to me."

"What? Why not start thinking about these things? If not now, then when? I mean, the legacy project doesn't have to be set in stone; it's just a way to get the ball rolling." I don't know why, but I stand up. My fingers steady me on the desk.

"Asking a high school senior about their legacy is lame. Boo. Boring," he says.

If I didn't know him better, I would believe him. But something's off. This doesn't make sense.

"You sound ridiculous." Ezra thinks he can fool me into thinking he's so blasé about life, but he can't. He doesn't respond, so I keep going. "Is this why you didn't apply to college? What are your plans after graduation, anyway?" I close the binder and take a step toward him.

"This is more of a second- or third-date conversation, don't you think?" He fakes a chuckle.

"Ezra Philip Davis-Goldberg, answer my question. Don't you try and humor your way out of this. You are the top of your class, and what, you have no plans after graduation? Make it make sense." We stare at one another for a moment, and I try another approach. "You're too talented not to have a plan. I just . . ."

But he won't even make eye contact with me. "Even in these photos, there's a lot of potential." He winces at the word.

"Fine." I give up.

"Fine." He echoes. Except I don't really want to give up, because I care. Not that it's Ezra but, you know, like, if it were anyone. Sometimes we all just need a little motivation. Encouragement or something.

Ezra hangs up a few photos near the baths, and I hand him the heavy binder. He gathers his stuff and steps to me, carefully removing his glasses, which have left small dents on the side of his nose.

"It's touching that you're concerned. Let's get out of here. We can talk about it over a donut. My treat."

And there we go. Another reminder that everything is a joke to him. Including the title and scholarship. "Hard pass."

"Oh, come on. I'm sorry about pulling you out of class. I couldn't help myself. I swear I didn't know how that donut stuff would go down. It's just that, SJ, I don't know why I'm like this around you." Ezra rubs a hand on the back of his neck. We both pause, and then he continues. "This is just wild, right? It's like I know you, but I don't know you, so I'm unsure how to act. You must feel like that too. I can't explain it, but maybe I can over food. What do you say? Tacos? Pies? Fries? My treat."

I shoulder my bag and head toward the door. I'm not falling for whatever this is again. "Thanks for the offer, but I'm busy."

"Studying?" There's a hint of mockery mixed with curiosity in his voice.

I shrug.

We stand in silence, taking each other in. What is the appropriate move here? More wit? More humor?

He gives his lips a small lick, and I don't like how much of his mannerisms I'm noticing.

"So we still good for bet two?" I ask as he sheepishly grins.

Good. Because I need to win this thing.

CHAPTER 16

QUICKLY, I HEAD TOWARD THE EXIT DOING MY ZOMBIE WALK, arms extended, as the red fades to black. My eyes adjust to the darkness as the soft folds of the curtain greet me. Get me out of here now.

My fingertips find the door first and I give it a push. But nothing. I inch closer, the smell of musty wood in my nose as I try again. The door doesn't open. I wiggle the long handle, the deadbolt rattles. It's locked.

"Fuuuuuck," I mumble. "Bad idea, worst idea ever." I lean my forehead against the door and close my eyes—not that it matters; can't see shit in here anyway.

My brain is about to start spiraling when a hand touches the small of my back, and I let out a piercing scream.

"Wow, wow, wow. Chill. It's just me." Ezra grabs my shoulders as I turn.

I can feel his breathing; the air tickles my upper lip. We stand in total darkness for a moment. My heartbeat begins to quicken. It should slow down, it's just Ezra, and I'm okay, but instead, everything inside of me begins to accelerate, like when I drink coffee without eating any food.

"Come on." Ezra grabs one of my hands and leads me back into the darkroom. He laces his fingers into mine, like I'm a balloon and he can't let me float away.

When we get back to the red light, he gives my hand a squeeze. "I promise you that wasn't intentional. I know how it seems."

Ezra makes a small puppy-dog face, somehow producing a glimmer in his eye, but I can't respond. Words are somewhere. Not in my mouth. All I notice is his touch, my hand, his fingers, still laced, connected.

He continues. "I swear I'm done with the jokes. This serves me right. Kevin—you know, tall Kevin with the 'fro? Well, whatever, we've been pranking each other all year. The darkroom locks from the outside. He's smart. This is good, very good. I didn't think he had it in him."

Ezra takes a small step toward me. My eyes scan up, and I notice a freckle on the tip of his nose. The smallest details about him come into a soft focus.

"I promise you, he's probably on the other side of the building, laughing his ass off."

Ezra chuckles to himself and his eyes widen. He tilts his head as if to say "This is funny, right?" but I can't think about that. The only thing I can feel is this connection between us. Waves ripple through my chest. I don't want to let go of whatever this is.

He keeps going. "I'm sorry. Really. I didn't intend to trap you in here with me." Ezra makes me look at him, and I let myself be fully seen. "And I meant what I said earlier. I'm not trying to be a jerk, pinky swear. Shit's been weird. My life feels off. I know I should use better words to explain myself, but *weird* is the best I can do."

"Um. It's okay, about Tall Kevin." My brain is partially on. I try again. "And I'm sorry that your life is weird right now." I cringe at my awkwardness. If there is a gene for being smooth, it seems to be absent from me.

"I just hate this part about senior year, you know? It's like I'm eighteen, but I'm also expected to be twenty-one, and twenty-seven, and practically thirty-five all at once." He shakes his head and lowers his chin. " 'You have to make a decision, Ezra. What are you going to major in? What about college? Graduate school? These choices now will affect the rest of your life, you know.' " His voice is proper, an imitation of all the adults around us. "The rest of my life? Word? For a moment, I just want to be eighteen. I just want to *be,* without any worries about the future. I don't want everything to weigh so heavily on this one decision. Is that not okay?" The only sound in the room is the water, flowing into itself. The perfect symbol for time, no beginning, no end, just continuously moving, whether we like it or not. In some ways, I think I understand his need to want to pause these small moments, to stop and really savor what we have, before it slips away.

Ezra doesn't stop. "My bad if I'm oversharing. And I know, I know what you're thinking. I'm a total brat. I know what a privilege it is *not* to be able to know. I have the luxury to fuck around and find out, and still know I'd be okay. I understand the irony. That I'm lucky to be able to take my time. That a lot of us aren't allowed the freedom I have. But it doesn't make my confusion any less real." Ezra turns away.

He is a brat. But also, he's not wrong. Senior year has been rife with intensity and questions and planning.

"Well, damn. I guess the darkroom really is where things come to light." He takes a dramatic pause. "What about you?" he asks, perking up. "Is your legacy project about the cathartic power of WeTalk dances?" He squeezes my hand again.

My stomach drops as Ezra lets out a little laugh. "Tell me I'm right. Please tell me I'm right, that would make my day. Scratch that—make my life," he says, the joy back in his voice.

I love that he remembers that. "I hate that you remember that." My words are barely audible.

He releases a smile that takes over his whole face. "You always had these big dreams. Of being an astronaut, a dancer, or a scientist—the sky was never a limit for you. It was dope to be around to hear them. You always made the impossible seem like it was possible."

There's a compliment or two in there, but I can't really receive them. I free my hand from his and grab my stomach, my insides upside-down. Ezra reminds me of a time when I used to dream, like, really dream about all that this life could offer. Before life got real—before bills and work and practical life stuff. When we were younger, I kept a secret idea notebook, which was full of all these wild and imaginative things. He was the only one I'd show it to, and he'd offer guidance and support where and whenever he could.

"Things change. Life put me on a different path. A realistic one. I dunno. I just don't think about those things anymore." My hands shake.

"Well, I'd like to hear about it sometime. Your life now, that is. You listened to me babble on. Let me return the favor." I feel light-headed. He continues, "And I told my mom we reconnected. She wants you to come over to the house for Shabbat dinner, like old times."

He mentioned me to his mom? I'm speechless.

Ezra leans in and a sweet scent fills my nose. "Can I?"

My voice is barely above a whisper when I ask, "Can you what?"

"Relearn you?"

I think I've stopped breathing. I nod, taking a small step closer to him.

"All right, all right, you're free," a voice booms from behind us. Tall Kevin. "What'd you think of that one?" Tall Kevin gives me a nod as he lifts his hand and greets Ezra with a slap and a shake.

Ezra takes a step back. "Kev, this is SJ—I mean Sasha." He flashes me a wink.

"Oooh. So you're the one keeping my guy up at night," Kevin says nonchalantly. Tall Kevin walks over to the pictures hanging up and points to a still in black and white. "Nice work, Ez."

From the corner of my eye, I can see the outline of Ezra. I

want to turn and face him, to ask him exactly what Tall Kevin means. My heart wants to know. But my brain won't push me to ask.

"Y'all want to get burgers or something?" Tall Kevin glances back and forth at us.

Ezra's eyes widen.

Something in me softens and I want to say yes, I really do, but I can't.

Instead, I blurt, "I better head out." But my legs are heavy. Ezra's face falls, but he doesn't speak.

"For what it's worth, I'm glad I got to spend some quality time with you," Ezra says, a rawness in his voice that almost makes me sad. Tall Kevin expresses his excitement with his eyebrows, which curve up, practically to the top of his afro. Ezra walks to his backpack and digs in. "Before you go, take these." He hands me papers. "A copy of the civics stuff, from the reader. Kerry's idea, not mine. I swear." I grab them and hold them against my chest. "Thanks for coming, SJ."

At Ezra's words, something inside me shifts, like a car changing gears. It's automatic and I can't stop it.

I pull at my backpack, the right words ready for once. "Me too, Ezra," I say, meaning it. Being stuck with him in a cramped photo room was . . . nice.

I savor one last look and then I head out to find the light.

CHAPTER 17

THERE'S JUST SOMETHING ABOUT FRIDAY AFTERNOONS, THE
closeness to the weekend, and torturing students. It's the last
period of the day, and I'm doing everything in my power to
stay focused, even though the hands on the clock seem to be
moving backward, seconds stretching like hours.

I'm at my desk, my setup (pencils, pens, highlighters, and
small Post-it notes) welcoming whatever is in store for today's
AP English lesson.

Mrs. Gregg strolls around the room, her hands in the
front pockets of her yellow gingham dress. I'd say she's one
of the more stylish teachers at school, like straight out of an
Anthropologie catalogue: dresses with pockets, cardigans,
Chuck Taylors. She heads to the front of the room and passes
my desk.

"Okay, how about a little Friday fun?" She tilts her head.

Note: Whenever a teacher says something is about to be
fun, brace yourself. Because more likely than not, it will not be.

At her desk, she hops up and sits down as she crosses her legs. "I was thinking we'd have a little impromptu conversation. You've finished *Hamlet*. You've completed your essays. Let me hear your uninhibited thoughts about it. Go for it. Be free." Her eyebrows bounce up and down.

Right, the essay and the bet. I frown, remembering my defeat.

Like he's been waiting for this moment his whole life, Carlos's hand shoots up. Mrs. Gregg nods, and Carlos coughs as if to clear his throat.

"On everything, I hated it: the play, the story, all of it. Detest. Do not recommend. Do not pass go."

Mrs. Gregg widens her green eyes. "Really? Carlos, elaborate, please."

By the glimmer in his eyes, he's been thinking about this for some time. "Come on. I know y'all agree. Hamlet needs therapy. Big time. The whole play is just a testament to grief— the power of grief and the side effects of grief. Hamlet lost everything, no cap, in his life because he couldn't get over his dad's death. What a bizarre legacy to leave behind."

Around me, students mumble under their breath. They agree. My stomach tightens.

Carlos continues, "Like, okay, it was shady that Claudius killed his brother, but Claudius is right when he says that we're all gonna die someday. Hamlet just can't come to terms with that reality, and in that grief, his pain just destroys him. He loses his mom, his girl, his friends, everything! Because he's chasing around a ghost. It's textbook psychology. He could have been prince in peace, but nooo. Had to act out. It's a clear case of when being too emo goes wrong."

Stacey Clemens stands and gives a slow, golf clap. All I can do is clutch my hands together. My skin is heating up, my throat is hoarse, and my heartbeat is strong, so strong and loud. I know he wasn't speaking about me, but his words feel personal. The word *legacy* strikes me in my stomach. Graduation, the tie, valedictorian, all the hard work I'm doing for myself and my family feel on the line, and the weight is massive. What if I have no legacy to leave?

Carlos stands up. "Let me back up. I guess there were parts of the play that were interesting. The play could have been one act if Hamlet had the courage to work through his shit— I mean, issues."

Some snicker. Carlos drapes his arm across his chest and says, "Thank you for coming to my TED Talk." He then gives a small bow and sits back down just as everyone else stands up. The room explodes into a balanced roar of claps and laughter from half of the room. Clearly, those who've never lost someone.

I can't be in here.

Without thinking, I'm out of my seat and through the door, walking down the empty hallway. I've endured way worse in class, but I've never gotten up and actually left because of something someone's said. But this, this hit different. I need some air.

As soon as I step outside, my eyes begin to swell, and a pressure I didn't know I was holding tightens my body. *Oh no, not now. Please not now.* But it's too late.

I tilt my head, chin pointed toward the sky. Maybe if I stay still, the tears won't come. Maybe gravity will hold them back. But they form. Small, warm pools at the edge of my eyes. I close my eyes tighter. *Don't cry. Do not cry.*

Carlos wasn't talking about you. Nothing he said was about you or your grief. It was about Hamlet. I shake my head, his words echoing in my brain. I'm just tired. It's been a long, stressful week. Especially with that damn essay score laughing at me.

I keep my eyes shut. Maybe if they were open, if I weren't holding a dam of tears, I would have seen him approach, and I could have made an escape.

"Hey, you good?" a smooth voice says from behind.

Ezra.

Nope. Not now. I squeeze my eyes tighter; maybe he'll just go away.

"I was taking some photos, and I saw you run out of the hallway. You good?"

If I don't speak, maybe he'll take the hint.

"It's okay if you're not okay." Seconds pass, he doesn't budge. "Listen, I'm going to do something I learned as a kid, a tried-and-true remedy for this type of feeling." He steps closer. "I'm going to give you a hug. I know I should ask for your consent, but since you're not speaking, and I don't trust you'd answer honestly if you were, I'm going to just go for it."

Is he for real right now?

I hear his footsteps, but I don't move. I can feel his body, and goose bumps ripple across my skin.

His arms wrap around me in the exact moment the air is sucked out of the atmosphere. I can't move. So I just stand, eyes locked shut, my arms by my side, like some sort of alien who has never received a hug.

Ezra squeezes me, and the pressure of his touch brings an unknown comfort through my body.

"So, small update. You're doing great. I'm going to keep holding you, okay?" His voice is soft and tickles my ear. "Science says that if you want your hug to be effective, to release oxytocin and whatnot, you need to do it for at least twenty seconds. So just stay with me a bit, I want to make sure you get everything I'm giving."

In the name of science, I let him hold me. Each moment is long and confusing; scary and heavy and floaty and expansive. My heartbeat follows his and begins to beat slower. My breath, too, seems more stable.

Ezra speaks first. "You know you can open your eyes now, don't you? It's over. Good job, you survived a Davis-Goldberg hug," he says, arms loose but still around me.

I squint and see the stubble on his chin.

"You're human. These are human responses, and it's okay to have them. You cry, I cry. It's cathartic and natural and important in our healing process. I get it."

Get it together, Sasha. I take my time to fully open my eyes, small blinks to reacquaint myself with the world, and there he is. A little blurry, but he's there. The afternoon sun is behind him and gives him perfect lighting.

He doesn't release me, so I don't move.

Ezra leans in and the world around me dims, but the closer his face gets to mine, I realize there's a part of me that wants to see what will happen next.

"You know, you think you're pretty clever, but I'm onto you." He pauses, his voice soft and rich like velvet on my skin. He waits for our eyes to lock, and when they do, his words tickle my ear: "You ever gonna answer my question from yesterday?"

"Wh-what question? From what I recall, there were many."

He smirks. "When's the last time you've been kissed?" It's not so much a question, but an invitation. There's magnetic pressure from his hand on my back that pulls me to him. His arms tighten around my body again. My heart stops beating and my lips part just as the fingers on my back melt into my skin.

Okay . . . I can handle this . . .

"Hello! Mrs. Gregg sent me out here to make sure you're okay," a familiar voice calls out. Ezra pulls back first, albeit reluctantly.

Oh my god. Again? What was just about to happen?

Stacey Clemens takes a long pause before busting into a grin that cannot be contained. "Take your time, Sasha. I'll tell Mrs. Gregg you're just fine." She gives me a wink, like a proud mother or a knowing best friend, before returning to the classroom.

I take a step backward, and then two more, just to be safe.

The blood in my body floods my cheeks as my face heats up from embarrassment. Ezra runs a hand across the back of his neck, and a sheepish smile forms on his face.

When Stacey is gone, I get the nerve to speak. "I. Um. I'm class. I mean, I'm fine. We should get back to class," I say. He locks eyes with me and gives me that pensive look of discernment, eyes serious but also steamy. I don't like it. It's too strong, like he has X-ray vision and can see what's inside of me. Or, like he's Professor Xavier and he can read my thoughts. It's brooding and powerful and *dangerous*.

Ezra shrugs. "Or not. Class isn't that important. We can stay out here, you know. We can leave, do what you need to do to take care of yourself. I can come with you."

My lips feel like they are on fire and we didn't even kiss. This is not okay. I feel naked, exposed.

"You want to get out of here?" he asks again, motioning toward the front gates.

Ditch class? With Ezra?

"I'm fine," I say, doing my best to mask in my voice the emotions building in my body. He holds my gaze, so I say it again. "School's almost over. Let's just go inside and pretend this never happened."

But I don't move and neither does he. Ezra stuffs his hands into his jeans pockets and just studies me, his eyes full. He's waiting for me to make a move, I realize. The ideas and implications run through my mind again. *He's waiting for you to make a move!* I cast my eyes to my shoes and move in the only direction I know how.

Back to class.

$$\heartsuit\heartsuit\heartsuit$$

Pretending an almost kiss didn't happen isn't easy. At all. Believe me, I've been trying. And to my detriment, it's now all I can think about. The almost, the what-if, the endless possibilities. Outside of today, and fine, maybe yesterday too, I've never thought about kissing Ezra, other than that one time in seventh grade when Ezra's cousin asked if I *liked* liked Ezra, but I pushed that thought to the side. We were friends, *just friends,* and—

"Hello? Earth to Sasha. Your good thing—you're up!" Chance cries. After school, we're at RJ Burgers, the place that started it all, this lovely tradition. Big booths and delicious, piping-hot steak fries.

I struggle to snap back into the moment. "My good thing?" I parrot. I left class and Ezra found me and we *almost* kissed. Is an almost kiss a good thing? Is an almost kiss a thing at all? I fiddle with my napkin. "I, um, my good thing . . ." This shouldn't be this hard to answer.

"Womp. I guess we're all in a slump this week," Priscilla says.

Oh shit, what did they say? I try to recall the last fifteen minutes, but nothing comes to mind. Guilt builds in my chest. An almost kiss has made me woozy, weak. Imagine if I actually kissed him?

I stuff another fry in my mouth, absolutely certain that *almost* had the possibility of making me trip up, and I refuse to let anyone get in my way of winning.

CHAPTER 18

THE NEXT MORNING, I WAKE UP WITH NERVOUS ENERGY. I'M groggy and antsy at the same time. I get out of bed to start my Saturday study routine, but when my mom begins to move around the house, I quickly slip back into bed and pretend I don't hear her. It's not until she knocks on my door that the pressure from the week returns in full force.

"Aigee-ya. You almost ready to go?" She hangs on my doorframe, her long black hair pulled up save for a few runaway tendrils.

I sit up and bite my bottom lip, but I'm too afraid to respond.

"What is it?" She walks toward me, her eyes scanning my face like a mom detective.

Instantly, nausea lurches up inside me, because for the first Saturday in four years I'm about to do something I never, ever, do. "I just . . . I have so much of my own work to do today," I say.

"Oh."

"I'm sorry. But I think . . . is it okay if I don't go?" I ask. The words fill me with a heavy guilt. My shoulders sink, like the Pattersons' large house is sitting on my back. I'm basically asking my mom to clean that all alone. The scrubbing, the dusting, the cleaning, all by herself.

I'm on a seesaw: the weight of one obligation bounces me up and then the other pulls me down. I just have to go into beast mode for the civics presentation, also known as Bet #2, so that Ezra and I will be tied. That way, I'm still in the game. Then once I win, I'll be back to my normal, regular self.

"It's fine, sweetie," my mom says, but it's hard to believe her; the hints of disappointment linger in her voice. Here I am, breaking a four-year standing date.

My mom leaves my room. I twist and turn, the blankets feeling heavier each second I stay wrapped in them.

I should change my mind and go with her, but I don't.

Instead, I hop out of bed, reach for my backpack, and begin taking out my planner and books. My mom fidgets at the front door; she doesn't say goodbye on her way out.

My body loosens up a bit and a wave of excitement picks me up because today is the day I unleash my secret weapon: the Walker Ross Lecture Series.

Next to the library there's a small, rustic building that used to be the first capitol building of California, before the capital moved to Sacramento. Now it's a museum and art space. And for the last month, it's been the home to select works of Walker Ross, the county's super-famous politician and philosopher. Okay, maybe super famous is a stretch. But he's popular around town. He's written dozens of books and can be seen on the evening news, depending on the topic.

Once, I saw him at the local grocery store. I wasn't sure if it was him, but another older woman stopped and stared like he was Brad Pitt, with no care in the world how hard she was ogling, so I knew it had to be. He's older, probably pushing seventy-five, with a head full of flowy white hair and an endless collection of chunky brown sweaters.

As of the last month, Mr. Ross's works have been on display at the museum as an ode to an anthology he's releasing. To promote the book, he's been having small lectures with question-and-answer sessions after. I saw flyers weeks ago and knew it would give me a leg up for Mr. Mendoza's presentation, though I pushed it out of my mind when I saw it was on a Saturday, because Saturdays are usually reserved for working with my mom. But that was before Ezra and the bets.

I settle in for a morning of the most extensive research I have ever done in my life. My desk is covered in Post-its of all sizes and colors. I take out a black pen and a yellow highlighter, then turn to a clean sheet of paper. The blank page is a canvas, and I am the painter. By the time I'm done, it will be an erudite masterpiece. I start by reading an article, annotating and asking questions on large Post-its, which I stick in the book. To reinforce the ideas, I say them to myself aloud three times.

After an hour my hand starts to tire, the muscles aching. I bring my hands together and clap. I've done some good work.

Around lunch time my brain begins to shut down and heads into rest mode. I peep at the clock, almost noon, then slide, stretching, to my feet. It's time to go anyway.

As I'm heading out the door, my phone vibrates in my pocket.

> Priscilla 10:15 a.m.: I'm single, and I'm sad. Before I call Gina and beg her to take me back, are you around? Let's go thrifting? Or get ice cream? Dye your hair? Cut my bangs? We can turn this tragedy into triumph! Let's make a memory.

My shoulders slump. The pain in her words hits me. I technically am available, but . . . I can't. She'd want me to do whatever I can to win the valedictorian title along with the hefty scholarship that comes with it, right? Nerves flood my body and I attempt to untighten my jaw, wiggling it side to side. I try not to deflate in self-pity as I respond.

> Sasha 10:16 a.m.: Sorry girl, I wish I could, but I'm working.

> Priscilla 10:16 a.m.: With your mom?

I don't think, because if I had, maybe I wouldn't have lied.

> Sasha 10:17 a.m.: Yeah, with my mom. Our usual Saturday routine.

Priscilla 10:18 a.m.: Oh duh, that's right. Maybe Chance wants to give me bangs. If not, I'll continue listening to "thank u, next" on repeat. Text me later. Tell ohmma hello. XO

I read the words quickly as I turn my phone over, as if maybe she can see me or sense my lie.

CHAPTER 19

WHEN I STEP OUTSIDE, I AM SURPRISED AT HOW VIBRANT THESE Saturday streets are. The sun shines, instantly warming my skin. The weather is a perfect, comfortable seventy-four degrees, and everyone in the city is out to enjoy it. I see a couple roller-skating while holding hands, and another in matching Adidas jumpsuits on a tandem bike. Every car that drives by is filled with laughter, its windows rolled down, letting the ocean water scents flow in and out of its passengers hair. Spring is the perfect time for a walk, and even though I'm not participating in this Saturday fun, it's good to see it happening in the moment.

With each step I make toward Ye Old History Museum, the more the good vibes start to fade. From my mom to Priscilla, my guilt is off the charts.

At the old brick building, I stall outside the door and grab my phone, a creature of habit. There's a part of me that wants to text Priscilla, because I need support, reassurance. But

Priscilla thinks I'm working with my mom, who is currently cleaning the Pattersons' large house all by herself. Something stronger than guilt drips down me now, swirling around my stomach and weakening my knees. The one thing I don't want—my mom to overwork—I'm actively making her do.

I hate this.

Priscilla must feel me thinking about her, because instantly, my phone lights up with a text from her. It's a video compilation of a French fry–eating competition and then a link to an article titled "What Happens When You Eat French Fries Daily?" followed by *"Worth it."* Another message comes in.

> Priscilla 1:00 p.m.: Update: I've got major updates. MAJOR. Call me after work plz?

I swallow the lump in my throat, shove my phone into my backpack, and enter the museum. The museum is old and made of cobblestones and smells kind of rustic. Mr. Ross sits near the entrance; he sips a cup of tea and nods his head at himself as he watches everyone's movements. I scan the room and notice I'm the youngest person in the audience by at least fifty years. But no matter, I'm just thankful that no one else from school is here.

Mr. Ross stands up and a hush falls over the room. He taps at a mic and then begins.

I take out my phone to record his words and a small notebook to write down important thoughts.

"I've dedicated my life to thought, a life of the mind, as

150

they say." His voice is deep, and his words stretch like taffy. He speaks in a way that makes everything sound intimate, like it's just us two, old friends having coffee. "People always ask what that's like, and I get confused, because aren't you doing the same? Haven't we all dedicated our lives to something? Hasn't everyone spent their entire life thinking? Among other things, of course."

It's almost too hard to write and record while standing, but I manage. I scribble a rhetorical question he asks, when a poke at my ribs sends a jolt through my body and causes my phone to drop out of my hand. The sound of hard plastic hitting against the wood floors is jarring, and almost immediately every head in the room turns toward me.

I scoop up my phone, relieved it didn't break. And then I find that Ezra's standing next to me, doing his best to hold in an uncontrollable laugh.

My face burns. I might die of embarrassment. I flash him my poker face, to which he simply holds up a finger and points ahead. The nerve!

We're like two middle Pringles stacked in a can, smushed together by the crowd. Our arms brush and my pulse races. What is he doing here?

Ezra watches Mr. Ross, engrossed, like he's hypnotized. He doesn't turn or talk to me for the rest of the hour; I know because I sneak glances at him every other minute. If we did make eye contact, I'm not sure what I would do. Ezra stands straight, his dark eyes almost stormy with thought. When Mr. Ross says something complex, Ezra tilts his head to the right and a curl bounces by his ear. Every so often, he shifts his weight and his hand bumps mine. His skin is soft and warm.

When he's finished, Mr. Ross stands and the audience explodes in applause, which makes Mr. Ross blush, his cheeks turning a deep pink. I gather myself, smoothing my shirt and my jeans against my skin. The room comes alive with chatter as Mr. Ross makes his rounds.

"Well, well, what do we have here?" Ezra asks, as if we haven't been grazing each other for the past hour. He turns to face me completely, the smallest space between our bodies. My chest is so close to his I can't help but notice all of him. He's in an old YMCA shirt with small holes at the neckline, black basketball shorts that are too long, and black high-top sneakers. His skin is radiant and warm, like he's been basking under a beautiful morning sun.

"I could ask you the same thing." I stuff my notes into my backpack. "Shouldn't you be at the gym? You really came here dressed like this?"

He puts a finger through one of the holes. "Like what?"

Like the attractive lead in one of those old-school movies where the captain of the basketball team takes the winning shot at the absolute last second of the game, renewing the team's ability to love or dream or hope, but he can't read or something equally traumatic and basketball is his outlet or maybe his prison or possibly both.

Ezra raises his eyebrows. "I have layers, SJ. Came here after a pickup game at the gym. I am also a fan of Mr. Ross and his work. I always come out to hear him speak, and guess what, no pens." He does jazz hands in the air.

"But why are *you* here?" Ezra asks. Why is he always so smirky?

My lips part and I prepare to speak, but he continues. "Oooh, let me guess, civics presentation?" He taps his forehead. "You're here to get some hot information, fresh from the source. You think that this will give you a leg up on bet two, and me. A little obvious, but I see you."

He lifts his chin, all smug-like, and I hate him for being right. This is like a terrible chess game and I'm always one move behind Ezra. Or maybe I'm playing checkers and he's playing chess. The crowd around us moves, so we follow and take several steps toward the exit.

"You want to show me your notes?" he asks. "Want to talk over your ideas? I don't mind."

I stop to glare at Ezra, holding up whatever traffic was behind us. Ezra motions to the doors, and we walk through the lobby and out into the street together.

"I'd show you my notes," he says. "But I don't write things down; I like to keep everything digital. I do my processing at home, where I can think in peace. There, now you know about the pencil-gate mystery."

So, what—he's just absorbing and storing information until he hurls the words onto his computer? I almost don't believe him.

He grabs the crook of my arm. "We should study together sometime, if you want."

Outside, the sunshine from earlier is gone. Gray clouds linger in the sky and small rain puddles cover the ground. We are held together by some unknown force. I focus on the change in weather; it's too hard to think with his hand is still on my arm.

I'm about to let out a sigh or a bashful smile when Mr. Ross walks up. He's shorter than I imagined, and he uses a shiny wooden cane to help him get about. He stops next to Ezra, and his eyes gleam in that joyful old man way.

"Why, Ezra, I'm so glad you're here. What did you think? Satisfactory?"

"A pleasure, sir, as always," Ezra says. "Thank you for taking the time. And, um, this is Sasha Johnson-Sun, my best friend and one of the brightest minds of our generation."

"It's an honor to meet you, sir," I say, even though my mind is still stuck on Ezra's compliment.

Mr. Ross greets me and holds my gaze just before he shuffles away. When he's out of sight, I squeal and give Ezra a pat. "You know him?"

"Eh." He shrugs. "Just from the lecture series. I've come a few times. I ask questions. He listens and answers. It's been chill."

Ezra and the locally famous Walker Ross chat and "it's been chill"? Let's call it what it is—Ezra is the biggest nerd on the Peninsula. Ezra is a super fan. That fact is almost enough to make me fall over.

"Also, best friend? For real?"

"What? I was gonna say 'best friend forever ever,' but I

didn't want to be too cringe." He jostles my shoulder with his hand, and the combination of his laugh and touch send a pleasurable jolt through me. "Can you spare a few minutes? For the sake of art and nature and the beauty of living in this very moment? I think you'll love it."

For the sake of art and nature and the beauty of living in this very moment, I nod.

Trust me, his eyes say.

My heart pounds. I let him lead me to his car.

CHAPTER 20

WE DRIVE IN TOTAL SILENCE AS I STARE AT THE OUTSIDE WORLD, everything a little hazy from the rain. They are the same streets I have known my whole life, but now nothing is familiar. We travel through the Monterey tunnel, and I close my eyes and hold my breath. It's a ritual. Except . . . I don't know what to wish for. I've always wished for the same two things—my mom's health and me being able to make my family proud. At this point though, I want to ask for something different, a little something for me. What does my heart want? The car buzzes, everything goes dark, and when we emerge on the other side, I open my eyes and exhale.

The car slows down, and Ezra scans the streets for parking. We're in tourist heaven: restaurants with clam chowder, the aquarium, and shops overfilled with marine life trinkets. Despite the weather, the area is busy. Tourist season is alive and well.

I've seen this viewpoint before, but I don't think I've ever been here.

Ezra's long torso twists, and his back is near my face. His body glides in between the small space of passenger and driver seat, front and back of the car. I can smell him—that woodsy- jasmine mix.

Then he pops back into his seat, beaming.

"Found 'em!" He hands me black binoculars. "Come on. You're going to love this."

He's right. As soon as I step outside, I love it. We stand near the water, the air crisp from all the rain. The ocean is a deep, dark gray blue; the waves swirly and powerful as they crash against the rocks. The sky is a silky gray; clouds linger as if to say there will be more storms.

I peer through Ezra's binoculars as he stands near me, his arm touching mine. I can tell he's watching me view the world. I try to focus on what's in front of me. It takes my eyes a moment to adjust to the small holes. I think about the ocean, the fact that it is 90 percent unknown. We think we understand a thing. But in reality, we have no idea. Because, like Ezra, most things have layers. And a lot of us are just scratching the surface, just beginning to comprehend the vastness of it all.

"You see anything? Dolphins? Whales?" Ezra steps back, I notice when our touch drops, like losing an important connection. With his camera in his hand, he aims off into the distance and takes a picture.

"No, nothing yet." I squint my eyes, which only makes

things worse. I refocus. "I see a seal, or an otter. Definitely an otter. Here," I say, handing him the binoculars.

The air is cool and clean on my face. I rub my arms and try not to stare at Ezra as he marvels at the world.

Ezra peers through the black plastic, his head hunched over, the only time I've ever seen him sort of slouch.

"I love to come out here and just get lost admiring the ocean, especially after big storms. Once, I saw a family of dolphins, just swimming. Another time I saw a double rainbow *and* a whale. It was epic. I swear I almost shat myself." Ezra puts the binoculars down and turns to face me. "There are some dope things here. You just have to take the time to find them."

My heart flutters and my cheeks warm at his insightfulness. Ezra's whole face lights up, sparkling. It does something to me.

"The lighting is perfect right now. Let me take a few shots of you. Please?" he says, bending over and grabbing his camera.

"What? No. Me? I don't think I can. I'm not ready," I let out.

It's too late. Ezra tucks a loc behind my ear and is smiling so big I think his grin might fall off his face. I do my best to fight off the joy, a literal contagion, that begins to seep over me, but I can't.

"Don't think too hard, just try. It'll be good. I got you."

The last words beat in my heart, and my chest swells.

"Fine. Ten minutes, tops." I can't believe my own words. Who am I right now?

"Dope," Ezra says, and his shoulders bounce in excitement. "Okay, I'm just going to have you loosen up a bit, get familiar with being in front of the camera." He walks backward and fiddles with his lens. "I want you to walk toward me, give me confidence, give me boss girl vibes. Be playful. Just walk," he says, his camera already clicking.

I take two confused steps toward him; I don't know if I've ever been so self-conscious of my movements before. The camera keeps clicking. I really try to loosen up by placing a hand on my hip, but that only makes me feel jerkier, like a robot who needs oil.

Ezra's face pops up from behind the camera lens. "Good start. That was awesome! But be more bold, *even more.*"

My lips pout. More? "I'm too awkward," I whine. "Plus, the ground is all squishy from the rain." Ezra notes our muddy shoes, then scans the rest of the area.

"You're right. How about you go . . . up there," he says, gazing at a big gray rock behind me. I could probably sit on it. There are small grooves in the side that I could use to climb up.

We walk to the rock, and after three attempts at what is the equivalent of one pull-up, my muscles finally get me to the top, some four feet off the ground. I sit, my jean overalls protecting me from the cold rock, my legs dangling, Ezra several feet away from me.

"Great. Just relax. Be natural. I'll ask you some questions, and you can answer. Change movements and body language, just be you. I'll capture it all."

I try to strike a pose like I've seen models do on TV, but it's way harder than it looks. Instead, I sit up straight and turn my head, gazing off into the distance like I'm on the cover of an indie album.

"Yes, there it is. Hold that," Ezra says, so I do. "Okay, would you rather . . ."

I let out a little laugh. "Oh god, you remember?" Of course he does.

"Duh. How could I forget? It was one of our favorite games," he says, raising his face from the camera lens. "Okay, would you rather have a pause or a rewind button on your life?"

My facial expression shifts from silly to more serious. "I think rewind. You?"

He doesn't hesitate. "Definitely pause, but you could have guessed that."

True. I think about his love for photography, his love of the darkroom, all the ways in which he holds on to time, to life, his commitment to savoring the beautiful in his photos. Whereas I know parts of me wish I could go back in time to savor a few old moments again.

I straighten up, quick to ask a question before he does. "Would you rather have the world's best pizza once and only once in your life, and no other slice ever again, *or* mediocre pizza whenever you want?"

"Ugh. The torture. How you gonna ask me that? You know how I feel about pizza." Ezra gives me a playful sigh. The boy always loved his pizza. I don't know why I'm so glad to know that he still does.

"It's supposed to be difficult. So, what's your answer?"

Ezra brings his hand to his chin, letting his fingers cover his lips. "This is like, is it better to have loved and lost than to have never loved before? Is that what you're asking me? Is this question metaphorical?"

I raise one eyebrow in interest.

Ezra continues. "World's best pizza, hands down. Hopefully, it's a whole pie and not just a slice. Same thing goes for love—give it to me, let me have it, drown me in it, rip my heart out if you must, but let me experience it while I can. I'd choose one phenomenal love over a dozen decent ones any day."

The wind picks up around us, and the leaves begin to dance in the air. Ezra's words settle in me. My eyes stare off into the ocean and I almost forget what we're doing.

"Awesome. Hold that right there," he says the minute my body moves. We both laugh.

Ezra gives me directions, and I do my best to act natural for several more counts. I smile and try to strike a pose. At every movement, Ezra praises my actions.

"So I've been dying to know. NYU or Columbia?"

"Huh?"

"Oh yes, that's the face." The camera flutters, capturing every move I make. "I've wanted to ask you ever since people

161

started getting acceptances letters. Just to see how past SJ and present SJ aligned."

Ezra lowers the camera again. "I remember all you talked about was attending college in New York. Living in Greenwich Village? Summers on Fire Island? I don't know, you said you were inspired to live in New York by some babysitter? Stephanie? Sam—Sar—, she had some *S* name, like you. That was, like, your big thing. You just had to go to college in New York. I know you got the grades and the test scores to get in. So what did you decide? What school am I losing you to?"

I frown, unsure how to handle this question.

He continues. "You're not going to tell me? If I had to guess, I would say NYU. But you know, maybe I'm wrong. You have a little bit of that elitist Columbia thing going on too. My parents are still pissed because I didn't apply anywhere. I don't know, I'll figure it out. I can transfer from the community college, if I want. College is going absolutely nowhere. I still have time to sign up for classes. I have time to figure this next step out."

His face becomes contemplative, his brows knitting. "Okay, but that's me. Now, what about you?"

I shake my head. "Again, I can't believe how much you remember about me."

Ezra is startled. "Why not?"

My chest tightens. It's like Ezra has some special remote control that can rewind and replay parts of my life I've so carefully tucked away. These memories are filled with excitement and hope. I spent a lot of time in middle school dreaming about college. The teachers used to dangle college in front of us, like some carrot, some big ticket to a new life. And at the time, I was all for it. I knew I could work hard, that I had power over my grades, that I could control how well I did in school. That I could be the first in my family to finish college. We did a research project and *Stacy's* (from *The Babysitter's Club*, Ezra was close enough) knowledge and my computer skills led me to New York City. I knew I had to go there the moment I saw all the bright lights, all the possibilities. I wanted to live in a big, fast-paced city, nothing like this sleepy coastal town. I wanted adventure and subway rides and endless bagels and views from atop skyscrapers.

Ezra's vulnerability pushes me to open up, just a little. "I kinda forgot I applied there, feels like so long ago. And yeah, I got in but didn't get as much financial help, which sucks because out-of-state tuition is no joke. I'm going to Monterey University. I made the decision to stay local, you know. I gotta help my mom with work. It's just more practical to stay here. It just is what it is."

My eyes are hot.

Ezra swallows and says, "You know, sometimes depression and anxiety can affect our memories. Our brains protect us by forgetting things."

This sucks the life out of me.

Ezra must notice my soul disappear. He speaks, softer and slower this time. "I don't mean to offend you. I don't. I just know that you've experienced grief, and I'm here for you. I've always been here, and I'll always be here."

My eyelids close, and when I open them again, he's near the rock, near me.

"Here." He offers his hand and I take it, pushing off and jumping down.

When my feet hit the ground, the mud engulfs my old Nikes and sucks me an inch into the earth.

"Oh no!" I yelp.

Ezra pulls at my arm the same time I'm trying to tiptoe out of the mud. My body falls into his, which surprisingly has the strength to support us both. It takes me a moment to realize he's still holding one of my hands, which is now on his chest, above his heart.

Ezra's other hand makes its way around my waist, and if I wanted to move, now would be the time. But I don't. The air around us warms and the city pauses; traffic stops. He tightens his hold on me. Our bodies are intertwined, his full lips close to mine. My brain shuts off, because my body already know what's going to happen next.

His lips are like silk pillows against mine, the kiss soft and slow before an increase in intensity. My body relaxes for a moment, and the world stops spinning.

His arm tightens around my waist. I press into him, matching his pressure. My body is floating. Our lips move together like professional dance partners, like we've done this before, like this is something we're exceptionally good at.

After several blissful seconds, I take a step back, releasing myself from his touch.

My eyes find his as he's biting his bottom lip, with a sexy

grin on his face. My lips, my cheeks, hell, even my teeth are on fire.

Ezra pushes his camera from his chest to his back. "Was that okay?" he asks.

I nod. *More than okay,* I want to say, but speaking is too difficult right now. I think my life will be split in two distinct eras—before and after this kiss.

"I've been waiting to do that since we were twelve," he whispers.

My eyes widen in shock.

Ezra quickly speaks up. "Wait, you knew, right? You must have known—"

My heart pounds. I shake my head, embarrassed.

Ezra grabs my hand and our fingers zip together.

"Come on. Let's get out of here. I can tell you more about my massive crush in the car."

CHAPTER 21

INSIDE EZRA'S CAR WE ARE QUIET AS HELL. ALL I CAN THINK ABOUT is his lips on mine, the way my soul floated out of my body, and how the words "since we were twelve" and "massive crush" sent a shiver up my spine. He turns the volume up in his car, which is good, because I'm almost positive he can hear my thoughts, they are so loud. H.E.R. plays in the background—between the melodic guitar and her warm voice, it feels like she's singing to us. It is the perfect soundtrack to this beginning. I might combust. Again.

"This is me," I sputter as the car pulls up to my building. Ezra inches near me, his eyes asking for more. Maybe he and I should talk first, before, you know.

"This is you," he parrots back.

Be responsible, I think. It would be so easy to sail away into this—yeesh, *what is this*? I've read one too many a romance novel about people getting swept up in . . . lust. But don't they also live happily ever after? Shut up, logic.

"Thanks for the ride, Ezra," I say, but I'm sure he can hear the uncertainty in my voice.

"Let me walk you to your door," he says.

"That's really not necessary." But he's already out of the car. Of course he's chivalrous.

Ezra walks behind me as we head up to my apartment. We turn toward the building, and my mom approaches from around the corner. She spots us, and her face lights up.

"Oh, mo mo," *oh my gosh,* she says. She must be truly surprised for the Korean to slip out. "Who is this?" She leans in, and then her eyes widen in recognition. "Ezra? Is that you?"

My mouth falls open. She remembers him? "Mom, you're home early?"

She ignores me and beams at Ezra like he's her long-lost best friend and they've been reunited after a war. I can't remember the last time I've seen her this excited.

"Anyoung hasaeyo," he declares confidently, saying a formal hello in Korean while bowing deeply at the waist. He does a deep insa, a show of respect. I narrow my eyes, unsure of what I'm really seeing. I don't even bow that low to my elders. How does he know to do that? My mom nods, impressed.

"Honey, it's so good to see you! I didn't know you were coming over. Sasha, why didn't you tell me? Come in, come in."

"Mom, can we—" But it's too late. The front door is already open.

"And when did you learn Korean?" she says, practically shoving us both inside. I try to give her a signal, to speak to her silently, but she's not having it. She's in full-on hostess mode, and there's nothing I can do to stop her. "I just need a moment to freshen up from work. Then I will cut us some fruit and we can catch up. Ezra, I want to hear all about you and your family. Give me five minutes." She rushes to her room, not waiting for an answer.

Ezra stands in the doorway with a satisfied smirk as he takes off his shoes. He's never been in this house before, but he remembers our house rules. He isn't shy. He immediately saunters near the walls, admiring the pictures, as if he's walking through a museum exhibit. He stops at our makeshift altar. I stand several steps behind him with my arms across my body. I'm not sure why, but I'm feeling overly exposed, having him here.

He bites his lip and releases a loud exhale through his nose. "Your dad was a really cool guy." He turns to face me and the taunting sparkle from his eye is gone. Something else has replaced it.

"Remember when he'd take us to play basketball?" Ezra asks.

My throat tightens. When Ezra would come over, we'd usually spend so much time reading or playing video games inside that my dad would beg for us—plead for us—to get out of the house. Except when we got outside, we didn't know what to do. It was only when my dad dragged us to the park with a ball that we began to play and do other things outside of reading anime and writing fan fiction.

I think about what Ezra said earlier. What other memories have I stored away? What else has he kept that I've forgotten?

Ezra has a new, soft light in his eyes. "I'm sorry. I hope it's okay that I brought that up. I . . ." He contemplates for a moment. "I have a lot of good memories with him. With your family. I bet it's hard. I just know he must be so proud of you, that's all."

Ezra and I are truly seeing each other for the first time in a long time. At least, that's how it feels. As if we've known each other all along. "People are like mirrors to the soul," my dad would say.

Ezra's not afraid of silence, so the moment stretches. Instinctively I pull at the end of my hair. Ezra tilts his head and parts his lips.

"Now, all done." My mom comes out of her room and interrupts our trance. She pats Ezra on the shoulders, rising on the tips of her toes to do so, and he laughs.

"Go. Have a seat. I'll bring some food," she says, shooing us to the couch.

Keep your cool, Sasha. This is called being hospitable, a good host.

Ezra and I sit on opposite ends of our old couch, sinking into the cushions. In the kitchen, I can hear the knife methodically hit the cutting board. Knowing Mom, she's going to come out with enough food to feed an army.

My emotions swell. He wasn't supposed to come over, and yet here he is, making my mom laugh and sharing kind thoughts about my dad.

Before I can parse through any more memories, my mom comes back into the room and places a large platter of sliced fruit on the table. She's got apples, oranges, Korean pears, and grapes. Not only is there fruit, but there's nuts, honey, and dried squid. I check to see if Ezra is squirming at the squid, but instead, he claps his hands together in excitement.

"Komawhoa." He says "thank you" with his best Korean accent.

"Your Korean is pretty good." My mom is acting like she's never heard Korean from an American before.

"You're too kind, Ms. Sun. I was fortunate enough to travel to Japan and Korea last summer for an exchange program." Ezra's sweet, make-you-melt voice is back on.

"His accent is oh-kay," I say.

My mom ignores me and talks to him. "So smart. And so handsome. Honey, you got so handsome."

My whole body lights up. Ezra searches my eyes for approval, and goose bumps run up and down my arm.

"So handsome," she says again, nodding. Mom shifts her attention to me. "Sasha, don't you think?"

"Oh my gosh, Mom!"

Ezra gives me a small poke, like the one from earlier at the museum. Except this time when he does it, I mentally relive the moment his arms wrapped around my waist and our lips met. And she's right—he is handsome. *So handsome.*

My mom grabs one slice of a bright orange. "Okay, okay. I'll stop, I'll stop. But it's true." My mom smiles at both of us. "Before I forget, you know the Pattersons? I was talking to Mrs. Patterson today, and apparently her daughter goes to Skyline too."

"You know the Pattersons?" Ezra asks both of us.

"Yes, they are a new client of mine. We've been cleaning their house. Nice family."

Ezra turns toward me. I've never been embarrassed of my mom and her work, and I don't plan to start now. Mom motions for Ezra to have more food and he does. He knows the cues. Because my mom would be pissed if he didn't have something to eat. She would consider it rude, and I wouldn't hear the end of it. Ezra takes a handful of nuts and throws them into his mouth, one by one.

"So, Ezra, how is school going?" my mom asks between pecks of food. Such a predictable mom question.

But Ezra is just as amused. "Awesome. Straight As. I'm kicking butt." Ezra chomps into his apple and grins at me.

"Did you hear that? Such good grades! He's smart and handsome, Sasha. I bet you study all the time like Sasha."

I can't help but roll my eyes.

"Oh, come on, SJ," he says, "I'm not that bad. Did you tell your mom about our current tie for—"

"No," I say. "Erhm . . . nothing. Nope. Stop right there."

Ezra raises his eyebrows but doesn't finish his sentence. Realization hits, and he bats his eyelashes. "Speaking of the Pattersons, did you know that Kerry is ranked third? Possibly fourth, but hopefully third, if she has her way in the end." Ezra says something else, but my brain fizzes out. Kerry is third? Shit. Of course she is. That explains the reader shenanigans. Everyone is fighting to be first. I've been so caught up with Ezra lately, I forgot about the rest of the senior class.

For one moment, could the world slow down? A fear knots in my stomach. Could I end up in . . . third? I am speechless. I should say something to ease this tension, but I don't.

"Okay. I'll let you two finish . . . whatever it is you were doing. Let me know if you get hungry, I can make some soup." My mom stands and pinches Ezra's cheek. "I'm glad you came by. Come back soon, okay? I'm glad you found each other again."

My mouth falls open. Is this what she really thinks?

Ezra nods and flashes me a grin.

I smile back, but his words are still at the front of my thoughts. "Does Kerry know about the bets?"

Ezra nods again and shrugs his shoulders. He reaches over and gives my shoulder a squeeze. But I have a hard time noticing him because, just like that, Ezra has unveiled another layer to this whole mess.

CHAPTER 22

ALL I CAN DO IS SHAKE MY HEAD, IN AN "UNBELIEVABLE, HOLY fuck" kind of way.

"Where's the bathroom?" Ezra asks, standing up. I point to the closet, or the bathroom, or a portal to another world, and Ezra walks over there.

Ezra's small truth bomb reminds me that this competition ain't over—far from it. The guilt from the day and Ezra's lips and my legacy project swirl in my brain, making me hazy. I tilt my head, staring at the space he just occupied. Ezra in my house. Ezra and my mom, reunited. It's all just confusing. Then something sparkles at me, calling my name. Ezra's keys. I reach for them and notice something silver and bright and it says, "Hello, Sasha, over here!" A silver flash drive. *Digital notes.* I recall Ezra's words from earlier. I check over my shoulders and listen for footsteps.

The coast is clear.

My hands are moving faster than I can breathe or think,

because before I know it, the flash drive is spinning, spinning, spinning off Ezra's key ring and is in my pocket. If Ezra has an unfair advantage—Kerry as backup—why shouldn't I? I expressly told Priscilla and Chance not to engage, but Ezra didn't stop himself. He invited Kerry into our . . . situation.

"You two okay?" my mom calls from the hallway. I stuff my hands between my knees and try my hardest not to appear suspicious.

"Fine," I shout back loudly.

As Ezra exits the bathroom, I paint on an innocent smile.

He sits back down, and I fidget with the couch pillows, fluffing them with my hand. I can't face him. If I do, he'll know. He somehow always knows what's going on in my head. It's like he knows me better than I do half the time.

Ezra's eyes burn my skin. The flash drive is hot and heavy in my pocket.

"You good?" he asks.

"Yeah, I just have a lot on my mind, with everything, you know." I motion with my hands.

"Got it." He clears his throat. "One last thing that's been on *my* mind."

Oh no.

He swallows. "I'm sorry I was shitty to you at the surprise party in eighth grade. I know that's what started our falling-out. That was never my intention, and if I could take it back, I would." Ezra leans over and grabs a handful of nuts from my mom's platter. He chews and then sighs. "I can own that I was a difficult thirteen-year-old. I took a lot of anger out on the wrong people, and I hate that. Because you were my friend, my best friend."

I take a deep breath. "I . . ."

"I'm sorry. I've owed you an apology for a long time. You may not believe me, but after our fight, I wrote you several messages. I was just too scared to send 'em. I dunno. Then I moved. Then it felt like too much time had passed. But hopefully late is better than never."

I thought I was prepared for a lot of things, but apparently, not this. This is . . . How long has he wanted to say this? How long has he been thinking about me? About us?

"SJ?" His tone is soft. I lean back into the couch's arm, hoping that space will slow my pulse. "Say something."

"I don't know what to say." That's a lie. That's the easy thing to say. I don't know how to tell him I'm sorry too. Or that I've missed him. That I want him around. That I want to hear about everything that's happened in his life since we've been apart. That I never want to fight again. That I want to pull him in close to taste his lips.

My brain won't let me.

Because any truth will feel tainted while his flash drive is in my pocket.

"It's cool," Ezra tells me before I can respond in some way. He rubs his hands on the top of his thighs. After a long moment, he gazes at me, his long lashes brushing his face. Ezra's eyes wander the room, and I eyeball the door.

"I'm sorry, I just—" is all I can get out.

"No, no. Totally understand. Let me get out of here. Tell

your mom it was nice to see her again and thank her for the food."

He quickly grabs his keys and the rest of his things. Then we are both up, and he is at the front door. He leaves without turning back.

I stand for a moment, the confusion settling in my body. Except my body doesn't feel like my body. This is not me. I am not this. The kiss, the apology, the news about Kerry. It all feels like too much.

I turn toward my room, and with each step a strong curiosity overcomes me, so by the time I'm at my door, I'm practically running. I'm frantic. I open my laptop, the adrenaline pumping so hard throughout my body, my heart feels like it's about to explode.

When the screen wakes, I shove the flash drive into the port and wait.

It doesn't take too long before I am transported into the depths of Ezra's brain. And it is one word: *magnificent.*

Or *meticulous.*

Okay, maybe three more words: *organized, detailed, thorough.*

"Holy shit," I mutter. My hand moves across the touchpad, my fingers click, opening a new world. I'm like a floating head watching my body violate his privacy. "Bad," I say under my breath. "This is bad." My hands are possessed; this isn't me. But I keep going, my fingers keep moving.

First of all, his flash drive is named Cerebellum. What a nerd. But inside Cerebellum, there are color-coded file folders for each of his classes. Inside the main folder, there are sub-folders: Reference, Personal Notes, Lecture Notes, and Projects. I click. Then I click. Click. Click. Delving further and further into his brain.

Inside each of the subfolders, there are pages and pages of outlines and notes and hyperlinks that lead to articles that lead to scholarly journals that lead to his in-depth thoughts. His notes make my color-coded lifestyle look like elementary scribbles. I am equally fascinated by the thoughtfulness and terrified by the brilliance.

Not to mention, there's *so much*. A digital encyclopedia.

I check over my shoulder, then lean into the screen. If I had any sense left, I would shut this, or hide this flash drive under an old board in the floor, or bury it outside, or throw it into the ocean. Anything but snoop. I shouldn't do this. It's not mine, and I definitely don't have his permission. I should stop. I could just give it back.

But I click and click again.

A blue folder named *Civics* catches my eye and my chest tightens. I need to find his presentation. Two more clicks, and his PowerPoint is open on my screen.

Ezra has gone to each of the Walker Ross Lecture Series, including today's. The boy has copious notes and recordings, in addition to pictures of himself and Mr. Ross. In one, Ezra is in a button-down shirt and khakis, cheesing so hard, his arm around Mr. Ross's shoulder, like they're besties. In another, Ezra has a copy of Mr. Ross's book *A Life of the Mind,* which he holds up as Mr. Ross smiles.

I lean back in my chair. A cold sweat covers my body.

I'm going to lose.

If he turns in his presentation the way it is now, I don't stand a chance. I want to cry, but I can't. Everything inside of me is too surprised to emote. My fingers tap nervously. I blink, and the demon that has possessed my body clicks on the folder and dangles it over the trash can on my screen.

I could just delete his work.

Just end him, this tie, this mess, right now. Things could go back to normal.

My fingers don't move. Right now, I have the power to be done with it all. Can I play this dirty? I shake my head and snatch my own hand, letting out a huge breath.

I can't. Not that. Maybe I can, like . . . remove *some* of the files? Delete some of his sources?

A knock.

Without waiting for me to respond, my mom opens the door, slowly. I fumble, trying to close the screen.

"Honey, where's Ezra?" she asks, peering around.

Can she sense my treachery? Am I wearing a scarlet letter? Does she know that I've become—*what have I become?* Is this worse than what Ezra's done?

My mom eyes me, trying to understand my silence and the way I'm wrestling my laptop and papers at the same time. "Well, it was so good to see him again. Your dad and I were always fond of him. I know his parents must be proud. . . ." Her voice trails off as she begins to shut the door. She pauses. "It's not often you find a boy like that, you know."

As soon as she leaves, I can hear my dad's voice, all ominous-like. I can imagine him standing next to me, his tall frame, his thinking face. I can see the three of us at the park. I think about graduation and the picture I've painted of me, being up on that stage. I can hear my dad's voice—so clearly, like he might be in the room—talking about integrity, character, and values. My chest tightens and then everything constricts.

What am I doing?

Daddy, what am I doing?

I can't . . . I can't win like this.

I reopen my laptop screen and the cursor on my screen hovers over one last file titled Misc. I click it open. The Misc. folder has other folders inside but the one that grabs me is labeled Legacy.

I gulp, that same fear beginning to build inside of me. I click to open the folder. A message appears on my screen: *Password Required,* and a cursor blinks in the box.

It's too late now. I can't back away.

I chew a fingernail, the tension in my body growing like I'm disabling a bomb. I enter his birthday. I pause before hitting enter.

Incorrect Password, the computer says.

I try another combination of his birthday.

Incorrect Password, the computer says again.

Fair enough. His birthday is a little too obvious. Shit. I am a terrible hacker. Think, brain. Computer passwords tend to be something unique, or very special to the user, something odd, but not so odd that you'd forget it every time you log on.

Then I see it, the EZYGZY11 black vintage CA license plate in his room, above his bed. For "Easy G," a nickname his grandpa gave him, and his favorite number. Ezra never got into cars like some of our other middle school friends, but he always said as soon as he got his license, he was going to make sure to have custom license plates with his nickname.

I type each letter in, making sure to spell it correctly.

I swallow.

My thumb hovers over the enter button. As soon as I press it, the folder opens.

"Jesus take the wheel," I mumble.

I did it?

I did it!

Inside the folder there are hundreds of photos, all in black-and-white, of Ezra and his family. *Of course he has something prepared.* Some photos are recent, the ones I saw in the darkroom. Some are super old, from when he was a kid, now digitized. I scroll through endless photos. But the ones that are the most striking are of his parents. There's a whole folder with Ezra, his mom, and his dad all together. It's the same photo, but different versions. He's modified the colors and tones. And each one is somehow more stunning than the one before. Why? To reveal something new, see a new take? I study the photograph, the way his parents' faces crease, the way they hug tightly together. I can't think of the last time I saw his family like this. Maybe Ezra can't either. Maybe that's why he has these.

"Holy shit," I say again, the magnitude of my discovery settling in my body. Why did Ezra lie to me?

We don't have too much control over our parents, what they do and how they behave. Or how they shape us. I close my laptop and wrap the flash drive in a scarf and stuff the scarf in my backpack. I don't know where to begin or what to think. Although Ezra is back in my life, there are some things he doesn't want to tell me. And by his emphasis on these photos, from the past, when his parents were still together, Ezra seems to be searching for something. A clue, a sign, something to make sense of where he is now. It doesn't take much for me to realize there's hurt in those photos, whether Ezra wants to admit it to me or not. Did I just add to it?

CHAPTER 23

WHEN PRISCILLA PICKS ME UP MONDAY MORNING, I ALMOST don't recognize her. In addition to new bangs, she is wearing round, black-rimmed eyeglasses. Her usual bright and peppy mood is heavy and pensive, from her jet-black fingernails to her black turtleneck and black jean jacket with spikes around the cuffs.

"When did you do all this?" I ask as I buckle my seat belt inside the Golden Girl. "No Chance?" But the answer is clear since I've got shotgun.

"Said he'd do a half day." Priscilla accelerates, the car jerks forward. "Do you hate it?" Priscilla paws at her forehead like a cat.

"Oh, no. I love them. But aren't you hot? It's literally May in Monterey; it's gonna be high seventies today." Outside the window, the sun is already glaring. Priscilla deflates, so I try again. "I didn't know you were really going to do it, that's all.

And glasses? But I'm feeling the overall aesthetic. You know you always look good."

"Straight up, this weekend was emotional. You never called me, and, I don't know, I needed to act, to let go and release. So Chance came over and helped me cut bangs. They aren't supposed to lie like this—and yet!" Priscilla lets out a nervous laugh.

"Stop. They're cute! Besides, it's just hair." I try to reassure her.

"Oh yeah? Says who? You've been wanting to do something new with your hair forever and you haven't." Priscilla side-eyes me. I want to push back but I can't. She's right. I've wanted to take a risk with my locs, like shave the underside, or dye them a bright color, or shave *and* dye them, but I can't bring myself to do it. My dad helped me start my locs, and while I think about trying something new, I just can't. I know I shouldn't hold so much sentimentality for hair, but I do.

"Gina broke up with *me*."

Well, damn. I didn't see that coming.

Priscilla doesn't look at me as she speaks, so I don't look at her. We sit in silence for a moment as she hits all the green lights and we coast to school, though the inside of the car feels like a ticking time bomb.

"Oh shit. I'm sorry." I do my best to recall this information. Was this a possibility? When is the last time we talked? Surely we spoke. I know the weekend was a lot for me, but it sounds like the past couple of days were worse for her.

"Imagine my surprise. Yeah, so okay, I wanted to break up too, but I still feel off. Like, I had no clue. Gina said she's been feeling this way for a while. We were both just faking it, I guess. But for how long? How could I be so blind? What does this say about me? That I can't see if someone else is unhappy too."

I pat her hand. "It'll be okay. And listen, I'm sorry I've been—" My phone vibrates and Ezra's name flashes on the screen.

Ezra 7:44 a.m.: Hey you.

I can't stop thinking about this weekend and this is random, but did I leave my flash drive at your house?

"Sweet baby Jesus," I mumble.

"Not the most present friend?" she fills in for me. "I know how you can make it up to me. All of us at prom? Chance said he could be persuaded. Imagine it, if you can."

"Oh hell," I say, mumbling again.

"What? What is it?" Priscilla parks the car, ignoring the lines on the ground. "Hello? Are you going to tell me? Say something, please."

"Sorry. Hold on, sorry I just . . ." My fingers start tapping back, eager to bury the angst.

Sasha 7:46 a.m.: No sorry didn't see it.

As soon as I send the text (the small, teeny tiny lie), I purse my lips, pushing down whatever in my body is trying to come up. It is not my intention to lie to Ezra, but I don't know how to explain the flash drive situation to him in a message. Honestly, so much gets lost via text. I can't just write *Yeah, sorry, I've got it. Stole it while you were doing your business.* I can be honest with him in person, and I will. When the time is right. I will give him back his flash drive and we can continue being cute and kissing. More kissing.

The thought of Ezra's lips on mine makes my heart beat with much more drum and bass. I don't notice Priscilla and her glaring eyes. "Fine, don't tell me," she says with an attitude. In one fast swoop, she hops out the front and grabs her stuff from the back seat, while I scramble for my things. She slams the car door as I tumble out, trying to catch up with her.

"Sorry. It was Ezra. I—" Even though we are outside, my voice is too loud.

"Why the hell is he texting you? At seven-forty-five in the morning, no less."

Okay. Fair question. I pull on my backpack's straps, but I don't respond. I haven't told Priscilla or Chance anything about Ezra other than the bets. Definitely haven't explained our moment of bliss by the water. I will, of course, once I know what it all means. Once things are clearer, once we've established what we are, I can tell them.

"Are you going to tell me or not? Because you're acting like you've seen a ghost."

"He . . . Ezra came over to my house."

"Excuse you? Like, where you sleep at night? What the

hell? Last I checked, we hate him? That doesn't make any sense, Sasha. Explain."

I scratch my collar. "I can. And I will. But now, we should—we should get to class, right?"

"Now, Sasha." Priscilla's voice is stern.

Around us students push by, heading to class, where we need to be. I rack my memory to recall the weekend and the weird events that transpired. "I saw him Saturday at the museum for Walker Ross and, and—"

"*Saturday?* When did you have time for the museum?" Priscilla asks.

"I went in the morning, but—"

Oh crap. My heart stops.

Priscilla frowns.

"I thought you were working?"

"I—I was going to go to work with my mom. But I got caught up in—"

"Yeah, yeah, yeah. *The bets.* I know." Priscilla's sharp voice pierces my skin. "So why did you lie about it? Or, specifically, lie to me about it? Why couldn't you just say 'I'm not going to work, I have to do this.' Or 'I can't talk this weekend, so I'll check in with you later.' Why not own what you're feeling instead of whatever it is you're doing now?"

"Actually, I'm right about to. Or I am, I just—"

"You know, that's really shitty. I'm trying to be supportive of you and all of this because I'm rooting for you. Really, I am. But you could have told me. You didn't need to lie. This feels like Gina all over again. Are we friends? Why can't you just be honest when it matters, Sasha? Who are you right now?"

Priscilla takes two quick steps ahead of me and I grab her wrist; her body slinks near mine.

"Okay, okay. I hear you. I will explain, I just need some time to process it all." To understand what I'm feeling first. Then explain after. But Priscilla doesn't buy it, or she can't hear it, or both. Her face is so empty of emotion it's scary. I've never seen her like this. She narrows her blue eyes; ice on my skin. Once Ezra and I talk, things will make more sense, I know it. Another painful moment passes and then Priscilla turns on her heels and heads to class.

They say professional athletes can go clear or empty their brains when they are playing. No thoughts, just sheer execution. I kind of feel like that this morning, in an odd way. When Mr. Mendoza calls me up to the front of civics class, it's officially go time.

Mr. Mendoza loads my presentation on the projector, and I remember what works—to keep my back straight and my chin up as I stand in front of the room. I hold on to the little black clicker so hard I'm sure it might break into a million pieces. But it doesn't. At least not while I have it. I gaze at the class, twenty-eight pairs of eyes all on me, ranging from excited to bored.

I take another deep breath, and I square my shoulders and examine the room. I push the weirdness from the last two weeks out. *I got this. It's show time.*

Once I start, everything begins to flow, just as I practiced. The slides, each embedded with at least a picture or a gif, keep everyone engaged. After six minutes of presenting, I say the easiest words: "That is my presentation, thank you."

The class claps, and Mr. Mendoza gives me an approving nod. Bet #2 is complete.

Well, for me, at least.

"I really love the additions with Mr. Ross," Mr. Mendoza says. I blink at him, realizing that I'm still up in front of the class.

"Any other students able to catch his lecture series?" Most of the students stare at him blankly, and those who are awake only shake their heads no. "No matter. Another excellent job, Sasha."

I sit at my desk, expecting some relief, but it never comes. All I can hear are Priscilla words about honesty and asking me who I really am and what I'm really about—and I don't know how to answer.

"Well, this is awkward," Chance says at lunch. We sit at our normal spot, near the quad and underneath a budding redwood tree. He's not wrong, the energy is off. Our trio has now turned into a duo.

"I wouldn't want you to feel stuck in the middle of anything," I say between chomps of my sad peanut butter and banana sandwich.

"I don't, trust me. But I told Priscilla I'd meet her in the quad for some games today. Apparently, you can win a class sweatshirt or something?" Chance shrugs and throws me a pity smile.

I do my best to match his energy. "You should go, then, totally. No problem," I say.

"Are you sure?"

I nod, and Chance slings his backpack across his body. He throws me a peace sign as he walks away.

I close my eyes, desperate to shake this weird feeling. I want to feel juiced about today's presentation, but I don't. I only feel more confused.

CHAPTER 24

AFTER SCHOOL, EZRA IS PROPPED UP AGAINST MY LOCKER, LIKE we are that it couple in some teen movie who can't stand to be apart.

"Hey, you." My ears perk up at the sound of his voice. It's one thing to think about him all weekend; it's another to have him here, after school, waiting for me. My heart swells. Could we kiss here? Could I kiss at school? I mean, I know people do it . . . plus a lot more—but could I? Just outside my favorite class with my favorite teacher?

He leans in like he wants a hug. His smell, a jasmine-and-sunshine-spilling-through-trees-in-the-woods mix, lingers in the air. It draws me in and my brain short-circuits. His fingers brush my cheek before he takes a small step back.

"Wanna hang with me in the darkroom?" His eyes glow.

I poke him right in his nicely toned stomach. "That feels like code for more than just processing film."

"You're not wrong."

I bite my lip, a small part of me wanting to just give in to temptation. "I do, but I can't today. Today is kind of . . . weird." I think about Priscilla, and Ezra's flash drive, and for a moment wish I hadn't gotten myself so caught up. Can't I just enjoy this chemistry? This hot bit of flirtation?

He nods as he places his hands ever so lightly on my hips. I meet him halfway for a small peck. *I could get used to this behavior.*

Ezra pulls on my arm again, wanting to bring our bodies together, but I stop him before we get too carried away in my favorite hall outside my favorite class.

"You sure?" His puppy-dog face emerges. "Just for a little bit?"

The dimple wins. "Just for a bit," I say, even though something inside me is telling me to take my butt home.

He links his hand with mine, so effortlessly, and we walk toward the darkroom. When we get inside, everything is just as romantic as before. The red light is brighter, and it makes Ezra hotter than he was two minutes ago. Ezra fiddles with a machine and something hums.

"I love it here," I say, because I kinda do. "But I would be traumatized if we were stuck in here again. Is there a way to make sure that doesn't happen?"

Ezra laughs. "Yeah, true. I'll be back. Don't disappear on me." He drops his backpack and spins on his heels, glancing back for a beat before he disappears.

Now is my chance to make things right.

Faster than I've ever moved, I take his flash drive out of

my pencil pouch, open the front of his backpack, and drop it in. Plop. There. Back to your rightful owner, Cerebellum. Ezra can think he just misplaced it. My conscience can be clear and I can pretend this never happened.

Without another thought, I zip the pouch closed and head back to my spot near the water bath.

I'm just as clever as he is, if not more. The donut and the book seem like child's play comparatively. A grin consumes my face, and I let it. I got the info I needed without hurting anyone or anyone knowing. Truly legendary. I give myself a mental pat on the back.

Footsteps cut my praise short, and then he reappears. "That's a nice smile," he says, stepping into the room.

I bend down and grab my bag. "Thanks! Anyway . . . change of plans—I actually need to go." I make my voice super sweet so he can't protest. "Rain check, okay?" I rise on my toes and place a small kiss on his cheek. Before he can respond, I head out the door and exhale.

♡♡♡

When I finally make it home, I'm greeted with comfortable silence. I kick off my shoes, and before I call out, I see my mom sprawled out on the couch, dead asleep.

What the hell? It's only a little after five. She doesn't move when I come in and close the door; that's how I know she's *tired* tired. She must have gotten up early for work today. Or maybe it's the way that her work rolls into herself—she's never had more than a day off in years. There is always some-one to clean up after. I worry she'll never find the time to truly take care of herself.

On the edge of the couch is a small teal blanket. I unfold it and drape it across her body. She twists slightly into the cushions but stays asleep.

I notice the coffee table, which is covered: a water glass, an empty bag of shrimp chips, a gum wrapper, and her phone. I grab the remote off a napkin to turn off whatever K-drama she has playing in the background, but then I stop, taken aback.

My Sassy Girl.

The familiar faces of characters whose love story I've grown up with my whole life bounce on the menu screen.

Despite the number of K-dramas my mom would talk about or try to illegally stream, my dad never got into them, but *My Sassy Girl*? The movie of his heart, a love story written just for him. My parents were always watching it, which means I was always watching it too. We loved everything about it, especially the way beginnings and endings are intertwined. And of course, the way the two people find themselves to-gether again, no matter what the outrageous circumstances. Love always wins.

My stomach dips.

I don't think I've seen her take this DVD out of the cabi-net in . . . a while. The fracture in my heart deepens because I know it means she's thinking about him and their love. A small part of me wants to wake her up, to sit on the couch and press play.

But that doesn't feel right. She needs the rest.

With one quick click of a button, the screen fades to black.

I pick up her cup of water to take to the kitchen, and as I turn in our hallway something catches my eye: there's a long white garment bag hanging from the closet door, perfectly camouflaged with the wall. I take another step forward. What in the—

My heart sinks. This isn't— I tug on the zipper just enough to catch a glimpse of lilac and lace—the dress from Anna's, the one in the window from the other day.

I sigh.

I study it, inhaling the plastic, that new-garment-bag scent. I pull the dress out slowly, like I'm touching glass. It's beautiful. The fabric is super soft, with small crystals sewn into the lace. The last time I put on a dress this nice, in eighth grade, every worry slipped away, and my life felt . . . perfect. My hand rests on the delicate collar, and a lump rises in my throat. Eyes stinging, I blink until some semblance of control returns to me. The dress makes me think of the father-daughter dance, which makes me think of my dad and my mom and The Plan, our happily-ever-after, together.

I touch the dress again, afraid to breathe on it.

Instinctively, I check the lining in hopes of finding a tag, but nothing sticks out.

It's expensive, I can tell by the stitching. Is this why we've been working at the Pattersons? I know she's always working hard for me, but this is too much, right?

There is no room for large, frivolous expenses like this. I don't want her picking up extra work for me. What am I doing for her? The scholarship comes to mind. I want her to know that all her hard work as a parent has paid off because I did it—I proved that I was the best at Skyline.

I stuff the dress back into its protective covering and zip it up. I open the closet door, and there I see something else in the corner: Mom's old backpack.

I tiptoe to my room, being mindful not to wake her up when I close the door. At my desk, I stare at the same faded photo of my family as my brain bounces between thoughts. I exhale and try to quell the guilt that builds in my chest. I lean back in my chair and shut my eyes.

Describe what defines you. The legacy questions scream at me. Have I let desire for school success determine who I am?

Think about your future: What does it look like?

Thoughts of Ezra flash in my head, in my body. He remembers so much about me, about us. And I've kind of just shoved our memories together to the back of my mind like clothes I know I'll never wear.

I let my thoughts wander; I try to recall things about myself that maybe I've forgotten, purposefully or not. The list starts small—reading comics, space exploration, my obsession with Hello Kitty—and then it gets bigger, more detailed. Dancing. Traveling. Ezra and I once talked about backpacking through South America for a summer. And of course, there's New York.

I know I wasn't always only about grades. I was full of lots of other things, other dreams, too.

That's the thing about futures: they stay ready to be created, mine included. Maybe my future can have it all—the school, the boy, the degrees. I spin in my chair, hopeful.

CHAPTER 25

"KNOCK, KNOCK," A FAMILIAR VOICE SAYS. THURSDAY AFTERNOON
we're in Ms. T's room when Ezra appears in the doorway,
cheesing, confident. I sit up straight and place my hands in
my lap. The students tilt their heads in curiosity. Chance and
Priscilla both bailed on tutoring (mostly likely to avoid being
around me). So at the last minute, I asked Ezra.

I clear my throat, but instead, it sounds like I'm choking
on food.

"Whoa—you good? Who knows the Heimlich?" Marquese
calls out, standing up from his desk. Juan side-eyes, like I've already started to embarrass him in front of important company. I
clear my throat once more, normally this time, before speaking.

"Everyone, this is Ezra," I let out, my voice raspier than
I'd like.

"Oooh. He's cute. Is that bae?" Khadijah doesn't miss a
beat.

"Wha—what? No, I . . ." My face heats. Ezra as my bae?

197

I mean, yeah, we've been kissing a lot, but we haven't established anything, like, official.

Khadijah makes a face that says "Answer my question, because I do not want to ask again."

"No. I just—I mean, it's Ezra."

Ezra laughs as he slides into the desk next to me. "Nice to meet you." He's smooth, even in the face of nosy middle schoolers.

All the students' eyes dart between us.

"Your what-if, then? Or it's complicated?" Khadijah presses, her eyes stuck on Ezra.

My tongue is in a knot. It's complicated, at the very least.

I don't mean to, but I eye him up and down, really taking him in. He's wearing light blue jeans that have rips across the knees, with a black cotton T-shirt that shows off the muscles in his arms. He sits tall, and his shoulders are broad, his back straight. And of course, there's his face.

Our eyes meet.

His lips split in a grin. "She's bae," he says to the room confidently.

"Everyone!" I throw up my hands, willing myself to regain some semblance of control. "Pause, pause, pause. This is Ezra. He's here to help with your homework and nothing more." I love the kids, but they don't need to know everything about me.

"If you're not dating, then how do you two know each other?" Khadijah asks Ezra across his desk.

Ezra turns to her. "Sasha and I go way back. We have

history." Khadijah is clearly intrigued. "She was my first real friend. My best friend."

"Ezra also happens to be brilliant and an excellent tutor, so he's here to assist. Now if my interrogation is over, can we *please* get started?"

Ben peers up at Ezra through his glasses. "Do you think you can help me with my math? Usually Chance teaches me." Ben is in eighth grade too, but he's the runt of the group. He's small and has the cutest baby face, with bright greenish eyes, and is always losing his work despite his massive SpongeBob backpack. "I just really hate math," he sighs, opening the large textbook.

"What?" Ezra walks over and crouches at his side. "You can't hate math! Yo, you ever heard of Benjamin Banneker?"

Ben shakes his head. The other students listen in. My ears also perk up; I don't recall that name.

"Benjamin Banneker was *that* guy. Back in the day, he was born a free Black man in Maryland and was practically self-taught. He was a math whiz and credited with inventing America's first clock. The clock! Where would we be without it? Wild, right? Imagine that being his legacy and your namesake."

Ben's eyes widen and light up his whole face.

"Whoa," the group says.

I have to stop myself from jumping up and inserting myself in their conversation. I am elated thinking about the connection that Ezra is making with Ben so easily. I almost forgot about Ezra's obsession with random facts. We used to watch

Jeopardy! and *Wheel of Fortune* together, and he'd joke, or so I thought, that when he grew up, he wanted to compete on the show, win a sailboat, and travel the world.

Out of the corner of my eye I can see Khadijah, her hands waving in the air. *Earth to Sasha. Hello, come back down!*

"Miss Sasha, can you help me with this?" Khadijah asks, her eyes wide.

"Huh? Yes, sorry. Algebra?"

"You already know." She opens the thick textbook and turns it my way.

After about forty minutes of polynomials with Khadijah and mitosis with Juan, the students are restless, shifting in their seats, releasing a chorus of yawns. We're at our limit. I don't blame them. An intense tutoring session after a long day of classes is a lot. Even for me.

"I'm getting hungry. Who has food?" Hector's round face and greenish eyes droop. He takes off his Dodgers cap, signaling the end of our work session, and checks the clock on the wall.

"I could eat." Khadijah drops her pencil.

Ben lays his head down on his desk, clearly choosing rest over food. "Miss Sasha, Ezra is really good at math. He's good at explaining it. Did you know that about him?"

Ben has struggled with math since we started tutoring. He's got dyscalculia, which means reading and writing are good, but math is pretty rough for him. But right now, Ben is cheesing at Ezra like he's unearthed a rare Pokémon.

"Nah, man," Ezra says. "You did that."

"Yeah, but . . . math is hard, and you won't always be around with the assist." Ben sits up with a yawn and closes his notebook.

Ezra nudges him with his shoulder. "We can do hard things." He gestures to the worksheet. "Proof. See? Don't ever forget that."

Ben brightens up. "All right, sure."

Khadijah watches, her eyes darting between Ezra and me.

"You think you can come back?" Ben asks.

Ezra blinks at me expectantly. The kids are awestruck, and so am I. He is kind. Gentle, even. Very go-with-the-flow. Easy to be around, I guess. He also has a nice laugh. And he's smart. God, he's so smart. He's not afraid of intellect; in fact, quite the opposite. Take his flash drive, for example—his files are detailed and organized, but naming the drive Cerebellum is a little playful, too. He knows he's got it, but it doesn't control him, which frankly makes me jealous.

I pull at a piece of my hair. Oh my gosh, has he always been like this? A perfect blend of smart, and generous, and funny, and handsome?

I can't believe I'm thinking all this about . . . *Ezra*.

"Yeah?" he replies.

Shit, did I say that out loud? "Nothing, I—was just, um, what were we talking about?"

"If I can come back?" He laughs.

"Erm. I mean, yes, if you want."

He lights up. "Of course I want to. This was the most fun I've had in a long-ass—a long time."

The kids mutter happily to themselves.

Everyone starts stuffing books in backpacks, dragging chairs across the room.

In another blink, they're all gone. Khadijah actually wiggled her eyebrows at me before she left.

Just the two of us now; Ezra scoots his chair next to me.

Hot. Is it hot in here?

I can see the slope of his nose and the fullness of his eyelashes. "I was wondering if you could help me with something?" He unfolds a piece of lined paper and slides it my way.

I'm scared to open it, but Ezra's giving me those wide, enthusiastic eyes, so I do.

SJ, would you go to prom with me? Check a box: yes or no. I stare at the two choices; the *yes* box is about ten times larger than the *no* box.

Ezra leans over. "Here, I even have a pencil for you." He hands me a sharpened bright-yellow Ticonderoga pencil that I know he got from Ms. T's desk.

I don't have to think, I just do it. I draw a heart in the *yes* box, shade it in, then hand him the paper back.

"Saturday, then?" he asks.

"Saturday." I lean in, sealing this note with a kiss.

CHAPTER 26

HOW I GOT THE CREW TOGETHER FOR ANOTHER FRY-DATE IS beyond me. Maybe I can turn on the charm too? In any case, here we are, at McDonald's, in our favorite booth in the back with our favorite foods: three large fries, two cones (the Mc-Flurry machine is still broken), and six apple pies (we each like to take one home). And thankfully, everyone showed up on time.

"Good things?" Chance calls out, squeezing a pool of ketchup from the packet. Priscilla swirls her straw in her cup, the ice swimming and clanking inside. I try to gauge her mood, from her black-and-white polka-dot cardigan to her pink floral print pants. . . . I don't know—it's a lot of patterns. What does that mean? Just how mad at me is she?

"I'll pass," she says.

Got it.

I reach for a fry and Chance swats my hand.

"Ow!" I yelp.

"Apologies first. Don't forget your manners." He shoots me a playful look.

He's right. "P, I'm so sorry. I know I haven't been myself. Chance, I'm sorry too, if I've been, I dunno, absent." Priscilla softens, her lips form a tiny smile. "For reals. I'm hoping we can talk it through right now. I'm here to answer any questions and make amends." I hold up the square napkin. "Here, it's me and a white flag." I wave it around.

"Very cheesy, but Switzerland accepts your apology," says Priscilla.

"I thought I was Switzerland?" Chance jokes.

Priscilla's shoulders relax. She dips a fry in the ice cream and replies, "Not today. I want to know everything"—she glares at me—"because why did Jessica with the shoulder tattoo tell me that she saw you and Ezra kissing? At school?"

"I heard that too," Chance says.

"So I guess Ezra is my good thing." I hesitate to say the words, but once I start talking, I can't stop. I fill my friends in on the weekend, our talks, kisses in the hallway. Then I remember the cherry on top. "Also, we're going to prom together," I say sheepishly.

"Wow." Priscilla grabs a handful of fries. I don't know what to make of her response.

"Chance, prom?"

"Isn't it tomorrow? Also, very unlikely. I'm still, ya know, on probation or whatever for attendance, or lack thereof. But!

I got my plane ticket. To England. It's official." Chance smiles like a madman; the exhilaration in his face is contagious.

"When?" Priscilla asks. "I've started making you a list of restaurants you have to visit. My parents and I want to go back there too. Go there, send me pics of you and the desserts. Oh my gosh, I can make you one of those Flat Stanleys, but it can be Flat Priscilla."

"Food, yes. The rest . . . we'll see," he says. "Get ready for the kicker—departure date is the evening of graduation. A red-eye landing at Heathrow."

"So cool, Chance, seriously," I tell him.

We nibble on fries for another moment before Priscilla brings her hands to her face, her fingers undulating playfully.

"Let us throw you a bon voyage party," she says.

Chance doesn't even blink. "I love it. Give it a European theme, but no soccer—I mean, football. Nothing sports-related."

"Absolutely brilliant," Priscilla says, the elation in her voice almost over-the-top.

I grab an apple pie and slowly open the box, noticing the perfect design, from the carton's shape to its ventilation holes to keep the pie crisp.

"P, you never said your good thing." I can't look at them; instead, I pick at the flap, freeing the pie.

"Well, I don't know. The week has still been shitty, but it's good to be back together. I've missed you both."

"We've got, like, three Fry-Dates left until graduation," Chance says. We avoid each other's gaze, too afraid to acknowledge what we already know.

"I guess all good things must come to an end," Priscilla adds.

Do they, though?

CHAPTER 27

"WELCOME TO THE PROM SPA," PRISCILLA SAYS WITH A BOW AS I open my bedroom door.

It's Saturday, prom night. Priscilla's standing in the middle of my room glowing, her arms held as wide as her grin. Her navy suit is tailored perfectly, and she's wearing gold cuff links and matching gold bracelets. Her hair is in big curls pinned back to show off her makeup: blue and gold eyeshadow and dark blue mascara.

My bedroom transformed into a fancy department store; outfits hang from every corner of the room. She's lit at least thirty tea light candles, and SZA plays in the background, soft and soothing. Maybe this really is a fresh start for us. She's even changed the lightbulb on my desk lamp, which is now blasting a bright red.

"What is all this?" I ask, bewildered.

"It's important we set the right mood. What do you

think?" she asks, doing a quick twirl as she gestures to everything nearby.

One of the great things about having Priscilla as a friend is that she demonstrates her love in some of the most unconventional ways. And when she shows herself, like now, it's impossible not to feel her warmth. It is nice to be cared for.

"I—I don't even know what to say."

"Say it's fabulous, like us." She winks.

I sit down on my bed next to a light pink dress with thin straps that could probably be a shirt. That's a hard pass. On my other side is a black faux-leather jacket-and-pants set. Also a no. These are very much Priscilla Gone Wild Outfits.

I'm thinking about the lace and the lilac when Priscilla cuts in.

"I'm not sure if you've picked up on the vibes, but the outfits go from moderate to a little risqué, if you know what I mean." Her eyebrows hop up and down.

We both giggle.

"Where am I sitting now?" I ask as I point to the pink dress and then the faux leather. "What do these outfits mean?"

"Great question. You're in the middle of the rough, messy-sexy kind of vibe. So think of soft pink with dark black makeup. Or faux leather and glitter eyes. Make sense? Tell me you see the vision." She waves her hands in front of her face.

I shake my head.

"It's fine. It will all make sense in a moment. Why don't you really check it out?" She motions to all the outfits, so I do. For a moment, I forget where I am. So many new clothes, so many new chances. Who could I be, in this plaid-skirt-and-jacket combo? Or this striped jumpsuit? Priscilla even brought a . . . a wig?

I hold the wig up to my face, and for a moment I wonder about the possibilities, the other Sashas that could exist in this world. What does purple-wig Sasha like to do? What is her life like? I can't help but think of motorcycles and fancy dinners and full hearts. I smirk at the thought.

"Oh yeah. That's Ruby. She's a keeper. Try her on." Priscilla gives me a nudge, so I indulge her for two minutes before we refocus.

"This is cute," I say, pointing to a simple black dress with sparkles on it. If I have to do prom, I think I should wear black. Timeless. Classic.

"Ah yes. That—that belongs to Janine, if you can believe it." Janine is Priscilla's mom. Priscilla has been calling her mom by her first name since she was a little girl. Priscilla said it made it easier to find her in the sea of other people who also answered to Mom. Mine would never claim me in public if I did that.

I hold up the black dress, and the chiffon fabric speaks to me.

"I knew you'd pick that one. Classic Sasha. Lovably predictable," Priscilla says, behind me.

"By predictable, do you really mean boring?" I ask as I sneak a peek at the time. We have about thirty minutes before Ezra arrives.

"Honestly, it couldn't hurt to step outside the box

sometimes," she says, sitting down at my desk. Without glancing my way, she adds, "You should know that I'm doing my best to not harp on the fact that you're only coming tonight because of Ezra. I'm going to ignore that for the sake of having fun and creating new memories with my best friend . . . and being the bigger person. Also, growth. I'm evolving, you know."

I groan. Clearly, she *is* still mad, then. "Hey, listen, I—" I start, my voice shaking.

"I'm not mad. I just want you to be comfortable telling me what's going on with you."

Priscilla glides around my room as I stand in complete confusion. I'm not quite ready to explain whatever it is Ezra and I are or aren't.

I like being around Ezra, yes. I like that he knows me, that we already have history, that I'm important enough to hold space inside of his heart. I do like the way he smells, and sure, his hugs are nice too.

"Are you okay?" she asks.

I drop those thoughts and nod.

Priscilla points to the dress. "I don't mean to rush, but you need to get ready so I can put on your lashes, and we can both go. Ezra is coming soon, and I'm meeting people at Alicia's parents' house—it's not what you think, not like a date or anything, it's just for pictures—and then I want to head over to prom to make a grand entrance."

Without saying another word, I shimmy into the black dress. But when I step in front of the mirror, my heart skips

210

a beat, and not in a good way. It's cute? Not what I imagined when I saw it on the hanger, though. It's too stiff or something.

Priscilla brings a finger to her chin, then squints. "Very sophisticated." But I can hear the hesitation in her voice, or maybe I'm imagining it. Thoughts of my dad nudge me, the way his eyes lit up when he saw me in my dress for the eighth-grade dance. The way he'd gasped like I was the most beautiful thing on the planet.

"One sec," I say, my voice hoarse, and I don't give Priscilla a chance to speak before I'm out the bedroom door. I open the closet door and scan the contents again; this time the space doesn't feel like an empty void. I grab the dress from Anna's. Maybe sometimes things just need to sit awhile before they are ready.

A knot forms in my throat as I run back into my room. I ignore Priscilla's stare as I slip out of the black dress and into the lilac one. The moment I zip it, I know. It's elegant but soft. Sophisticated but warm. My mom knew.

This is it. This is the one.

"Oh my god," Priscilla croons.

"Is it . . . It's too—"

"It's *perfect*," she says. "Why didn't you tell me you got a dress?"

"I didn't," I say, scratching at my neck. "My mom did. Long story."

"Adorable. Well, that's the one. Sit down and don't move. I need to put on your lashes."

We spend the last ten minutes polishing up, or Priscilla polishes me, rather. And when she's done, I check myself out in the mirror. I look nice. Beautiful, even. My long locs are braided to the left side. Priscilla has applied simple lashes and a soft pink lip that makes my brown face sparkle. She's even let me borrow a pair of diamond earrings—real diamonds—that make me feel like a movie star.

"We look like a million bucks," she says, snapping a quick selfie. "Now let's go. Your *ride* will be here any minute, and I have places to be."

We head toward the door the moment it bursts open. My mom stumbles in, dropping her bags, and when she sees us, she freezes. For a moment, she can't speak. And when I see her trembling smile and the way her eyes glimmer, I swallow hard.

"Meet you there." Priscilla says hi and bye to Mom before slipping out the front door.

"I rushed home to see you," Mom says. Her hair is a mess, and I can see a full day's work in her face. "You are so beautiful." Her voice is soft. "Turn. Turn around."

I do a quick twirl.

"Thank you for the dress, Mommy," I say, pressing a kiss to her cheek. "I'm sorry I—"

"Oh, honey." She wraps her arms around me in a tight squeeze, her voice cracking.

"No, no! Stop. Don't make me cry. Priscilla just did my makeup." I dab the sides of my eyes, careful to avoid ruining the Fenty eyeshadow on my lids, even as I'm grinning.

"Dad is smiling right now." She clutches her chest.

My phone lights up.

"Ezra's here. I should go."

Her brows dent in confusion. "Isn't he coming up?"

"No, it's fine." I can just go meet him. I kiss her cheek again and ignore her confused expression as I head outside.

CHAPTER 28

I STEP ONTO THE SIDEWALK TO SEE EZRA JOGGING TOWARD ME.

"Hey, what are you doing? I would have— I was going to come up," he says, slowing down as he approaches. He runs a hand over the back of his neck. He's in a fitted dark blue suit that is ironed crisp. He has a white shirt underneath, and one thin gold chain hangs around his neck.

I almost can't believe it's him. He looks *good*. Damn good, like straight out of *GQ*. Did he have a growth spurt overnight? He suddenly seems even taller and sexier.

"I didn't want you to have to wait."

Ezra rubs his chin, which is freshly shaven. "I don't mind waiting for you."

My cheeks burn, and I study my feet. He gestures for us to walk to his car. Beside him, my arm brushes his, and my heart thunders like it does every time we touch. He doesn't move, so I don't either. Ezra clicks the alarm and the doors unlock.

"I've got my mom's car tonight," he says. It's a sleek white

Volvo that just got washed. "Here you are." Ezra opens my car door, bowing like a chauffeur, and I can't help but giggle. I don't think I've ever had anyone open my door before. Except maybe my dad.

"Thank you. Such a gentleman," I say.

He blushes before sliding into the driver's seat.

"You look—"

"Thanks for—"

Our words tumble over each other. We fall silent.

"Sorry, you go ahead," he says.

"No, no. It's okay. What were you going to say?"

"No, it's okay. *You* go. I'm sorry, I didn't mean to interrupt you." Ezra turns in his seat to face me directly. I peer out the window, back at my apartment complex, for a brief reprieve. I shake off my nerves. God, why does Ezra make me so nervous?

I take in a deep breath. "I was just going to say thank you for picking me up, for asking me to prom."

Ezra leans into me. "My pleasure," he says, and I'm tingling all over. "I was going to say you are, uh, super dope. I, um, I mean—beautiful. Beyond."

His words fill my heart and heat my cheeks. "Thank you. You look really nice too."

Ezra grins and then grabs something from the back seat.

"I hope this is okay, I got you this." Ezra holds a clear plastic box, and inside is an array of lilac, white, and gold flowers. "I was going to give it to you inside, but—"

My breath catches. "They're gorgeous."

Ezra takes the corsage out of the box and holds it up. It's the size of my palm. The flowers are arranged perfectly, a bouquet for my wrist.

"I—I didn't know what you were going to wear. But I remembered your favorite color is lilac, right? I just . . ." He chews on his lip and scrunches his nose. It's so cute, I have to hold back a laugh. Is he also *nervous*?

"It's perfect." I extend my hand, and Ezra slips the corsage on my wrist. His fingers brush my skin lightly, and goose bumps shoot up my arm.

We stare at one another again. My eyes drop to his jacket; then I reach into my small purse.

"I . . . I made your boutonniere." I hold it up, the cream paper and black ink folded into a single rose with two small paper green leaves behind it. "It's a book boutonniere—I used pages from *Fullmetal Alchemist,* but now that I'm seeing how well you clean up, maybe I should have gotten you real flowers. Your suit is so nice, I just thought—"

Ezra shakes his head in bewilderment. "I can't believe you remembered my favorite book."

I shrug, and in my best rusty Alphonse Elric voice, I say, "Some memories *are* meant to leave a trace."

I offer the flower, which he plucks lightly from my fingers and holds up to examine the small details.

"It's ridiculously perfect," he says, his voice raspy. "This is . . . Nah, you did good, real good." He leans over; his words leave me wobbly. It takes all the concentration I have to pin the flower to his jacket and not prick either of us. Imagine if the pin were old and rusty and we got a weird case of tetanus or something? I shake the thought away.

Ezra turns on the car and we head toward downtown. We chat about the little things, like the pink of the sunset and the new twinkle lights in the trees, and when we can't think of anything else to talk about, we listen to music, as if each song were crafted for us. Every time I peek over at Ezra, he's beaming, and I catch him sneaking glances at me too.

"What? What are you smiling about?" I ask.

"I just—no, nothing," Ezra starts.

"Tell me."

He grins. "I just haven't stopped smiling since you came back into my life."

CHAPTER 29

WHEN WE GET TO PROM, I ALMOST CAN'T BELIEVE IT. EZRA OPENS my door again, and I'm beginning to feel like . . . like . . . the happiest I've ever felt in . . . my life?

We walk through the hotel lobby under the bright lights and mellow music. Tourists admire us with nostalgia on their faces, the words "We used to be young too" hanging off their lips. When we get inside the banquet hall, I gasp. The room is full of soft pastels and 3D clouds that sway from the ceiling and bounce off the walls. There's a large balloon arch, and the lighting is fancy and high-tech.

"Wildest Dreams," I whisper when I see the theme on the back wall, next to big cursive phrases like *Dream Big* and *You're a Dream Come True*. The decor is perfect—dreamy, wispy, floaty. Priscilla and the prom committee did a fantastic job; this decor is legit. I can't believe I almost missed out on seeing this in real life.

"It's so whimsical," I say to Ezra. A group of people

move around us, so I lean into his shoulder as he hooks his arm around mine. Then he lifts my hand and kisses the top. I take note of his moves; he must be watching more romance movies, because everything he's doing is . . . *extremely effective.*

From across the room, Priscilla and I find each other. She shuffles toward us.

"Oh-em-geee!" she shouts the closer she gets. She grabs my arm, drooling over my corsage. Then she elbows Ezra with a wink.

"What can I say? Your boy's got style." Ezra bounces his shoulders and grins.

"Someone call 911! She's hot, you're hot—together, you're on fire! Paramedics!" Priscilla shouts, waving her arms, pretending to cool us down. Her movements cause several chaperones to crane their necks at us, making sure there's no real medical emergency.

"Not in a million years did I expect to see you here," a voice calls from behind me. I turn to see Kerry approaching me. She's in a fitted white bodycon dress with big, chunky gold jewelry, and her hair is in a high ponytail with curls.

"You look nice," I say, doing my best not to be a hater, because she does.

Kerry gives me a small curtsy. "You do too," she says. We stare at one another for a moment, mouths slightly open, like there's more we want to say. Like maybe we could sit down, and we could gab and be silly together. Like maybe, perhaps, we are more alike than different. Maybe some of the things that I worry about, she does too: That sometimes being eighteen is just . . . hard. That maybe we missed out on a friendship by competing against each other. But we don't talk about any of that. A tall blond guy in a white tux comes by, grabs her hand, and pulls her away. She peers back at me over her shoulder and waves. I lift my hand and wave back.

Ezra and I make our way to one of the tables near the dance floor, watching as everyone sings loudly to Bruno Mars. I'm about to eat another monstrous cookie from the dangerously delicious basket of baked goods on the table when Anderson .Paak comes on, causing the room to go up in a roar, the dance floor immediately packed. The teachers, too, head toward the action. I can't help but gawk, my mouth wide open at the realization—educators by day and video vixens by night? Because right now, the teachers are letting loose, their hips shaking and shoulders moving in unison. I even see Ms. T drop it low like a professional. Scratch that—she *is* a professional. She gets even lower as students around her cheer. Now I'm certain she's done this before.

Ezra tugs on my hand. I bring my fingers to my mouth and wipe away any cookie crumbs.

"You're here, I'm here. The dance floor is over there. Shall we?" Ezra puffs out his bottom lip and widens his eyes, his go-to puppy-dog face. It should be illegal to be this cute. How will I survive him? I bite my lip and let out a small exhale. I've come to the conclusion that I simply won't.

"We shall," I say, surprising myself.

Holding my hand, he leads me to the action. The moment I

step onto the dance floor, my brain shuts off and my hips find the beat. Ezra has more rhythm than I remember, bouncing his shoulders while throwing in a little two-step and a twirl, kinda like dad dances moves, but they're cute on him. The DJ plays Doja Cat and then another pop song. Soon, small beads of sweat build on my brow.

"Should we get something to drink?" Ezra cries out over the loud bass.

"After this—" But I don't finish, because the crowd is too lit. The DJ begins playing a mash-up collection of popular WeTalk songs, and like our brains have some programmable chip in them, we all begin dancing in sync. The dances aren't hard—they are mostly hand gestures and some neck rolls—but I get into them, adding a stank face here and an extra dip there. Ezra matches my energy, and before I know it, there's a small circle around us, cheering us on like we're in a dance battle. I even seen a few students take out their phones and begin recording us. Something in me begins to freak out, but Ezra grabs my hand and spins me into him. And I let that potential fear roll off my back.

We do this for about thirty more minutes before I notice that the sweat is making my edges frizz on my face and my dress is now plastered to my body.

"Okay. Sorry, Megan Thee Stallion. My knees need a break," Ezra calls out between exhausted breaths.

I snort. "Come on." I grab his hand and lead him back to our seats. Getting off the dance floor is its own type of special skill, ducking and dodging beautiful dresses and moving body parts. Without saying anything, he grabs two water bottles off the refreshments table and hands me one. We guzzle them down while we sit, our bodies wobbly, like we've just finished a marathon.

We take loud recovery breaths, just smiling at one another. Even in this dim lighting, Ezra glows. And when I see my joy reflected in his own face, I brighten, too. Has this light always been in me, or has he just helped me remember how to shine?

I'm about to speak, when the lights in the room dim low and the DJ's smooth voice comes on. Small bits of white foam release from the sky, sprinkling down. I extend my arms to catch the magic.

Every senior is now in the clouds, in this magical snow. Me, full of enchantment. Ezra, straight out of a dream—his jacket is off, his sleeves are rolled up, a bow tie hangs across his neck, and his top button is undone.

Ezra wraps his arm around me, but this time it feels different. There's an urgency in the embrace that makes my heart beat faster and louder as we head to the dance floor. I squeeze back and let our bodies intertwine. He doesn't say a word. He just holds me close, and I note just how well we fit, how there's space at his collarbone for my head, how my arms make their way around his neck comfortably. He moves his hands to my waist and touches my back, which causes me to laugh because it tickles. Ezra takes his hands off, and my entire body misses him already. Then he touches me again, intimately, and my body rejoices. Sound has been sucked out of the room, because I only hear his heart beating through his chest, like a metronome.

Ezra keeps one hand on my lower back, and his other hand comes around, brushing my bare collarbone.

"You look really beautiful tonight." His lips graze my ear as the words chase down my spine.

Ezra runs the tips of his fingers across the side of my face. "Can I be real for a moment?" he whispers. Behind us, the room twinkles; gold and silver bounce off the walls like light refracted by diamonds.

"Yeah, of course."

He is like all my favorite things: a new book, pages untouched; the beach in the early morning; fresh flowers in bloom. He grazes his thumb down my back, making small circles.

"I can't believe how we've found each other again, you know? After all these years," he murmurs. "I don't think it's a coincidence. It can't be. When I realized how much time I let pass, I almost wanted to kick myself for being so dense. Maybe I'm not as smart as I think I am."

I nuzzle my face in his chest before responding. "What are you saying?"

"Just that . . . you're my best friend, you know? You're the brightest star in my universe. That I don't just think, but I know that I've . . . I've loved you for a very long time, SJ."

His eyes widen, probably mirroring mine. Because it's like we've been waiting our whole lives for this. And maybe we have. This moment feels worth the wait. He smiles, a dimple denting his cheek. We gravitate toward one another, and our lips meet. This kiss is unlike any of our previous kisses. This is a kiss built on a love sanctioned by the cosmos. This kiss is love coming home to its rightful owner. It's a passionate one, so much so that I can feel us both grow taller, stronger, together. When we pull away from each other, I know I have unlocked a new superhuman power.

Our heads spin for a few seconds. Before either of us can let out another word, the DJ plays some hip-hop loudly, way too fast and upbeat for the moment we've just come out of. The lights flash obnoxiously, and a crowd of bodies flood the dance floor.

Hand in hand, Ezra and I walk to our table. I sneak a peek back at the scene, the clouds, the smiling faces, the traces of fake snow, the excitement. Never, ever could I have imagined any of this. I've been too caught up in school and grades and the idea of being the best. I didn't think I could exist in this world, be here, with this human by my side. Freely.

Maybe this is my wildest dream.

CHAPTER 30

Ezra has changed the name of this conversation to 😋 💋 👧 💜 👦

SUNDAY

Ezra 12:45 p.m.: I have a prom hangover. I wish we could go back.

Sasha 12:47 p.m.: Me too. It was . . . perfect.

Ezra 12:47 p.m.: It was perfect squared. Perfect to the perfect degree. Pick you up for school tomorrow?

Sasha 12:48 p.m.: Yes please 😋

MONDAY

Ezra 9:15 a.m.: Would you rather be an alien or a zombie?

Sasha 10:00 a.m.: Alien. Closest I can get to space travel, duh. You?

Ezra 10:11 a.m.: Zombie. But only if you'd be a zombie with me. Wanna go out and eat some brains? I'll bring the hot sauce.

Sasha 10:12 a.m.: So tempting . . .

TUESDAY

Sasha 11:00 a.m.: Would you rather be able to speak any language you want or speak to animals?

Ezra 11:11 a.m.: Animals. You? Also, make a wish.

Sasha 11:12 a.m.: Okay, Eli Thornberry. I'll say any language. I really hate how bad my Korean is.

Ezra 11:13 a.m.: Maybe you could take a class next year in college? It's never too late to start. Try something new, surprise yourself.

WEDNESDAY

Ezra 8:15 p.m.: Would you rather read the book or watch the movie?

Sasha 8:15 p.m.: Do you even know me?

Ezra 8:16 p.m.: You're right. Read the book. I'm the same. Just checking!

Sasha 8:17 p.m.: We should bring that old thing back?

Ezra 8:18 p.m.: Pick the title and I'll be your living, breathing, walking audiobook.

THURSDAY

Ezra 7:30 a.m.: Tutoring today, right? I have something for Ben.

Sasha 7:31 a.m.: Awesome. What is it?

Ezra 7:33 a.m.: That's confidential information.

Sasha 7:33 a.m.: Fine. I'll just eavesdrop.

Ezra 7:34 a.m.: Dope. See you soon.

Sasha 7:34 a.m.: xx

Sasha 10:00 a.m.: Would you rather be kissed or hugged every day?

Ezra 10:02 a.m.: By you?

Sasha 10:02 a.m.: . . .

Ezra 10:03 a.m.: You know how much I love a good hug. But I'll take whatever I can get.

SATURDAY

Ezra 1:15 p.m.: I'm gonna go to the gym and then maybe a movie. Wanna come?

Ezra 1:15 p.m.: Or get dinner?

Sasha 3:45 p.m.: Sorry, busy with mom today.

Ezra 3:45 p.m.: Tell ohmma hello.

SUNDAY

Ezra 9:15 p.m.: I don't wanna go to school. I think I'm gonna take a day off. Join me?

> Sasha 9:17 p.m.: I can't. But I can get a ride with
> P in the morning.

> Ezra 9:18 p.m.: I'll miss you. Love you, SJ.

My fingers hover over the keyboard on my phone. Ugh, it's so easy for Ezra to say "I miss you" or, when he's feeling super affectionate, "I love you." It just rolls off his tongue or his fingers. Whenever I try to type the words and I see them staring back at me, I panic.

Do I love Ezra? I mean, I know I love spending time with him. I love being with him, and of course, kissing him is just as nice. I type the words again, and as soon as I do, my thumb hits backspace, deleting my thoughts. I know it's weak, but I drop a heart emoji instead. Ezra never presses me to say it back. Not yet at least. One day I want to; I want to be able to tell him how I really feel.

My throat tightens. Relationships don't come with manuals, and right now, I kinda wish they did. I guess I haven't loved anyone new in so long, or in this way, that I've forgotten how to do it.

CHAPTER 31

THE POST-PROM GLOW AND GIDDINESS LAST FOR TWO GLORIOUS weeks. Two perfect weeks of Ezra and SJ, of school, of incessant texting, of the things that were once mundane now being delivered with a special twist. The love glow-up is real.

The following Thursday morning we're in Ezra's car headed to school, his hand in mine. Ezra pulls into the parking lot, and before turning off the car, he leans over with a hard stare. "Do you trust me?"

I smile. "Yeah, I do. Why?"

"Let me borrow you for the morning."

I peer outside the car window, confused. "But we're already at school. What do you mean?"

"I can have you back by lunch and of course for tutoring," he says confidently. He raises his eyebrows and rubs the top of my thigh. I melt into him like butter on hot toast.

"Okay, but we need to be back by the end of lunch." I try

to sound more confident than I feel. I'm allowed to have a case of senioritis too, right?

Ezra puts the car in reverse, and then we are the only car exiting the lot.

We sit in a comfortable silence for ten minutes as he gets on the highway. I exhale, and Ezra chuckles.

"What? What's that about?" I ask.

"I know you hate surprises, so I won't make you suffer any longer."

"Low-key . . . thank you." To know me is to love me.

He points to the glove box. "There. In there." Then he puts both hands on the wheel.

I lean forward and press the cold plastic button. The front drops down, and a bright white envelope sits on top of a pile of napkins and papers.

"Go ahead, open it." Ezra steals a glance at me and then his eyes refocus on the road. I pick up the envelope—it's light. I turn it over and pull out two tickets.

"No way," I say, reading the words once, twice, three times. "An Alvin Ailey matinee? How did you?"

"My mom and the pit conductor are pretty good friends; they used to play together in San Francisco. She pulled a favor."

"This is incredible. I've always wanted to see this dance troupe perform, I just—" I examine the tickets again, trying to ignore the price in the corner. "Ooh, orchestra seats?!"

I grab his hand and kiss it. Doja Cat fills the car, and Ezra does a small shoulder shimmy on beat. My eagerness can't be contained, so I let go through my favorite dances. My head and arms move in sync, and even though my seat belt is on, I'm able to move my arms and deliver small body rolls while Ezra drums on the steering wheel. We car dance for thirty minutes, until the windows begin to fog and Ezra flips on the AC, reminding us to breathe.

♡♡♡

For the next hour, I sit at the edge of my front-row seat, mesmerized. I am in awe of the beauty, the mastery, the joy in the dancing, as well as the physical expression of my people and our history. I feel connected to something larger than myself, like my soul is speaking to other souls through some time portal. I don't think I blink the entire time. I watch the show more intently than I've ever watched anything in my life.

The house lights come up, and onstage the dancers hold hands and take a synchronized bow. I'm the first on my feet, applauding loudly. Ezra follows, and then, one by one, the other guests do too. The dancers bow again, and I clap louder, harder. Each clap contains all my enjoyment, my pleasure, my gratitude, so I make sure they can hear it. The doors open and a wave of feelings ripples through my body, high tide. Small tears form. Tears of joy. I let them fall, salty in my mouth. I pat my eyes and turn to Ezra.

Ezra leans into me, eyes wide. We stand, hand in hand.

"Hold up," I say as the other people make their way toward the center aisle to exit. I survey the crowd—who are they, what type of magical lives do they lead to be able to go to a dance show in the middle of the day? How awesome to be able to take time out of your life to honor and enjoy the things you love.

"That was so dope. You wanna get going?" Ezra asks, squeezing my hand.

I'm giddy; my eyes dart around the room. "What if . . . what if we wait? Give it two minutes, maybe three. The dancers are gonna come out after, I know it. We could try and get a photo?"

"Hell yeah! I love this energy." Ezra begins walking down the aisle. The audience dissolves quickly, and sure enough, two dancers walk down as if to join us. He gives me a squeeze, and I go a limp, just a little.

I spot one of the lead dancers, Michelle Simon. She stands, long and lean. I remember her from all the routines, up in front, commanding the audience. Her skin is a deep, flawless brown, warm and glowing. She's in a black tank-top leotard with short brown Uggs. She runs a hand over her head, which is freshly shaven. Each step she takes toward us, I swear the ground beneath me shakes. Behind her, the other dancers follow.

Ezra doesn't waste a second. "Excuse me," he calls out. Michelle stops in front of us and smiles. On her collarbone there's a small tattoo, a butterfly with wings in the shape of Africa.

Ezra says, "We're big fans. Would it be okay if we got a photo?"

"Absolutely," she says; even her voice is beautiful, soft and melodic. Without hesitation, she puts her arm around my shoulder, and we pose, proper at first, and then, as if on cue, we throw up peace signs and duck lips.

Ezra rejoins and the other dancers join too. Just us, hanging after the show with the Alvin Ailey dance crew. No big deal? Huge, huge, biggest deal of my life.

"Y'all from around here?" Michelle asks. There's something Southern in her voice; she kinda sounds like my dad's big aunt. Ezra gives my arm a shove.

"Close by," I reply. "The show was absolutely amazing." Now they smile, proud.

Alvin Ailey dancers, in the flesh, in front of me.

Do it, Sasha. Just ask.

"How did you, um, how did you do that?" The words barely make it out of my mouth, but I have to know.

"The dances?" another asks. She has a slight foreign accent, but I can't place it.

"I mean, yes, but also . . ." I pause again. I need another moment to align my thoughts. "It was more than dancing. How did you, you know, where did you learn to . . ." *Shit*. "I'm sorry. It's just there was so much emotion, so much history, so much passion in every movement. I've danced before, but I've never, I've never been able to—"

"That fervor is already in you. The spirit you need to break free is all there. You just have to trust your gut, you know?"

she says as we lock eyes. She gives me a small nod and then she removes her palm. From behind her, more of the dancers begin walking toward the front exit.

There's a dance in the show called "Revelations," and I feel like that's happening now to me. Like she's just given me the key to unlocking magic in my own life.

"All right, it's time to eat!" someone in the group calls out. Michelle does a small but extremely graceful twirl, waves her hand, and walks out.

I turn to Ezra and kiss him, a light peck on the lips. "This was perfect. Thank you."

CHAPTER 32

"I JUST DON'T WANT TO BE LATE FOR TUTORING," I SAY. I FIDDLE with my fingers to hide the irritation in my voice, but it's hard. What is it about Murphy's Law and the one time I decide to ditch school? What was supposed to be an hour car ride has turned into two, the highway bottlenecked due to a flat tire on a semi. I stare out the window as we inch toward our destination, afraid to show Ezra the worry on my face.

"Shit, I know. It's out of my control. I think we'll make it just in time for tutoring according to the GPS. Not so terrible if you're a little late, right?"

I don't answer him. Being behind schedule's not the worst thing in the world, but it's not my favorite.

We pull into the school parking lot five minutes before the final school bell rings.

"Back just in time." Ezra unbuckles his seat belt. He presses his back against the door, facing me.

"Thank goodness." I grab my phone and out of nervous

habit pull up GradeSavR, our school's app for grades and attendance. I check it daily, because, well, you know.

"Oh shit." I freeze. "Mendoza posted our presentation grades. He must have gone over that today."

"Word?" Ezra unplugs his phone from the aux cord and taps away at his screen. It takes a moment, but then his grade appears. I do my best not to peer over his shoulder, but I can't help it.

"What'd you get?" The eagerness in my voice fills the car.

"A ninety-five!" Ezra relaxes. "Dope."

Something in me shifts and my stomach tightens.

Ezra jostles my shoulder. "And you?"

I blink. "A ninety-nine."

"Go off. She's pretty and she's smart." Ezra winks.

I wait a moment, hoping Ezra will say it first. My body stiffens. He doesn't say anything, so I go for it.

"This means I beat you."

"What?"

I swallow and lean back, the space shrinking. Outside, the final bell rings, and doors bust open.

"I said . . ." I make an effort to soften my tone. "I said, I beat you. I won."

Confusion fills Ezra's face, which annoys me. He forgot about the bet? Or is he choosing to act dumb? "Well, yeah. Great work on your presentation." But his voice is bristly, like those yellow-and-green sponges I scrub with on the weekends. "I guess you win a thing too. What's it gonna be? Ice cream date?"

I pause. "Not exactly. This means we need to decide upon a final bet, for . . . you know, the scholarship and stuff. Since we are, well, tied again."

He doesn't hide the irritation in his face, his eyes cold. No, disappointment. "Seriously? We still doing that?"

I throw up my hands. "That was the plan, right? What we had agreed to? Come on, we didn't make this deal that long ago." I recall the last four weeks. Sure, we haven't been discussing the bets, but we sure as hell didn't call them off.

His shoulders slump. "Yeah, I just kind of assumed we were off that. You know, since we've been together." He motions between us with his fingers. "I honestly haven't been thinking about the scholarship or the title."

"Why doesn't that surprise me," I say without thinking, shocked by my own snark. Ezra sighs but thankfully doesn't respond. The awkwardness in the car puts a sour taste in my mouth. We sit in silence for another moment, and then Ezra perks up and grabs my hand.

"I have an idea. What if we share the title and the scholarship?"

Oh hell no. "What? We can't share. It's not a pizza," I say.

"Try and imagine it, Sasha. It's actually not a bad idea, if you really think about it."

My name, not my nickname. His brown eyes burn into mine as if they are trying to find something. I'm so taken aback I almost forget he's holding my hand.

"What? I'm not good enough to be co-valedictorian with?" He fakes a laugh, but I don't respond. This is not about him.

His eyes are glassy, but his jaw is firm. "Okay, here. You want a bet? For bet three, instead of some ridiculous legacy project, bet your heart, Sasha Jalisa Johnson-Sun." His lips quiver but his words are sharp; he does his best to smile.

"What does that even mean, Ezra? You're not making sense."

"It's just a feeling! It means, you know, lead with your heart and not your head for once. Bet on you and me. Trust that love will guide us in the right direction. It got us here now, right? Put your heart on the line, and I'll do the same. The final assignments will be what they may. School is school. Whatever happens with the scholarship, just let it happen. We've got something good here, I know it. You do too."

I can't move. My chest squeezes. I'm dumbfounded, and anger begins to build inside me.

His eyes dart between mine and the school, a test within the test. This is a trick question. There doesn't feel like there could be a right answer.

Silence.

Ezra drops my hand. "You've got to say something," he says, with pleading in his voice. The tone drives a wedge into my heart. "I know I was a jerk at the beginning of all this. I just wanted to shake up your work ethic a bit. I've seen the way that singular focus can destroy relationships, you know? Maybe you haven't." He pauses, then starts again, slower and resigned. "That was definitely true for my parents. Their obsession with work tore them apart. Have you ever seen a ninety-hour workweek in a relationship? Maybe that's extreme, but I just—I want to *be* with you, Sasha. But that means we have to be open to whatever happens with school. What if I win the scholarship? Are you—"

The dam that was holding my emotions back breaks, and suddenly everything inside me rushes out, flowing into whatever is in its path. "And there it is. Admit it, Ezra. You want to win just as much as I do." There's an edge to my words that's unrecognizable to me. "And you know . . . how funny, because you don't even need the money. . . ." I shake my head.

I can't believe this. We agreed to the bets, and I still want to win. Why is this so confusing? How can he not understand?

My brain pounds, so I don't respond. Right now, we are standing in a river of emotions—confessions, love, fear, and the brink of hurt. I don't know what getting swept downstream will mean.

Ezra's voice goes raw. "SJ, you're missing the point. I don't really give a damn about those bets. I'm here for us. The bets were just— I only agreed to them to reconnect with you. I thought you were doing the same. Say you care about *me* more than the damn title and scholarship. Please."

An unfamiliar rage begins to build inside of me. "Don't ask me to pick between you and my future, Ezra."

"Why do they have to be mutually exclusive? Am I not in your future?"

My pulse picks up, louder and faster, like my heart is beating in my ears. "That's not what I'm saying. Ugh. You have no idea what it's like to do something for other people. To carry this constant pressure on your back."

"And you don't know what it's like to do something for yourself! News flash: Self-care is important." He sighs. "This is what I mean about you. Could you ever put us first? Could you put yourself first?" Ezra snaps, his voice cracking. I ignore it. He tries to soften his eyes, his tone, but the bitterness is still there. "I'm not asking you to *not care*," he says, throwing his hands in the air. "I know how you feel. I actually really love how passionate and dedicated you are. I just want to know that you *could* care about me as much as you do your work and school and your grades. You're allowed to be happy in life, you know? You can work hard and have passions and—"

"Not you giving out life advice right now. You're a hypocrite, you know that? The worst part? You can't even see it."

Ezra pulls back. There's a wall between us that's thick and impossible to climb. We stand on our separate sides.

"What the hell does that mean?"

My heart is telling me to stop, but it's too late. It's like we are thirteen and fighting all over again, making sure to hit all the most painful points.

So I spill it all. "A lot of talk about doing the things we care about, right? Well, I took your stupid flash drive and saw what was inside your legacy folder. The one you said you didn't have anything prepared for. Which was a lie—you have enough photos to fill a warehouse. Yeah, I saw that one."

"But . . . there's a password . . ."

"I remember more things about you than you think, Ezra," I say sharply. Something in me keeps going. "There's a lot of talk about me. What about you, huh? What are you so afraid of? It's a freaking high school project, so what? And why are you so blasé about your plans after graduation? Huh? It's fine if you don't want to go to college, but to have *nothing* planned, is just . . . Let's say I'd rather care about something too much than pretend to not care about anything at all. You want me to care about you? *You* care about you." My voice is strong, maybe too strong. Honesty is supposed to be the best policy, right? Except right now it feels like the worst thing.

Ezra rubs his ear. "You— I asked you straight up. You lied about the flash drive?" Bafflement fills his face, his eyes narrow, his expression stern. Heat creeps up my neck.

I don't respond.

"So you took my stuff, lied about taking it, violated my privacy, and what, you were just going to pretend you never saw my work? Until what? Until we had a fight? Now you're holding this information over me?"

His hard expression pierces my skin, so I focus on the ground. He reaches behind him and grabs a large manila envelope. He faces me, his eyes empty. "Here, give this to Ben and take these. I sure as hell don't want them." He shoves them into my hand and I press the envelope against my body as he continues to speak. "You talk a big game about legacy, but you're totally missing it. I know you and your family, including your dad. He would have wanted you to be honest with

yourself and those around you. And to live, like truly live."
His voice is low and cold. My stomach sinks.

The tension between us is thick and heavy.

"Well, likewise, Ezra. I think you're missing the point about *your* dad, his accomplishments and all the sacrifices he made for you."

It's not something I ever meant to say, but I've said it. The words have left my mouth. I don't even know how much of them I mean. Either way, it's too, too late to take them back now.

He shakes his head. "Just for the record, this is not how I wanted this conversation to go, Sasha. I wanted us to be able to make all this work. I guess that doesn't matter now."

"No, I guess not," I mutter, the anger in my voice dissolving once I notice the redness in Ezra's eyes.

My tone, my delivery, too rough.

Ezra clears his throat, searching for his voice.

"Okay, Sasha," he says, defeated. "Maybe you were right all along. I don't know you. Maybe I never knew you. Because the person I thought I knew . . ." He pauses, and I swear I see every version of us—every instant, every secret, every laugh—flash through my mind, like the ending credits of a movie.

Oh, shit. Is this how we end?

He shrugs. "Maybe I knew you, but I don't anymore." The words hang in the air, enough to reveal the hurt on my own face.

I grab my backpack and press my hand on the door handle.

I sling my legs outside. Inside, my body lingers, waiting for one of us to stop this train before it's completely wrecked, to undo the damage before it hardens and solidifies, but we don't. Ezra turns his head away from me and stares out the window. I take that as my cue to leave, giving the car door a strong slam behind me. I walk to the sidewalk as Ezra's car backs up and drives away.

CHAPTER 33

THE SUMMER I TURNED EIGHT, I GOT THIS EPIC NEW BIKE. PINK AND silver stars scattered across the thin frame. One day, I was doing my usual tour de neighborhood, when I fell off my bike and broke my arm. I was in so much shock, I rode around for an hour after the fall before finally going home. Only when I got home did I realize how bad it was. I cried, of course, and screamed. I probably would've fainted had my parents not acted immediately.

I feel that now—that shock, the uncertainty of not knowing what is real and what actually hurts. How bad it all is, and most importantly, how I'll survive.

I'm in the back of Ms. T's room, watching Priscilla and Chance tutor, watching the kids, but nothing makes sense. That conversation with Ezra stretched for what felt like years, when only minutes had passed.

Once tutoring ends, after I've put on a cheerful face for an hour, the kids leave and I collapse. Chance snags a chair near me, flips it around, and sits backward, like teachers do before they give a pep talk. Priscilla sits on top of a desk as they home in together.

"What the . . . what did we miss? You look like your body has been taken over by some alien species." Chance waves his hand in front of my face.

I shake my head and blink back tears of sadness, or frustration, or both. And then I replay the day for them, from Alvin Ailey to our fight. I give them every detail, a word-for-word playback, leaving my bias out of my impersonations and tone. Chance and Priscilla are attentive listeners, nodding along to the beat. My friends get me.

Or so I thought.

When I finish, Priscilla doesn't even try to hide her confusion. "Hear me out . . . I don't think sharing would be terrible, would it? Sharing could be cute, right?"

Here we go. Again. "It's not like your strawberry milkshake or a rideshare. It's not something we can just split."

"Well, I don't know. It doesn't sound like such a terrible idea." Priscilla raises her eyebrows. "Chance? What do you think?"

"Honestly? I see both sides." Chance folds his hands together and attempts to sound neutral, even though I know he's siding with Priscilla.

"No need for diplomacy," I mumble. "You can be real with me." Chance prepares to speak, but I cut him off. "But before you say anything, try and remember that this stuff doesn't matter to him. Like, his life is just—his grades are—I mean, he doesn't *want it* like I do. He doesn't deserve it."

Chance leans in. "But if he wins the title, won't he be as equally deserving? Has he not done the same schoolwork as you? For him to be tied, it must matter, even somewhat, to him, even if his reasons for wanting it are completely different than yours."

"If he wins? What? Why would you even say that? Why would you even put that out there?" I reply. Chance lifts his chin, and I can tell he wants to say more.

Priscilla jumps in. "School work aside, you love him, right? Alvin Ailey was such a thoughtful and perfect gift for you. Very specific. Something only someone who truly knows you would get. Did that cross your mind? Maybe you should try and make it work. He loves you, it's super obvious."

Ezra says "love" one time at prom, and suddenly I'm supposed to give up what is practically my life's work? And *why* would Chance even suggest a reality where Ezra wins? I'm baffled.

"Do you two not hear me?" I throw my hands up in the air. "Yes, getting tickets to an Alvin Ailey show was nice, but does that mean I should give up on what I've fought four years for? Over a couple of hours? That's ridiculous. We agreed to finish the bets and suddenly we aren't. I still want the title. I still want to be able to fight for what's mine. I'm not a bad person for wanting to—to—" But I'm flustered. I'm standing my ground, but it feels like I'm on quicksand. The people I thought would support me only seem to let me sink further and further. Best friends shouldn't do this. "I wish you two could hear me—"

"No, I think we hear you just fine. You're choosing not to hear us," Chance is quick to respond.

This is utter and complete bullshit. Again. People say they understand you, until they don't. I shake my head. "I hear you, but I don't know if I want to." I shake my head again and again until I realize that maybe I just need to stand up for me. "Respectfully, Chance, what do you know about school and doing well? Like academically working toward something? You won't even do the bare minimum to graduate." I turn to face Priscilla, who's next to receive my wrath. "And what do you know about love and making things work? You didn't even know Gina was over you. Last I checked, you both were kind of struggling in these areas. Maybe you both could just be on my side and keep your unsolicited advice to yourselves."

The room goes painfully flat. My words saturate the air, the space now muggy with hurt.

I twist to straighten in my seat, but I don't feel good. But it's true, right? I'm right, right? Everyone wants to put me under the microscope, but what about them?

Chance whispers, "Huh, this is how you really feel? About . . . us? About me?" He looks at Priscilla, who is already off the desk, bag on shoulder.

I don't know how I feel about anything anymore. But I'm too afraid to admit that, so I don't.

With her phone in her hand, she points at me. "Why did

you even come here? You don't really care about tutoring or about us anymore. I've had it with your bullshit, just so you know. It's too much. You're too much right now. Do less." Her words are cold.

Chance makes sure I see him, the hurt in his face seared into my brain, into my soul. I've . . . I've done some damage.

But I hate backing down in arguments, especially when there's some truth in them. "I just—I don't think what I'm saying is so far off. I wish you could understand it from where I'm at."

Chance props his chin in his hand and his sadness turns into something I don't know. "Good luck making your life, and your legacy . . . meritorious, Sasha. Truly. I wish you all the best on your vapid, lonely path forward." He pushes the chair out and stands, walking toward Priscilla. Neither gives me a second look as they leave the room.

Time moves forward.

I stay in Ms. T's room until the janitor comes by, flipping on the bright white lights in the dark room. We acknowledge one another as he begins to pick up paper balls of trash. I stand, my butt and legs tingly from all that sitting. In one swoop, I grab my backpack, and the manila envelope falls to the floor.

Ezra.

Slowly I bend down to pick it up. My finger runs across the back flap, and without much resistance, the envelope opens. I'm tempted to sit again, but the janitor has a mop in hand.

I take two shaky steps toward the door.

"Good night," I say as I exit the room. He nods politely and continues his work.

I'm too afraid to peer inside. What if it's something that completely wrecks my heart, and the janitor sees me crying? I'm one human interaction away from crumbling. Somehow, I make my way outside to an empty corridor.

Here, open it here.

I turn the envelope upside down and out slide several matted black-and-white photos of . . . me.

They say that if you were to run into yourself on the street, you wouldn't be able to recognize, well, you. That we have such a distorted view of our true selves that we wouldn't be able to recognize our own being. Not to mention, we rarely see ourselves how others see us. That's how I'm beginning to feel. Who am I looking at? Who is this person staring back at me?

The first photo is from a few weeks ago outside Principal Newton's office. Our reconnection. I'm wearing a stupid grin, but I'm relaxed, sure of myself in a way that's so foreign now.

The next couple of photos are of me by the water, the day of our first kiss. When I see them, my body betrays me; nausea creeps in my stomach.

The contradiction of these two Sashas, night and day. In the photos I look good. Great, even. Ezra has been able to capture a playful side of me that I kinda forgot existed. For the first time in a long time, I'm seeing myself . . . Seeing myself joyful.

How dare Ezra use his art to remind me that . . . that I could be happy. That I *was* happy, with him.

Another bout of sadness steals my breath as I think of the things we said to each other today. His words about my dad and legacy ring in my ears. What would my parents want most for me? Isn't it the scholarship? If not, then I pushed away the three people I care most about for nothing. I can't accept that. And yet, the things that I thought I wanted for so long don't seem to make much sense anymore. Pain shoots through my body, starting from my heart and spreading to the tips of my fingers to my toes. The pain of losing your best friends not once, but twice in a lifetime.

CHAPTER 34

AFTER TWENTY-FOUR HOURS OF RADIO SILENCE FROM MY FRIENDS, I think that maybe, just maybe, I know how to repair what I've done. I take out my phone and create a genuine message to send to Priscilla and Chance in our group chat.

> Sasha 2:45 p.m.: I'll be at Spudsy today for our second-to-last Fry-Date. Please join me? I know I fucked up, and I want to apologize.

As soon as the school day ends, I rush to Spudsy.

"Table for one?" the hostess asks. She makes it sound so depressing. I fake a smile.

"For three, please. Is it possible to sit over there?" I point to our booth from our first visit, when life may have been uncertain, but I had friends who loved and cared about me, and I cared about them.

252

"No problem." She smiles. I follow her through the bustling restaurant as she leads me to our spot.

Ten minutes later, I order our favorite foods.

Twenty minutes later, the food arrives.

Forty-five minutes later, the server comes by and asks if I'm okay, and I fake another smile. It's scary how good I am getting at these.

I check my phone again. No missed calls, no new messages. I'm the last person to write in our group thread. I'm also the last person to, ahem, fuck it up.

Intense dread creeps into my body, followed by a wave of sadness. I push the basket of fries away, my body unable to stomach anything other than deep feelings.

After an hour of staring at the door and my phone, I pay the bill, leave a nice tip, and head out.

As I walk home, the realization is painfully simple: Without the people in my life who I love, I have no good thing. I just have an A+ on a presentation no one will remember.

CHAPTER 35

ON SATURDAY MORNING, THE HURT FROM THE WEEK WEIGHS me down. I only have the energy to burrow in my sheets, hiding. My mom knocks on my door, and I don't respond. She takes one long look at me, my puffy eyes, the mess on my desk, and understands. I'm thankful she knows me well enough and leaves for work without asking me if I'll be joining her.

Sometime in the early afternoon, I hear the front door open.

My mom heads to my room.

Knock, knock. "Honey," she calls. "Are you in there?"

I groan quietly. "I am. I just— I don't feel good." Which is true.

I sink into my bed. Maybe I won't go back to school. Maybe I won't graduate. What's the point? My best friends hate me, and the situation with Ezra is . . . more complicated than ever. Or over. I'm not sure which is better. I can still feel his hands on my skin. He said he that he's loved me for a long time. Could he still love me after what I've said? Do I even deserve it? If I spoke the truth, why do I feel so guilty about our conversation? And why is the valedictorian title still on my brain?

Sometime in the late afternoon, my mom knocks again with a little more gusto.

"Okay, honey, I thought—"

"Mom, I just need to be by myself, please! I'll be out of this funk soon enough, but I need to be alone today, okay?" My voice cracks, betraying my pain.

She waits before answering. "Okay. I hear you. . . . I will be back, then," she says, and before I can even respond, her footsteps lead her out the door.

Great. Now she's probably mad at me too.

I fall back into my blankets and let myself float off into the dreamworld, the only place I seem to be safe.

Around seven p.m., I leave my room to burrow on our couch. I snuggle into the cushions, but the location change does not trick my brain into being cheery. I space out for another thirty minutes, until I hear my mom rattle her large key chain, and slowly she opens the door.

"Oh good, you're up." She waddles in, a large paper bag in her hand.

I do my best to sit up, but even my bones are tired. "That smells delicious," I admit. My stomach grumbles. "What is it?"

She walks over and places the bag in front of me. "Open and see." Say less, Mom. My mouth begins to water at the aroma wafting from the container. I rip into the white box as she heads into the kitchen.

Large mounds of white rice, vegetables, kimchi, tempura, and bulgogi greet me. I give the bag another quick glimpse, and yep, it's from Sushi Time, our go-to spot. This is like a blessing in a bag. When I was younger, my parents and I used to go there on special occasions.

I gnaw at a piece of shrimp tempura and chew too fast. It's delicious; it's crispy. This food is everything I need to return to my senses.

My mom comes from the kitchen and sits near me. Her face is red, her eyes a little puffy. Something is written on her face, and when I begin to decipher the meaning behind it all, my heart drops.

The air is sucked out of my chest when I realize—too late, of course—the reason for my mom's trip to the restaurant, the special meal she's brought home to me, the incessant requests from her that I ignored. The way I've let everyone and everything important slip away from me. I've been so blind.

My heart twists into itself, then falls right out of my chest.

Today is my dad's birthday.

I forgot—how could I forget?

Sushi Time was his favorite restaurant.

That is where Mom and I have gone the last four years to celebrate, honor, and remember him.

Our tradition.

My dad, who always let me blow out the candles on his

birthday cake. My dad, who made sure that on his birthday he spent a moment "celebrating us." My dad, who stuffed a second birthday card inside your main birthday card so you knew how important your born day was.

His day, today.

That's why she was there, that's why she was trying to get me to come—the realizations flood me.

My mom gets up and lights the candle on the bookshelf altar. The match hisses and the room is illuminated in soft yellows. I collapse into the couch, forgetting the food.

How could I be so selfish?

I begin to cry.

Not small, delicate tears either. But the big, exasperated, headache-inducing kind. I almost can't breathe. The tears are thick, made for Ezra and Priscilla and Chance and for my parents and for me. I cry until all the pain is wrung out of me.

My mom sits down beside me and hands me a tissue, her hand on my back, comforting me. When the tears slow down, she pulls me in. Her arms hold me up; they give me a semblance of strength.

"I'm sorry. I really hate myself for this. I didn't mean to forget. I just . . ." My voice breaks. This is the last thing in the world I wanted.

She pats my back, and the touch is healing. "Oh, honey," she says. "Are you okay? You can talk to me." I shake my head. She reaches for my hand and rubs the top, her way of inviting me to share, to be open.

So I do. I tell her. And once I start talking, I can't stop. I start with the legacy project and my original goal to win valedictorian for Daddy. Then Ezra. Ezra, the reason for prom and mastermind behind the Alvin Ailey show.

"I didn't want to worry you. I've been so caught up in school and finishing strong and I think the title is slipping away from me. I'm sorry. I don't want to let you down. I've been trying so hard. I'm always trying—"

"Shhhh," my mom says, and now she's crying with me. "I am—we are proud of you, no matter what, you know." She grabs my chin and makes me look at her. "We couldn't have asked for a better daughter." Her arms wrap around me, and I hug her back.

My mom takes a shaky breath, wiping her tears away with a small grin. She pauses and her eyes soften. "You could have told me about you and Ezra."

There's a lot I wish I could tell her, things we've never spoken about. But where would I even begin? Should I tell her that life can be unfair, that I think it's unfair she couldn't finish school? That being tied with Ezra for the title has led to one of the most confusing relationships of my life? That I miss Ezra, and I'm afraid I've lost him forever? That I don't know where I stand with my friends, that our lives are going in such different directions, I'm not even sure we can hang on?

"I know. I'm sorry. All I've ever wanted to do is to help you and do the things in school you two didn't have a chance to . . ." But I can't speak anymore. The tears are back. They are the heavy rains of monsoon season.

My mom rubs circles on my back. "You work too hard, too much. That's my fault."

My eyes widen. "No, it's my fault. What I do matters—"

"This does not matter more than who you are. You are so much more than a title," my mom says. She points to cleaning supplies still on the kitchen counter. "You think I'm just a housecleaner?" Her voice is shaky.

"Of course not, Mom. I didn't mean it like that."

She holds my hands in hers. "I never want you to think your work is all that you are. You are so much, to so many. Including me. And your father. Okay? So never forget that." We both laugh a little when we reach for a tissue. It feels like my dad is here with us.

My mom's words pull at me and ground me at the same time. She's everything to me. Not because of the work she does, but because of who she is, how she chooses to live her life. If I can be like her at all, if I can remember that, I will always be okay.

She grabs my chin. "You know, maybe it's a good thing that you forgot."

I straighten.

"How?"

She stares into the distance; the candles flicker, and the light bounces off the walls. "I don't want us to be so tied to the past, tied to things we can't change. Maybe that's my fault. Maybe I've focused on the past too much. There's lots to enjoy right now, in this moment. He would want that for you, you know. To be happy and alive, and so busy living that you didn't get lost in these little things. Memories are good, but we can't let them haunt us."

She laughs, which sounds happy and sad and a little manic. "Forgive me. I'm rambling. Your dad would nag us for not enjoying every precious moment. He would've been thrilled to see you off on prom night; he would be overjoyed to know that you're enjoying as much of this life as possible."

I search for a response, something to tell her I understand what she's saying. Every word sounds counterintuitive to so much of *us*. Who we've become since Dad's passing? Is she sure?

"He would be mad if we had . . . what's the word? Regrets. Life is for the living," she says softly.

As much as this lecture is my dose of sage motherly advice, the way she fiddles with her hands lets me know that sometimes the things we say out loud to others are also for ourselves.

"Are you—do you have regrets?" My voice is so quiet, I'm not even sure she hears me.

Her head bobs, and she brings a finger to her eye, drying her remaining tears.

"Some. But I don't want to have them anymore." She gives my hand a squeeze. I roll my shoulders forward and lift my head. Mom hops to her feet and goes to the kitchen, where I hear her rummaging around for a minute.

When she returns, she's got a lit candle in a chocolate cup-
cake with a perfect swirl of white frosting. Dad's favorite.

"We can blow it out together?" I offer.

"Yes. Don't forget to make a wish. He'd want us to." The
candle has a small but mighty flame. I close my eyes tight and
breathe in. Then I blow and make a new wish.

CHAPTER 36

TODAY I'M MORE LIKE A HUMAN BUT STILL NOT FULLY MYSELF. I'M at my desk, staring at my legacy project.

A familiar knock rattles my door.

"Come in!"

Mom stands by my desk, eager, the excitement in her face almost terrifying. She looks revitalized, refreshed. Her hair is up in a white scrunchie (wait, is that mine?), and she's even got a little makeup on—mascara and blush, by the way her face glows.

"What? You're scaring me."

"Ha! Happy people shouldn't scare you."

"What's up?"

She takes her hands from behind her back and pushes a stack of old photos into my hand.

"Check out what I found in a box in the closet." She peers over my shoulder. I flip through photos of my dad, of my parents, of their life before . . . me. How dare they have lives and interests before I existed? But also, this is like gold.

"Holy shit," I mutter. Her motherly reflex kicks in, and she gives me a gentle but firm shove.

"Language."

"Sorry," I say. "Where did you—"

"These were waaaaay in the back. I don't know if we ever showed you."

I quickly sift through the photos, eager to take them all in. There are about thirty. Then I start again, slower this time, examining for clues. Each photo feels like it could be a moment for story time, an afternoon of laughs and sharing family secrets. I'm smiling uncontrollably. My parents are so fucking radiant in these photos. And cool. My parents were cool before they had me? I find it hard to believe, but the proof is right here, staring me in the face.

"Mom, your perm is kinda sick. Also, this midriff? Okay, abs." She's in a bright yellow tank top that stops above her belly button, and dark jeans. Her hair is in big curls with even bigger bangs.

"We did what we could." She rubs my shoulder.

The last photo is of my Dad, an old Polaroid, with *Lover's Point* scribbled at the bottom in his handwriting. He's so tall and handsome. There's a cheesy grin on his face, and he's showing all his teeth, which he rarely did.

"I took that one," my mom says proudly.

It's almost uncanny. It's déjà vu.

Or maybe not. Maybe it's time flowing into itself.

"Hold up." I hop up from my desk and dig into the bottom of my backpack. I pull out Ezra's photos, searching for the one of me by the water. "Come see this," I say to my mom.

She leans in. "Ha! Practically twins. When you were born, you looked like me. Next month you started to change, and suddenly you grew into his carbon copy." We hold the two photos side by side, and we are like twins. Well, if my dad had long locs and wore skinny jeans, or if I grew a mustache, but still. In both photos—us by the water, savoring the moment—the energy, the smile . . . it's there, same-same.

Seeing my parents' joy, my old smile, a large part of me wants to cackle at how foolish I've been. I want to call Ezra. I want to hug my dad. I want to do so many things at once, because the realization is both enlightening and terrifying. Because now, now that I know I can want more from life, I can't unknow it. It all makes sense: I feel free, and light, and a little wild.

"Are you all right?"

"Yeah, I just . . . I think I finally figured it out." I turn to face her.

"The meaning of life?" she jokes. Or I think she's joking. Maybe not the meaning of life. But the meaning of the big pieces of my life. Or better yet, what *I* decide to give meaning to in my life. This epiphany is tingly. My face heats up, and I feel like I could go downtown and get in people's personal space to spread my discoveries scribbled on large cardboard signs.

"Mom, do you ever, you know, think about dating?"

She chuckles. "How do you know I'm not?"

My jaw drops.

"I'm kidding," she says. I see an opening, so I take it.

"No, but seriously. Do you want to? Do you feel like your life just stopped sometimes?"

She pulls back, and I try to replay what I just said. Was it too much? I just—

"I . . . I know life keeps going forward, sweetie."

"Yeah, but are you still going forward? I wouldn't be upset if you wanted to date or whatever. Like, what would you want to do if you weren't cleaning houses?" The words tumble out of my mouth. Pre-revelation Sasha might've been upset at first if Mom went out on a date. But eventually Mom might meet a nice guy, right? I don't want her to be alone, in that way, forever. Isn't it good to talk about these things to prepare? Because Mom is still a baddie in her own right.

"I've always loved math. Maybe be an accountant. Or a nurse. I don't know, good question. Good to think about these things, I guess. I enjoy thinking about the future." She smiles and ruffles my hair like I'm a five-year-old. My body straightens and my eyes widen. She's not wrong.

Mom pauses before speaking. "What are you thinking about?"

"I . . ." The last month runs through my mind. "I just wonder if we can really have it all, you know? As women? Do you ever feel like you're picking one thing in your life over another? Who has it all? Besides Beyoncé?" I don't know how to articulate it. Not yet at least.

She just leans forward. "But I have it all. I've always had it all, silly." There's a playfulness in her voice that makes me think that she truly believes what she's saying. Which gives me an idea.

My mom lingers near my desk, but I'm already opening a new Word document, my fingers tapping the keys. I'm having a flash of brilliance; one I can't let slip away. My mom watches me for a minute more, understands that I'm in a zone, and then leaves my room, closing the door behind her.

My eyes toggle between the two photos of me and my dad. My brain thinks about the past week, the painful moments I caused and endured, which leads me to think about the last four years. Then I think about my life as a whole, my entire timeline. I write. I write write write, pouring myself onto the page. I thought I knew my legacy, but I was wrong. After this month and these bets, I understand myself and my legacy better than I ever could have imagined. I can't help but chuckle, because to my surprise, my life and my legacy have nothing to do with the scholarship.

CHAPTER 37

MY LIFE FEELS LIKE A GAME OF TETRIS. I'M DOING MY BEST TO move things around, to get things to fit, to score some damn points for a win. On one hand, since our talk on Dad's birthday, things at home with my mom are the best they've ever been. I don't know if we've ever been this honest and open with one another. We're all expressive and vulnerable vibes. Two days' worth, but still. It's a foundation to build on.

On the other hand, everything at school is a gigantic dumpster hellfire of a mess. Priscilla and Chance still aren't speaking to me. Which, duh, is the right response, given that I was a total bitch to them. I replay our conversation, and I'm surprised at my own behavior. I can be uptight, but cruel?

Meanwhile, Ezra hasn't been in class, and I'm too chicken-shit to call or text him, even though I've been staring at his photos and thinking about him constantly. *Constantly*. Every little thing reminds me of him: the way the light fills the room, or certain smells. Hell, sometimes I even think I hear his camera clicking in the background. Honestly, I now know that it's for the best we didn't kiss sooner; otherwise, I probably wouldn't have made it this far in life. I used to make fun of those old-school nineties R&B videos that showed singers in excruciating pain, missing their loved ones, but I get the point now. I truly understand. I am singing in the rain, hoping my person will come back to me.

Because I'm running out of time: graduation is in a week and a half.

♡♡♡

After class, I take out my phone and send my mom a text: *Where are you? Want some help? I'm out of school early.*

As soon the message sends, I shake my head. My mom isn't great at texting; she's definitely from the generation that likes to talk on the phone. It would probably be faster for me to send a carrier pigeon or a message in a bottle. When anyone sends her a text, she responds out loud, answering the question like they're in the room with her, then never writes back.

I slip my phone into my pocket, where it begins to vibrate. I check the screen and see her face flashing. Wow. Weird.

"Hello?" I answer.

"I'm at the community college. Can you come by?" Her voice is shaky, almost inaudible.

"Uh, yeah, sure. Are you okay?"

"I'm okay, I just—" She pauses, afraid to proceed.

"I can get there in five minutes. Hang tight."

"I'm near the library."

I hop in an Uber and try to keep my mind from spinning out of control. Why isn't she at the Lawrences' house, working? I take deep breaths and try to focus on what's in front of me: the trees, the buildings, the sky. I count down from one hundred until my driver pulls up to campus.

He drops me off in front of the library, and I don't see my mom. I walk through the building, and the expansive, silent space warms my heart, if only for a moment. There are several students deep in their books, taking notes.

I push through the back doors, which open to a manicured lawn with several wooden chairs and tables. Then I spot her, in a gray V-neck and black leggings with her floral backpack on the ground in the shade.

"Hey," I say as I approach warily. I claim the empty seat next to hers. "What are you doing here?"

She shakes her head like a young girl, timid, afraid. Her backpack peeks out from behind her.

My heart pauses, waiting for her answer.

She exhales.

"I'm scheduled to take the English and math placement tests." She motions to the library. "Just to make sure, you know, I enroll in the right classes. The last time I was here, it was so long ago . . ." Her voice trails off. How many times has she felt like a foreigner in these academic spaces? I wonder.

I grab her hand as I search for the right words. I had no idea she's been thinking about classes, or school, or anything like this.

She sniffles. "I'm scared. To go back in there. To try again."

My face gets hot.

She continues, "I'm a little old. Maybe it's too late for me."

"It's never too late," I whisper, hugging her.

"Aiya, you're going to make me cry. I don't want to cry today." She holds my hand and shakes off the tears.

I dab the corner of my eyes. "What time is the test?"

"In five minutes." She straightens. "But I don't have to take it. We can go home."

"How would that make you feel?" I say, almost shocked at how much I sound like Ezra.

My mom rolls her eyes. "Not good. Fine. Yes, I'll go in. You're right."

"I'll stay right here and wait for you," I say. My mom rubs her arms, and slowly, confidence returns to her. She takes the campus in.

"Okay. Wish me luck," she says.

I squeeze her hand. "You don't need luck. We got you," I say, and we both smile.

She grabs her backpack and slings it across her shoulder as she heads inside the building. She's trying. No regrets.

CHAPTER 38

I'M RUNNING OUT OF TIME. ON THURSDAY, I LEAN THROUGH THE doorway of Ms. T's classroom, hands full, unsure of my next step. I could back up, turn around and just go. I could leave things unresolved and pretend this part of my life, my best friends, never happened.

Or.

"Why you lurking, Miss Sasha?" Ben locks eyes with me. He gives me a frantic wave as the rest of the group shifts their focus to me. I take a small step into Ms. T's room. "Come in, we already got started." Ben motions for me to stop being a creeper and enter the room, so I inch forward.

I walk toward my usual desk and put down the large bags, my heart beating so hard my chest hurts.

"I smell food!" someone shouts.

"This is the last tutoring club, right?" My voice is meek, but I came here to try, so try I must. "I brought some goodies, to, you know, celebrate." I dig into the bag and take out the boxes. "I've got lots of fries and croissants. An odd combination, I know. But I wanted to share a little tradition with the group." Priscilla's eyes are cold, but she makes eye contact and Chance peers up from his book. "On Fridays, the three of us get together and eat French fries and share the good things in our lives. So I wanted to do that here. The croissants are in honor of Chance, my best friend, who is taking a big, brave step by going abroad and backpacking around Europe after graduation, alone."

My voice is shaky. I watch as the kids exchange confused looks. "I wanted to celebrate, but I also wanted to apologize." I stuff my hands into my jeans pockets and gaze into the eyes of everyone in the room. "I'm sorry, everyone. I never meant to let tutoring take a back seat in my life, and I know I have these last couple of months, but this group brings me so much joy. And, Chance, I'm so sorry about what I said the other day. I didn't mean it, not at all. I admire you so much . . . that you know yourself, and you know your worth without needing validation from anyone or anything." We lock eyes, and I swear the corners of his lips turn upward, just slightly.

I keep going. "Priscilla, I'm sorry. You aren't afraid to try, you aren't afraid to put yourself out there, and I admire that. To spin that as a bad thing was unfair and untrue. I'm really sorry. My life has been empty without you two in it. And I know we don't have much time together, so I definitely don't want to spend it fighting."

The silence in the room is loud. If they don't want to talk to me again, I have to understand. Words have power. I can't just go popping off whenever I'm upset. Chance stands from his desk, and Priscilla walks over. The kids look at us, mouths open, like they are in the front row of a TV drama.

Chance speaks first. "I don't want to spend any time fighting either."

"Agreed," Priscilla chimes in. We lean in for a group hug.

"Does this mean we can eat?" Hector calls out.

"Help yourselves," I say, but the students are already up, filling their plates. Chatter fills the room, and for the first time in a long time, I feel good. Great, even. Chance passes me a plate with fries on it, and I swear the act is so beautiful, I could cry.

"All right, so how this works: We're gonna go in a circle and share one good thing that's happened this year. How about that?" Chance's voice is booming. "Who wants to start?"

Khadijah starts talking and the rest of the group follows. And this is how we spend our last tutoring club—sharing all that's good in our lives.

After tutoring, we take our time gathering our things. I think each of us is storing a memory of the afternoon, of our last time spent with the kiddos.

"So what are you gonna do about Ezra?" Priscilla asks.

My heart flutters. "He's up next on the great Sasha apology tour. Maybe we can figure something out about valedictorian? If it's not too late. I don't know. We turn in our final assignments next week. Maybe . . ."

Priscilla stands up and throws away the last of the fry remnants. "What if you win? What if you lose?"

"I haven't gotten that far. I just . . . First I need to talk to him. We need to just talk. I think that's a good place to start."

Chance nods in approval. "As Drake once said, you only live once. Better give it all you've got."

Which is why on Saturday night, I think I know where Ezra may be: at the final exhibit for Walker Ross. I'm scared to see him again, to talk to him, but I gotta try. My heart beats so fast I'm sure it will explode, but my legs move, and I'm propelled forward.

I walk through the entrance, and any thoughts in my brain are drowned out by the excitement in the room. The usually rustic space is fancy tonight, with black tablecloths on round tables and twinkle lights hanging from the ceiling. Everything feels different from the last time I was here.

I turn in a circle, my feet twirling in my shoes. A sea of faces, some that I recognize from Skyline, but none of them has those seductive brown eyes or that singular dimple. None is Ezra. I have to push this disappointment down.

"Ladies and gentlemen, good evening," a melodic voice singsongs through a microphone. Like a wave, everyone in the room takes a step toward the stage.

Mr. Ross appears, and the room claps.

"My wonderful daughter, Willa," he says, pointing to a woman with dark brown hair and funky red glasses. She helps him with his seat, and when he's comfortable, she sits next to him. "Thank you all so much for joining me tonight." The crowd claps again. "To those of you who have made this event possible, thank you. I thought we could do something different, as this an intimate gathering of—what? A hundred people, I don't know, is that right?" A generous laugh ripples through the room. I grin. The lights dim, and on the stage, to the right of the daughter, a screen drops down.

"To know me and to know my work is to know my heart, the people of my affection." Mr. Ross grabs his daughter's hand and gives it a squeeze while the first image appears on the screen. "My Joanie, God rest her soul," he says. He and his daughter share a gaze that I know too well—one of love and loss, of remembrance. "It'll be ten years without her Earthside," he says in a low voice. His daughter flashes a knowing grin, and he straightens.

The slideshow begins with several pictures of Mr. Ross as a child, portraits in black-and-white. He flips through more, of big families and young children. Of the mountains. He tells quick anecdotes related to the photos, Willa nodding along.

I stare at the images, trying to focus on his words, but my mind begins to wander, some thoughts louder than others: *I hope Ezra is here. He should be here. He'd get a kick out of this, seeing Ross's life documented by photos.* Suddenly, Ezra's passion for photography, his love for capturing the moments that highlight the joys of life, that say, "I was here!" and provide proof of a live well lived, fills every ounce of me.

A warmth rushes over my body and an excitement builds in my chest.

Then yet another a lightbulb goes off, not in the room, but in my heart, and it's bright—impossible to miss. I realize his memories of me were never actually about dancing, never about New York or college, but always about supporting me. And my dreams, and my happiness. Ezra, cheering me on as I've changed and grown, all the while being excited for me. Ezra, wanting me to find myself and my passions; Ezra, by my side. Even through the damn bets. Ezra truly loving me for me.

The lights in the room come back on and the white projector screen retracts

My breathing picks up and my heartbeat accelerates. I do a slow turn one last time, to make sure he's not here, behind me, waiting to discuss what I've been too afraid to say but what my heart has always known—my epiphany: *I love Ezra.* I always have.

An urgency fills my chest. I need to tell him before another moment goes by. I scan the crowd, bumping into too many people, hoping to find the face I adore so much. But I don't see him. I scan again, too afraid to believe the reality of the situation.

Mr. Ross walks by and pauses when he sees me. "Why, Sasha, hello." He stops and straightens with his cane. "Wonderful to see you again," he says. I wave as they walk off. I scan the room one last time before deciding to leave. So what he's not here? I'm not giving up, not yet.

CHAPTER 39

"ARE YOU NERVOUS?" CHANCE ASKS FROM BEHIND THE STAGE, THE bright auditorium lights on his face. It's Friday, Senior Legacy Night is here, and the time has finally come—I'm up next to present. Priscilla gives me a look of concern, sweat beading on her face, and then answers on my behalf.

"She's terrified. You don't see the high tide on her forehead?" Priscilla has never been more right in her life. I'm beyond terrified. But it's too late now. It's one thing to have a new outlook on this project; it is quite another to panic, pass out, fail the project, and not graduate at all. Now, that would be— You know what, let me stop my brain right there.

"I'm really thankful you're both here with me." I grab their hands.

For the past year, I've been thinking about this project, working toward this milestone. Now that I'm here, ready to declare myself and my legacy to the school, this night, this feeling, is completely different than what I imagined. But I think it's better.

I'm about to say something else to Priscilla and Chance when a wave of clapping from the hundred or so students and parents floods my ears and Ms. T motions me to the front. I say a prayer under my breath. This is one of those moments where I think maybe I am in some kind of matrix, because without my consent, I find myself at the front of the stage, microphone in hand.

I clear my throat and the mic returns a little feedback. I survey the audience; faces smile back at me. Ezra shuffles through the crowd and turns my way. I feel stronger knowing that he's here, that he can hear my speech—and my apology.

I inhale a strong breath and begin:

Dear Younger Sasha,

You're going to be asked about your legacy, about how you want to be remembered come graduation. They say that the best way for you to think about your present is to go back and talk with your younger self.

So here I am.

I'll get straight to it, because there's no easy way to put it: life will be filled with challenges and heartbreak, yours included. I wish I could deliver better news, but I can't.

Now, you're going to spend a lot of time with this pain, wondering how to process it, thinking of ways to

honor those who grieve with you. You're going to want
to remember those you've lost; you're going to work
hard to dedicate everything you can to them, like your
grades and awards, to show your love, but that's not
your legacy.

Not because your accomplishments aren't great,
because, trust me, they are, you should be proud of
what you're able to do. But, simply put, you are magic.
You are the trophy. Your life, your brilliance, the way
you exist in the world, is one-of-a-kind. And that,
dear Sasha, is your legacy.

You were born from love, from strength, from
courage. You come from resilience, but you also come
from joy, from laughter, from happiness. The more
you realize that there is no better gift than living,
truly living your life beautifully, the better you'll be.
You're only eighteen, you have a lot to figure out.
Whatever your next steps might be, make sure that
they will be taken loudly, boldly, courageously. Let
your love be your legacy.

And if you're here, I just want to say to my very
first best friend, Ezra . . .

Somewhere in the crowd a chair shifts, grinding against
the floor. Necks crane to get a better view of me. Okay, brain.
Just refocus. You've given plenty of presentations before.

Ezra, what I want to say is . . .

Wow. Okay this is a lot harder than movies or books make it out to be. I want to say "I love you and I'm sorry," but, um, the words are . . . Where are they?

Sorry. I lost my train of thought. I'm a little . . . a little nervous.

No duh, girl. Get it together! Don't you dare mess up now.

Ezra. Friend. Best friend. What I'm trying to say . . . Wow, it's really hot up here.

Someone chuckles in the crowd. *Oh my god, you are really doing this now.*

What I'm trying to say is . . . Ezra . . .

I find the spot where he was just standing, but I don't see him. Panic and nervousness shut off my brain. He's . . . he's not here anymore. I stuff the mic into its holder, and I don't need to look up to feel the energy in the room. I scoot offstage and release a shaky exhale. He's not here; he doesn't want to hear what I have to say.

I shuffle past several students and head outside to the patio, where a jumbo TV screen plays what's happening inside. I exhale loudly, and then I let myself laugh at myself, and for once, it feels good. I tried. And sure, the end was a little rough, but the beginning was solid.

After several other students, Chance goes up to the mic and presents his legacy project. He gives a powerful speech about learning and living a life dedicated to the mind. It's almost too esoteric, because Chance; but then he does something unexpected at the end. He starts singing. And he sounds good. Damn good. Who knew the boy could sing? I didn't. When he's done, the crowd goes crazy applauding.

"Holy shit, that was amazing," Priscilla says once Chance gets off the stage. We all regroup in the back of the main room.

"Truly. That was epic. Where did that come from?" I ask.

Chance just shrugs. "I don't know. I just wanted to spice it up a bit. If I'm going to deliver this performance, might as well give the fans something exciting." A few students I've never spoken to walk by us and give Chance small nods.

"And that you did! You met the requirements to graduate! I'm super proud of you." I hug him.

"Yeah, well, I'm not decorating my cap," he says.

Priscilla scoffs. "Like I was going to let you do that alone anyway."

I laugh.

"I'll be right back," I say, already moving away from my friends. I need to find Ezra. I walk into the middle of the room, near a large crowd of parents and teachers.

As if the universe knows I'm searching for someone with answers, a chill runs down my spine, urging me to turn around. There he is, almost the same as I remember—tall, dark, handsome. Except now his black hair and mustache are peppered with gray.

"Sasha, hello. What a pleasant surprise." His voice is just like Ezra's—melodic and raspy—but deeper.

"Dr. Davis?"

"At your service," he laughs. "You're giving me the same look Ezra did."

"I didn't know you'd be here," I say. "It's wonderful to see you."

Dr. Davis nods. "Yes, likewise. These legacy projects, they are . . . interesting? Impressive? Yours is certainly a different generation than mine but engaging nonetheless."

Warmth swells in my chest. How long has it been since I've been able to chat with Dr. Davis?

"Did Ezra present?" I ask.

"He did. And I've never been prouder to call him my son. I should probably show him, tell him that more often," Dr. Davis says, more to himself than to me.

How did I miss Ezra's presentation? Ugh. Probably when Priscilla and Chance and I were in her car, charging our phones.

"Is he . . . here?" I ask, hopeful that Dr. Davis can't sense the desperation or urgency in my voice.

"He was."

"He left?" My heart drops to my stomach. Dr. Davis gives a small nod and cups his chin with his hand. "That was a very heartfelt speech."

Holy fuck. I'm mortified.

Dr. Davis lightly chuckles to himself. "You just missed him. Maybe by fifteen, twenty minutes." Shit. Shit. Shit. "I'm still here because I'll be giving the closing speech tonight. Alumni duty calls."

I sigh. "I see. Do you happen to know . . ."

He smiles. "The hospital. His mother began having contractions. I think Ezra will probably be a big brother by morning."

A mix of happiness and sadness rushes over me. Fuuuuuuuuck. Fifteen or twenty minutes? What a cruel joke.

"Don't worry, you'll have your time." The expression on his face is kind; his brow furrows just a bit. I make a strong effort to conceal my disappointment.

Priscilla and Chance rush up to me, and Priscilla grabs my hand. "That was epic. So don't freak out, but you need to check this out." She holds up her phone, and I see a small image of a girl who looks just like me onstage. Priscilla's finger taps the play button and there I am, giving my speech from her phone. "You're already online."

"Who posted that?" I grab Priscilla's phone and zoom in on the screen. "Oh, wow, the school did." I hand the phone back to her and shove down my urge to scream.

CHAPTER 40

IT'S OUR LAST FRY-DATE, EVEN THOUGH IT'S A SATURDAY afternoon. So we're having a combo feast to celebrate finishing yesterday's Legacy presentations and a goodbye party for Chance. We're at Priscilla's parents' house (they make sure Priscilla knows the distinction) in their backyard, lying across blankets in the grass, our heads propped up on pillows. The June sun is high and warming, a little tease of what the summer months will bring. From today's preview, life is going to be epic. Inside, her parents are drinking wine and making spaghetti, listening to soft jazz, their usual Saturday routine.

Priscilla spent all morning watching videos on how to make and elaborately design different types of food boards (I had to google the term *food board:* apparently, it's just a fancy way to display food). So we've got a board with French fries (obviously), as well as tacos, pizza, and desserts all displayed in a meticulous "Do you admire it or do you eat it"–type way.

We admire and take photos of the display, and then we eat like teenage queens and king.

Between nibbles, I reach into my bag. "Here, I come bearing gifts." I hand Chance and Priscilla both a perfectly wrapped silver box with a black bow.

Chance takes the package. "Should I open it now or later?"

Priscilla doesn't wait. "Now, always now." Before I can respond, they both tear at the washi tape and find their treasure.

Priscilla holds up the gift. "Shut up, this is amazing."

Chance's jaw drops. "Okay, please tell me you have one too?" He points to the black shirt I made with our faces on them. Last Christmas, we drove an hour to one of the remaining JCPenneys around and took photos at their portrait studio, our hands resting on our elbows, like we were in some vintage fashion catalogue. I picked one of the photos and plastered it on shirts. And they came out good, like hipster mixtape album good.

"Keep digging, Chance. There's one more thing in there for you."

In one swoop he holds up the black Moleskine journal, the sunlight creating a beam around the edges.

"For your travels. And your thoughts. Come back and teach me the secrets of the universe." Chance smiles big, holding the items to his chest.

We pick at the board in silence, the mark of true friendship, where we can gab and laugh one minute, and sit and be bored together the next. I take one of the last fries and give it a dip; a drop of ketchup falls off and stains my shirt.

I blot my shirt with a napkin.

"You wanna know how many likes you've gotten in the last hour?" Chance asks, penetrating the quiet.

I shudder. "Going viral is just . . . not the life for me." I grab a curly fry and douse it in ranch dressing. "Okay, fine. Really quick. I don't want the fame to go to my head."

Priscilla takes several fries and wraps them around a flattened donut hole, like she's building a taco, even though she has donut fries on the end of the dessert board. "Try this. It's the perfect salty-sweet combo." She lifts it near my face, but I just shake my head. I'm kind of a purist when it comes to mixing my carbs.

"Fine, more for me." She stuffs the food into her mouth. "Also, I hate to be technical, but I don't know if we can call the video of her speech 'going viral,' right?"

Thank you. "Technically, it's not viral, but it's more exposure than I'd like," I say. I don't know if I should be proud or embarrassed. I've had WeTalk for six years, and all my posts only get twenty likes at most, with five usually coming from the people right here (Priscilla has several fake accounts that keep the number above three). My legacy presentation is making the proverbial rounds. Some folks on the internet find it charming. Others think it's a bit cringe. To be honest, I'm somewhere in the middle.

"You're at four hundred and eleven." Chance lifts his shoulders, like he's proud or something.

I sit up, cross my legs, and steady myself on one arm.

"Four hundred!" I scream. "You think . . ." I'm kinda afraid to say it out loud. "That Ezra might be one of those views?"

"Or maybe all of them?" Priscilla asks.

"Four hundred would be borderline obsessive." Chance turns to me, laughing. "No shade, that would just be a crazy amount of viewing the same thirty second clip."

I nod. "No, I agree. I mean . . ." *Does Ezra think about me like I think about him? Does he replay our time together? Does he want to talk? Why haven't we talked? Maybe four hundred views is a lot, but also maybe he's watched it to make sure he knows that it's, um, about him.* "I just mean, it's very likely that he's seen the video, right? Seen me?" Professing my love.

Priscilla hands me a fry. "Yes, it's very likely he's seen the video. Isn't he tagged in it? You know what? Don't answer that. And ignore the comment section while you're at it. Folks on the internet will say anything to ruin your day."

I stuff the fry into my mouth. "Damn. Then why hasn't he called me? Or sent me a text? Or done anything? I thought . . ." *I thought I could win him back with a grand gesture.* "So what? That's . . . that's it?" When I say the words out loud, I know the answer. That yeah, we are done. Of course, I've thought about the possibility of that day in the car truly being our end—how could I not? Our last conversation replays like some annoying commercial jingle stuck in my head. And every time I hear it, I wilt just a little. It wasn't good. Scratch that—*I* wasn't good. Ezra tried to be vulnerable, and I shut him down. But I don't know, something in me thought that . . . maybe . . .

"Love is a great mystery," Chance says, ironing out the mix of emotions in my heart.

Like the clouds in the sky, the conversation drifts and floats from things we think we'll miss about high school, like being together, of course, to the things we're looking forward to—freedom. And time to really figure ourselves out, to try new things, to start a new chapter.

Priscilla sits up and straightens her legs. "I think I wanna visit you in Europe, Chance. What do you say, Sasha? Maybe we can both go for spring break."

I clap in excitement. I've always wanted to go to Paris, to travel through Europe, to see the world. I guess now I have a good reason to. I feel one step closer to being able to do the things I want in this life. "I can start saving now. I would love that." I eyeball the fry board, which is damn near empty.

Priscilla's parents come out to say hi and talk to us about graduation. When they head back inside, we all zone out for a moment. Priscilla picks up a golden-brown cookie the size of her face with colorful M&Ms bulging out. "You're not the only one with gifts, Sasha. I got us something special to celebrate." She turns the cookie in the air.

"From a Parisian bakery?" Chance asks.

"Close. Try the weed dispensary near the grocery store. You know, the one that kinda looks like an Apple Store." Priscilla breaks off a piece and extends her arm. "What? It's legal."

Chance stares at me. I know what he's thinking. He's waiting for me to say no so that he can bow out because I did first.

"It's *legal*," Priscilla repeats for emphasis. "Gina's brother got it for her, and she gave it to me."

Gina. A name I haven't heard in a while.

I turn to Priscilla. "How is that going, by the way? You know, I—"

"With Gina? It's better. You know, we're actually pretty good as friends."

Chance grabs the last sweet potato fry. "Just friends?"

"Just friends." Priscilla wiggles her eyebrows. "So, any takers?"

"It's an edible?" I ask.

Priscilla is already giggling. I could overthink this. Really, I could. But I decide today I just . . . won't. Easy.

"Fine. I'll eat it." I ready my hand for a piece.

"Gasp!" Priscilla pops up onto her knees, her eyes about to explode from her face.

Chance leans my way. He checks my temperature. "You're lying?"

Priscilla inches toward me. I grab the cookie piece. "Why not? We're just going to stay here, right?"

"Right! Exactly. We can be responsible and have fun." Priscilla's already broken off another third of the cookie and is extending her arm toward Chance.

Chance grabs the cookie and gives it a quick examination. "Cheers," he says. We lift our cookies and give them a small tap before stuffing our mouths.

Not bad. Not good, but not terrible. Definitely looks better than it tastes, but it doesn't matter now, because it's already in my mouth. I do my best to feign excitement while eating. Priscilla does a little dance while indulging in hers. Chance— classic, diplomatic Chance—keeps one hand over his mouth as he politely chews and swallows.

Twenty minutes later, I don't feel a thing.

"So I've been thinking about cutting my hair," I say out of nowhere. I mean, sort of, but why did I just bring it up now? Maybe I do feel something.

"Want me to get my dad's clippers?" Priscilla asks.

Oh. Um. I hesitate. "I mean like soon. Not necessarily *now* now."

Chance gives my head a quick size-up. "I could do it, easy. Two minutes tops."

I instinctively clutch my locs. "Excuse me? You know how to—"

"Cut hair? Yeah, don't insult me. I'm a Bell. And the third. It's practically a rite of passage in our house. What do you want done?"

I pause. "Just, um, maybe shave the back a little?" Before I finish my words, Priscilla is up, rushing toward the sliding glass door.

"Daaaaad, do you know where the clippers are?" she screams, loud enough to reach everyone inside her house.

Which is how two minutes later, I find myself sitting in a black folding chair, under the twinkly patio lights. My head is tilted forward, and my front locs cover my face.

"Don't worry, it won't hurt. You won't feel a thing."

Chance flicks on the clippers, and they hum to life. My

skin warms, and I imagine I can hear my stomach growl. Or wait, it did growl. Loudly. My body relaxes, and I think about the day I started my locs, all the time I've spent growing and maintaining them, and the ways they have evolved. Out of one eye, I peek at my feet, the first loc already on the ground. Several others begin to fall, and I release a smile, because for once, I don't fear change or growth. And I'll never be defined by just one thing, not even my hair.

"Okay, all done." Chance turns off the clippers and sets them down on the ground. Priscilla hands me a small mirror.

I examine myself. "I love it," I say, running a hand over the freshly buzzed space. I feel lighter. My neck swings side to side as I give my head a shake.

"It's very becoming on you, Sasha," Priscilla says.

At least, I think that's Priscilla. Her face looks a little funny. When did she start . . . glowing?

Chance lets out a little yelp.

"Was that a laugh or a cry?" I ask. I smack my lips together. My mouth is suddenly dry. Like *so* dry. Have I always lived like this? Wow. Words are so difficult to speak. Has it always been this way? "P. I need water. And maybe a—"

"Hi," she says.

Wait, what?

"Hi?" I respond. We've been together for a minute. The twinkle lights behind her duplicate, and what was one source of light is now three. Scratch that, four. Now try forty. I tilt my head to the left and to the right, the lights trailing in the air. No way. I squint.

"Did you see that?" I point to the air. Or the light. Or Priscilla?

Chance cackles. "Get it? *H-i-g-h*. High!" he says. Priscilla laughs at that. She's laughing so hard her arms are across her stomach, holding her body together. It must be contagious. Because within seconds, I'm on the ground, squealing and wheezing so hard I know the whole city can hear us.

We laugh more than I think I have ever laughed in my life. We giggle so much I cry, and I have moments where I can't breathe because of all the giggling and the crying (I even pee a little).

A bell rings, snapping me out of my hysteria. "Did you hear that? A bell?" We all turn toward the house. So, I know I didn't just make up the sound. Priscilla's mom is standing there with a small metal bell in her hand.

"Spaghetti's ready!" She gives us a knowing smirk, like maybe she's been high with her friends days before graduation too. We rush inside to her kitchen and end the night with the best damn spaghetti I've ever had.

CHAPTER 41

TODAY IS GRADUATION.

The day I seem to have been waiting for all year. I spend the morning getting ready, retwisting my hair, putting on makeup and even some of Mom's treasured jewelry. Around noon, Priscilla and Chance show up at my door, but I almost don't recognize them. Chance is in a fitted black three-piece tuxedo. He's always been handsome, but damn! This is something on a whole new level. "Okay, baby Idris. I see you." He shoves me playfully but keeps a smirk on his face.

Priscilla, too, has thrown me for a loop. Not because she's done something extreme, which I was totally expecting, but because she's toned down. Everything. Her long brown hair is braided loosely to the side, her fingernails are a light pink, and she's not wearing any makeup. Actually, maybe just a touch of mascara. She's spent all her time on skin care. Her complexion is glowing. No big jewelry, no diamonds, no rings, no earrings. Priscilla, undone.

"Wow, you both look great—not what I was imagining, but fantastic nonetheless," I say, letting them in.

"You know, I thought about wearing a face full of makeup," Priscilla tells me. "But I want today to be all about stripping away the layers. We are finally here. The last step, you know? I wanted that to be . . . simple." She gives my shoulder a quick rub. "But also, my graduation cap is *ex-tra*. Wait until you see it. It's three layers. It's like the Leaning Tower of Pisa tall."

We burst into laughter. I hold my stomach as small tears start to form in my eyes. Not that anything was especially funny, but this feeling of togetherness—it's joyous.

"Picture time! Let me take a photo of you three," my mom calls from the hallway. She heads toward us, all smiles. I do a double take of her, too. She's stunning in a fitted black skirt and white blouse. Her hair is lightly curled, and she's wearing makeup and her favorite diamond earrings. The sight of her makes my heart swell. I'm an occasion for her to bust out the good jewelry.

We take our usual positions by our bookshelf—Chance on my right, me in the middle, and Priscilla on my left. Mom snaps several photos and then we pose for some silly, back-to-back ones, and a few in a squat with our hands in the prayer position.

"Okay, don't be late. You should go. I will meet you later with the rest of the aunties," my mom says after she's pleased with the hundred or so photos she's taken (with or without our feet or heads, we'll see).

"Wait," I say. Priscilla and Chance stop at the door. "Priscilla, can you take some of us?"

My mom tilts her head. "But I don't want you to be late."

"I know what you're trying to do, and it's not going to work." I grab her and we stand near our altar. I wrap my arm around her shoulder, and she drapes her arm around my waist. Priscilla snaps several photos, and I cement this occasion in my mind, in my body, forever.

"A few with Dad, too." I stare at our light in an effort to blink back tears. My mom grabs his photo, and we place him between us. The room pauses and Mom and I say our own personal incantations. I know that Dad is watching over me, us. I revel in how full my heart is, how much love and support I have, and how thankful I am to have made it this far. My life is perfectly imperfect.

My mom puts Dad's photo back, and I bend down to hug her. I squeeze her tight in hopes that she can feel the intensity of my appreciation.

She squeezes back and whispers in my ear, "My greatest gift in life is being your mom. We are so proud of you, Sasha." She pats my back and lifts my chin. "Now go. Don't be late to your own graduation," she says as she opens the door for Priscilla, Chance, and me.

We slide into Priscilla's car for what will probably be the last time in a long time, with Chance leaving tonight and all. Chance sits up front, head leaned back against the headrest, his window slightly down. The salty ocean breeze flows in and dances on my face. Oddly enough, I'm not afraid of us closing the door on one chapter of our lives and opening the door for the next. The thing about endings is that they are also beginnings. It would be easy for me to get lost in the finality of this day. Instead, for perhaps the first time in my life, I'm eager to see what's ahead. I'll miss them; I'm going to miss us together, sure. But I've learned a lot about the power of love, the way it can transform and change shape. Love is like energy: it never really goes away. And if it does, was it ever really love? I just think about those who have loved me and how their love will always be a part of me and vice versa. When I think about how I want to define myself and what I have in my secret recipe for future success, the ingredients are mostly the same. A life built on love.

For so long I thought I had to make a choice between my head and my heart, but it turns out I need both. Not either/ or. My worth as a person will never be tied to the things I do or what I am able to accomplish. I exhale. I'm worthy. I'm enough, simply being me.

CHAPTER 42

ONSTAGE, EZRA AND I ARE SITTING NEXT TO ONE ANOTHER IN those torturous foldable metal chairs. We haven't been this close since the Alvin Ailey show. I try to make eye contact, but he's wearing black Ray-Ban sunglasses and his face is pointed straight ahead. His lips are pursed; his super-serious concentrating face. I haven't seen him this tense in, well, ever. I'm annoyed at myself for wanting to have small talk here, because it's clearly not the time or the place. So I keep my eyes forward, on the large crowd, waiting patiently.

Principal Newton pops up from his seat and stands at the microphone. "And now, ladies and gentlemen, it is my great honor to introduce our class valedictorian—Ezra Davis-Goldberg." The crowd cheers, and Ezra fiddles with his cap and inhales loudly before standing at the podium.

I smile big and with all my teeth because, fuck it, I'm proud of Ezra. And who cares that we haven't spoken since the argument in his car? This is still a special time for both of us. He deserves this moment, he's worked hard, and he's earned the title. Hell, I'm proud of myself, too. Salutatorian is damn good.

Ezra gives the mic a tap. "Microphone check, one two, one two," he says as the crowd answers back in hoots and several seniors stand and shout, cupping their hands like megaphones. Phones are held up high, recording history, the conclusion to this Skyline chapter.

At his voice, my body tingles, and goose bumps cover my skin. I fiddle with my hands just as he begins to speak.

"Ladies and gentlemen, esteemed guests, faculty, family, friends, and my fellow graduates, welcome to the next chapter." He pauses after thunderous applause.

I do my best to keep a straight face, but there's something charming—no, it's more than charm—something hypnotic about the way Ezra engages with the audience, not a worry in his voice, not a care in the world. Just talking and laughing with old friends, as opposed to the two thousand people in the audience on one of the most anticipated days of our lives.

He continues, "I'm very honored today to stand before you as your class valedictorian and humbled to receive such a generous scholarship. I am fortunate—privileged, even. And I am grateful, extremely grateful. If I've learned anything this last year, hell, this last month, I've learned this—that we are all connected. That my life is inspired by those who came before me, paving a path so I could walk a little easier. Thank you, Dad, for helping to make that possible. I'm inspired by those I haven't met, the kids who will come after me. And I'm lucky to be seen and challenged by those around me today. Thank you to my best friend, you know who you are, for modeling a life of dedication and of love. Because of your push, your challenge, your light in my life, I know the power we have in shaping not only our lives, but the lives of those who will come after us." He pauses, and I don't breathe.

"With that said, I'm excited and humbled to announce that I will be donating a portion of this year's class valedictorian scholarship to help fund an after-school program here at Skyline High School. The program will provide staff for tutoring, and extracurricular activities like photography, cinematography, and other forms of art—all for kids in the community." Ezra pauses at the exact moment the crowd goes absolutely wild. Principal Newton nods, impressed but not surprised, while the other staff members onstage all turn to each other in awe.

I'm stomping my feet and cheering with a wide and warm smile on my face. My eyes mist a bit—the tutoring club will get funding to live on, now with ample resources. I think about Khadijah, Juan, Ben, and Hector and what this could mean for them. Joy fills me up.

He can feel it, because he continues, his voice stronger than before: "As the saying goes, we are the ones we've been waiting for. So on that note, let's graduate!"

It's faster than I ever could have imagined, because in another instant, we do. They play that song, we grab diplomas, and our caps fly up in the air. We graduate. We've graduated. We're graduates.

As soon as the ceremony ends, organized chaos ensues on the football field. I'm afraid I won't find my people, but before I panic, Kun emo yells a distinct "SASHA-YA!" like I'm a lost child in a shopping mall. She and the rest of my family run up to me. Each of their hugs is full of enthusiasm and joy.

"Congratulations! We are so proud of you," my aunts squeal, pushing a large bouquet of red roses in my face. I give the flowers a squeeze; they are breathtaking. Together, we take like a hundred photos. And though I'm happy and relieved, something nags at me. Something is missing.

Out of the corner of my eye, I see his family first. Ezra's mom, her long silvery blond hair flowing freely, with a small bundle of joy tucked warmly away in a pouch like she's a kangaroo. Dr. Davis, in a fitted blue seersucker suit, an easygoing look on his face. A man with shaggy black hair and round-rimmed glasses holds flowers. I've never seen him before, but he's most likely Ezra's stepdad.

My mom notices me watching and nudges me. "Go say something. Don't be rude and stare." She's giving me one of her classic expressions, the one that says "Yes, she's my daughter; yes, she's a bit clueless."

I am grateful for her encouragement. "Fine. I'll go and say congratulations. I'll be right back."

"Bali bali"—hurry—my mom says, a grin on her face. I take two steps forward, rolling my shoulders back. I can do this. I'll just say congratulations and thank him for helping the tutoring club. It's the decent thing to do. This is graduation, after all; a congratulations here or there doesn't have to mean anything big.

I'm about five feet from Ezra when two large men with cameras and a woman with a microphone step in front of me, obstructing my path.

"Ezra Goldberg? Hi, we're with Channel Five news. Do you have a moment?" I hear the reporter's high-pitched voice as I approach. She's with a whole crew, so I stand on my toes, doing my best to get a glimpse of him.

Ezra nods and the woman sticks her mic in front of his face. Defeat floods my body. Maybe this is a sign to just let it be. We tried. I know I tried. But I still inch forward; something pulls me closer to him, not away.

A cameraman sends a hand signal, and the woman lights up on cue. "I'm here at Skyline High School with this year's class valedictorian, Ezra Davis-Goldberg. Ezra, we want to hear about this donation—and about your future, of course. What was the impetus behind such a selfless act? It's rather unusual, wouldn't you say?"

I take two small steps forward, my view of his face becoming clearer, those lips, those eyes. Around me, a small crowd begins to form, also interested in his on-camera appearance.

Ezra straightens and grins for the camera like he's done this before, that same confidence from earlier onstage back. "It's actually a little complicated, but I guess you could say it all started with bets."

The reporter's eyes widen as she lets out a fake chuckle. "Bets? That's odd. Do continue! You gave away part of your scholarship. I don't understand. Did *you* win anything from these bets?"

Ezra's face falls; he's clearly taken aback by the question. Was there a winner? If so, there's a loser, too. We both had moments of victory and loss; we both had moments of love.

Ah, fuck it. I can't let another second go by. I don't want to waste any more time, not with him. Because how much time do we really have? If I had to describe the last few months of us being back together, I'd say that our connection was never really about the bets; it's always been about one thing.

I step closer. "My heart! He won my heart!" I yell. The crowd parts, like I'm Moses at the Red Sea. One of the cameras pans to me. Ezra turns around and the world around me seems to fade. The noise is gone, and suddenly it's just us. Maybe it's always been just us.

"Can you give me a second, please?" he says to the news team before making his way toward me. I move forward too, until we are an arm's length apart. This close and all the feelings of the last couple of months rush over me; all the happiness that came from relearning him floods back to me.

Ezra stands in front of me in a white button-down shirt, green cap and tassel in hand; a comfortable smile forms on his face.

I swallow.

"I'm sorry—" we both blurt at the same time. Ezra's hands cover his mouth, but underneath, there's a smile.

I grab his hands in mine and give them a small squeeze. "No, listen, I'm sorry about what I said. I just—"

Ezra only shakes his head. "No. I wasn't being fair. I shouldn't have pushed you so hard to change. There was truth in your words."

My throat clamps up. "No, *I* definitely wasn't being fair. I never meant to push you away. But what's with—the program? Your scholarship? Are you sure?"

"I'm beyond sure. I get to allocate half my earnings for the tutoring club and half for . . . for me. For college. I'll do a gap year, but then I wanna try and get serious about photography. I can get my portfolio together in the next year." My body freezes. Ezra comes closer, and I feel light-headed. He continues. "SJ, even if we never spoke again, I wanted to show you, and hell, show myself, that I understand the greatness in acts of service. I learned that from you." He winks and I'm frozen, sheepish. "Seeing how much you care about the students and what they were able to accomplish, I really got the importance of the program and what we all are really capable of." Ezra beams, his eyes twinkle. "And my dad told me he talked to you. I really liked your legacy presentation, by the way. Well, and I kept getting tagged on WeTalk too, but that doesn't matter."

I nod and I nod again. It's all I can do.

Ezra blushes, his dimple deep. "I'm sorry I didn't respond to you sooner. What do they say, actions speak louder than words? I hope you know I get it now. Well, I understand you and your dedication better, let's just say that." He pauses and gives my hand a light squeeze. "And I know what it's like to really care about something. And someone."

I'm cheesy grinning but I let myself feel this. "Just so we're clear . . . the best friend in your speech?" I have to ask.

He closes any distance between us. His smell elicits memories of our time together, of being close to him.

"Oh, you know, just this girl I met in third grade. She didn't know I existed, even though we were reading the same books and in the same class. Then one day, our teacher let us pick our own seats, and I rushed to snag a desk right by her. I think I've been in love ever since."

Holy shit—I know her.

"Who me?" I ask.

"It's always been you."

I nod again, my heart fluttering. "So, will you be here next year . . . in Monterey? For your gap year?"

"Yeah. Principal Newton created a new role for me—after-school program coordinator. I'll help set up the art clubs and make sure your tutoring program stays afloat in the fall. Will you—"

"I'll be here too. Monterey University starts end of August. I'll take some typical freshman classes and maybe a dance class or two."

Ezra pulls me to him. I wrap my hands around his waist. "I was hoping," he starts, "maybe we can try again—" But I don't let him finish. My hands slide up to his neck, and I bring his face to mine, my lips eager to be near his again.

There's a lot I could tell him, so much I could say and intellectualize. I could pinpoint the moment of falling in love, of challenge and frustration, the second I knew Ezra might be my person. But I hope he can feel all that in this kiss. That he can understand in the way life has brought us together, time and time again. The way true love brought us back to what truly matters, and yeah, "will guide us in the right direction." The way love will help us to grow—to be better than we ever thought we could be.

Inside my heart, fireworks go off. This, he, us, together, is the best bet of my life.

EPILOGUE

I . . . DON'T REMEMBER HIGH SCHOOL BEING THIS . . . SMALL, LIKE I'm in a museum for dolls or something.

Almost three months have passed since graduation, and for the first time, I'm back on Skyline's campus. The chairs, the hallways, the classrooms, they are tinier than I remember. Or maybe I've grown?

I'm early, so I wait in the doorway to the photography room, admiring Ezra.

He floats around, in his element. He's in his teacher attire— fitted khakis and a blue button-down shirt—somehow more handsome than when I saw him two days ago for his mom's Shabbat dinner. Ezra shaved his head this summer, but the new growth is strong, and budding curls ripple across his head. I chuckle to myself when I see the red and green dry-erase markers sticking out of his back pocket, the smeared ink stains on his hands. He's really getting into this photo-teacher-tutor thing.

When he sees me, he gives me a quick nod, then jumps back into helping Khadijah, a newly minted freshman, with a roll of film. Once she's set up, he walks to the front of the room and holds up two ancient bulky black cameras, gives a quick rundown about them, then passes them around the circle. The head count has doubled, the number of students larger than our tutoring club. Even a couple of people from the year below us decided to pitch in and volunteer. The students fiddle with the buttons, curiosity on their faces, excitement in the air. He lectures for about ten more minutes before ending the lesson. After, the kids and other tutors rush out the door.

"Can you believe that used to be us?" I walk into the room, where Ezra is gathering the last of his things into fancy black leather bags. With his cameras draped across both sides of his body, he leans in for a kiss.

"Only a few months ago, I was here, just a boy trying to woo a girl."

I grab his hand, and our fingers interlock, his touch as comfortable and familiar as home. We walk out of the classroom, down the hallway to the staff parking lot.

"Where should we go?" Ezra asks. His eyes have a sparkle in them that melts my heart.

"Surprise me," I say as I slide into his car.

"All right, bet." He nods and starts the car. The engine roars to life, and we take off, ready to conquer the world.

ACKNOWLEDGMENTS

A big, heartfelt thanks to the incredible team at Park and Fine Literary and Media. To my agent extraordinaire, the one, the only Pete Knapp. Pete. Pete! I'm trying to write a clever metaphor to describe everything you encompass, all the talents you possess, all the ways you've helped me grow, both personally and professionally, but I'm having a hard time. Simply put—you're the absolute best. Thank you for building with me. Jerome Murphy, from the very beginning, you understood this story and these characters, and in turn, understood me. Working with you has been such an honor. Thank you so much, Stuti Telidevara, for keeping everything running behind the scenes. And to Abigail Koons and Kat Toolan for all their hard work in the foreign rights department, thank you.

Bria Ragin, I am in constant awe of you. Your versatility, your patience, your expertise, your kindness and support. You're an amazing editor and I am fortunate that we are a team. Thank you for your insight and for helping Sasha and Ezra soar.

I'm grateful for all the wonderful folks at Random House

Children's Books who help bring stories into the world. Thank you to Wendy Loggia, Beverly Horowitz, and Barbara Marcus.

Thank you to the lovely Trisha Previte and Kgabo Mametja for bringing the cover to absolute life. Endless thanks to Cathy Bobak, Tracy Heydweiller, Alison Kolani, Colleen Fellingham, Tamar Schwartz, Jillian Vandall, and Cynthia Lliguichuzhca. Publishing a book is really a group effort, and I'm so grateful to be a part of this team.

I stand on the shoulders of giants and am forever grateful for those who've paved the way for me to be here. To Nicola and David Yoon, thank you for your words. Thank you for welcoming me to the publishing world and for believing in me and giving me this opportunity. Finger hearts.

Thank you to Brenda Drake and the staff, volunteers, mentors, and mentees, past and present, who have made Pitch Wars such a magnificent, inspiring space. To my class of 2020—yo, we really did that! During 2020! This is for us.

To my Pitch Wars fairy godmothers/godmentors, author J. Elle and editor Emily Golden: I don't even know where to begin. I'm forever grateful to you both, for your big hearts, your brilliant ideas, and your love for Sasha and Ezra. Thank you for guiding me.

Thank you to Kacen Callender for the generous editorial critique of my very first, very messy draft. Thank you for your kindness and words of encouragement. I appreciate you.

Thank you to Elise Bryant for all the texts, the sage advice, the Real Housewives convos, and for showing me that this could be done. I owe you lots and lots of Susie Cakes.

A big shout-out to my fellow author Jade Adia. Being in the publishing world with you has been dope, but having you as a friend? The gift of a lifetime. Can't wait to plot our next projects together over Forage.

I'm forever grateful to Maurene Goo, Julia Drake, Samantha Markum, Elise Bryant, and Jade Adia for the generous blurbs. That part of the process was terrifying for me, and you each brought such excitement and warmth. I'll never forget your kindness. ILY.

It has taken me an extremely long time to feel comfortable enough to share my work (haha, just kidding, I'm still working on this). To some of the readers who've helped me at various stages—Maureen "Mo Song" Porter, Mo and Sarah Li, Kassandra Garcia, Tina Canonigo, Lane Clark, Myah Hollis, and Isadore Hendrix—thank you for all your help and for cheering me on.

I have lots of love for the group chats and text threads that hold me down and keep me going. Shout-out to my earth sign crew Tussanee Reedboon and Angel Valerio. Y'all ground me and give me space to grow, you love me and laugh with me, and I could not have asked for better friends. To the Hicksville Support Group/Bad Teachers Club, meet me in Joshua Tree at Zombie Haus. To the Ladies Who Lunch—Kathy Koo, Raquel Laguna, Tina Canonigo, and Elise Bryant (again!)—can't wait to celebrate our next life milestones together.

Rachel Lawrence, soul sister, BFFL, FingerPark Forever. Angel Maldonado, mister, thank you for your friendship. Jane Mina Akins, my soul mate. Sasha Alcide, one of the brightest and funniest folks I know, I admire you so much. Jennifer

Paschall Rodgers, thank you for the guidance and best visualization exercises of my life. Melissa Gonzalez, Michelle Kurta, and Alexa Martinez, y'all are the best. I appreciate the ways you all have helped me along the way and all that you do to keep me going. Thanks for checking in, for sending cupcakes, the voice memos, coffee, and for believing in me. Lots of love to my Monterey and Seaside fam.

To the staff and students at Alain LeRoy Locke High School and Animo Jackie Robinson High School, especially Rachelle Alexander and Kristin Botello. I. LOVE. YOU. To my Day One colleagues: Ms. Ruff, Mr. Walsh, Mr. Mendoza, Mr. Ramirez, Ms. T, Mr. Maldonado—once a Saint, always a Saint.

I would be nothing without my family and their many sacrifices. To my dearest mother, Mommy, Ohmma, I love you beyond words. I remember going to clean houses with you (and Emo) and saw just how much you'd do to provide for me. I'm eternally grateful. Speaking of family, we're large! To the Parkers, Husseys, Johnsons, Whites, Paks, Koppelmans, Browns, Sibonys, and Christophers: We did it! This book is a family affair. 😊

A special shout-out to Charles Koppelman, who has dedicated his life to the art of storytelling. Thank you for sharing your wisdom with me and reminding me that I have it all under control (even when life made me feel otherwise).

To our dearly departed: Daddy, I hope I've made you proud. I *know* you've been looking out for us and protecting us all. I miss you every moment of every day. Aunty Marie and my little cuz Ryan, I love you. Uncle Jeremy Pettas, my meter for kindness, thank you for helping me grow at such a pivotal time in my life. Ms. Ella, we are missing you and your pound cakes earthside. Dave Christopher, I'm going to miss sharing books with you. A lot. Tandy Messenger, you were the first person to ask me about my writing— challenging me to be accountable to my dreams. Thank you for seeing that side of me before I saw myself. I finally did it. We miss y'all. 🖤

Walker, you turn my sorrow into silk. My heart of hearts. Thank you for sharing your life with me. And for letting me tell my awful jokes.

To Miles, my greatest joy and deepest love. In the words of Lauryn Hill, "I know that a gift so great is only one God could create, and I'm reminded every time I see your face."

Big shout-outs to: My therapist, for helping me navigate this life. Solange Knowles for music that feeds my soul. I think I've listened to "Things I've Imagined" at least a million times, and every time, I feel infinite. To all the food service workers and delivery drivers who helped feed my family because I was deep in edits and because I hate cooking. Diandra Linder for the many inspiring and reassuring readings. Chani Nicholas for reminding me I am magic. Crissle West and Kid Fury and all the lovelies that make up *The Read* podcast, in my loneliest hours I knew I still had community with y'all. Toni Morrison, the queen, I am thrilled that we existed in the same universe at the same time.

And to you, dear reader, many thanks.

XO,

dP

ABOUT THE AUTHOR

Danielle Parker was born and raised in California. She has a BA in English from the University of California, Berkeley, and an MA in education from the University of California, Los Angeles. She has over ten years of experience as a high school English teacher, during which her greatest pleasure was helping reluctant readers find a novel they absolutely loved. Danielle now lives in the Pacific Northwest with her family. *You Bet Your Heart* is her debut novel. When she's not writing, Danielle can be found looking for a pool to splash in, thinking about dessert, or taking a quick nap.

danielleparkerbooks.com

7.6.2023